Date Due

A Commodity of Dreams
& Other Stories

by HOWARD NEMEROV

Simon and Schuster · *New York* · *1959*

PUBLISHED BY SIMON AND SCHUSTER, INC.
ROCKEFELLER CENTER, 630 FIFTH AVENUE
NEW YORK 20, N.Y.

FIRST PRINTING

The following stories appeared originally in these publications:
"*Yore,*" Hudson Review
"*A Secret Society,*" Virginia Quarterly Review
"*The Web of Life*" and "*The Amateurs,*" Furioso
"*The Twitch,*" Gambit
"*Beyond the Screen,*" Sewanee Review
"*Tradition,*" "*An Encounter With the Law*" and "*A Delayed Hearing,*"
  Kenyon Review

LIBRARY OF CONGRESS CATALOG CARD NUMBER: 59-6015
MANUFACTURED IN THE UNITED STATES OF AMERICA
BY AMERICAN BOOK-STRATFORD PRESS, NEW YORK, N.Y.

To William Abrahams

CONTENTS

Yore   1

A Secret Society   15

The Guilty Shall Be Found Out and Punished   37

A Commodity of Dreams   51

The Web of Life   71

The Ocean to Cynthia   89

The Twitch   105

Beyond the Screen   119

Tradition   143

The Amateurs   163

A Delayed Hearing   185

An Encounter with the Law   201

Visiting the Sick   215

The Sorcerer's Eye   235

Yore

OVER THE LAVISH *Forgeterie* of the Beauldvoir Hotel rose the bone-china moon, rubbing all things to a hard beauty that looked permanent. Tomorrow would be the war, and everywhere in the hotel people accordingly rose and fell in value; meanwhile here was the moon swinging over the lovely gardens and the pool.

Alone at a marble-topped table, Mr. Luc le Mesurier bent his ancient head, baldness tipped in moonlight, toward the small ivory radio which murmuringly kept him company; from time to time he drew out of his coattail and consulted his memorandum book, a thin, tall volume bound in calfskin. Here with a gold pencil he made a note now and again, or placed a mark against the name of some acquaintance, or crossed off a name entirely; then with a slight contortion and a sigh he would turn to slip the book back into the tail of his coat, but always a remark made by the radio could cause him to get it out again almost at once.

Mr. Luc le Mesurier was a lean, elegant old gentleman, whose subtly gleaming black and white clothes fitted him like a second skin; when he arose, as he now did to welcome his expected companions, the tails of his coat curled slightly but deftly up and back as though they belonged to his own muscular arrangements. The dark tan of his face left off at the brow, for on bright days at the Beauldvoir Beach he was accustomed to wear, besides a black loincloth, a skullcap against the sun, and for this reason he looked, as he bowed and nodded, like an old priest or haloed saint.

After turning off the radio he drew out a chair for Mme. Mastaba, who with care placed her enormous backside between its arms and pressed down. The black sequins of her dress writhed with moonlight as, emplaced, she shook herself into comfort. Mr. Aiken Drum, the American millionaire, sat beside her and opposite to the place which Mr. le Mesurier now resumed. Mr. Aiken Drum was a large shaggy man with a full head of gray hair, rather unkempt. In this company Mr. le Mesurier resembled a whangee cane placed on exhibition beside a knobkerry stick and a pillow—an exhibition, perhaps, in a black museum, of instruments employed in the commission of long-forgotten crimes.

"It is hard to believe," said Mr. Aiken Drum, "but it has happened at last."

"It was bound to come sooner or later," said Mr. le Mesurier. "I suppose none of you knows where Great Coco is? This is something the announcer has neglected to inform us of so far."

"It will be very quickly over," averred Mme. Mastaba. "Atom bombs, hydrogen bombs, very quickly over."

"No, no, this will not be very quickly over," said Mr. Aiken Drum somberly enough yet with a certain tone of pride. "It will be a long, bitter struggle. At least," he added, "we have seen my daughter married before it began."

Felicia Drum had been wed that very afternoon to Sir Lay-amon Brute, Marquess of Yore; the Bishop of Norfolk had been flown in to preside. It was now in the interval between the service and the wedding supper that the three elderly friends had gathered in the *Forgeterie*, at a table beside the pool.

"She does not love him, poor thing," said Mme. Mastaba. "A great shame."

"Well, no," replied Mr. Drum. "But she is a good girl, is Felicia, and knows that first things come first."

"He will perish in this war," said Mr. le Mesurier.

"Well," said Mr. Drum, spreading wide his hands, "that of course can't be helped." He snuffled slightly, and brushed the end of his nose with delicacy on the back of his wrist. "They will be down in a few minutes. Let us be cheerful."

A waiter now took their orders. Mr. le Mesurier had been drinking a wine which he persuaded the others to try, a very fine wine expressed from seaweed, tasting something like io-dine, dry, reddish-brown and puckering. As an afterthought, he instructed the waiter to find out where in the world was Great Coco.

"It will doubtless be an island," he said, "for the announcer speaks of 'the air base *on* Great Coco.' "

"Who would have thought," said Mme. Mastaba, "we should have lived to see the day when we had to feel respon-sible for an air base on Great Coco?"

"But reality is always improbable," observed Mr. le Mesu-rier.

Great Coco, the waiter told them, was in the Bay of Bengal.

"I am scarcely any the wiser for that," said Mme. Mastaba.

Mr. le Mesurier suddenly snapped on the radio again. After a silent moment they heard a chorus of young voices repeating the Hail Mary over and over again with the swaying emphasis of a roller coaster which takes a deep breath at the top of its initial climb, then rushes downward.

"No news as yet," said Mr. le Mesurier, turning the radio off.

"But that is more frightening than anything I have heard so far," said Mme. Mastaba. "During the First World War I was at the School of the Sacred Heart in Grenoble."

"I really cannot understand," said Mr. Aiken Drum, "why man cannot learn to live at peace with his fellow man."

"It is possibly because, my dear," returned Mme. Mastaba, "man living at peace with his fellow man would use considerably less oil than he will have to use under the present circumstances."

"My dear Andrea," said Mr. Aiken Drum in a dignified manner, "I did not want this war to happen."

With a slight wiggling motion Mr. le Mesurier now reached around to his coattail and drew forth his memorandum book.

"I was reflecting before you came," he said, "on where in the world one might go next. Doubtless everything will be destroyed in a few weeks, or the hotels will have no food and the servants will have been conscripted. Tananarive, possibly? But there will of course be an air base there as well. Mukalla? Porto Alegre? Toby Lustig has a small inn at Misurata, but will it still be there? And will any sort of transport be available? On the other hand—Kristiansund? Or a farm near Stornoway? Ireland may be neutral; a visit with Salvadi at Castlebar? I fear life will not be made easy for the traveler."

"I shall go to my cousin at Denderah," said Mme. Mastaba. "No one ever bothers with the Upper Nile."

"And I return to the States tomorrow," said Mr. Drum. "Not exotic, but quite safe if one stays far from the cities. You are both invited. It is the children I am worried about."

"They will be evacuated, poor things, in droves," said Mme. Mastaba.

"It was my children I meant," said Mr. Drum. "Felicia and Layamon."

"She will go to Yore, I suppose," said Mr. le Mesurier, "and he to join his squadron."

"But they are coming in now," said Mme. Mastaba, raising her massive white head and peering toward the entrance.

2 —

Over the black water of the pool, moon-whitened in rippled streaks, an orchestra hidden in an island grove began to play The Wedding March. Felicia Drum advanced on the arm of her new husband the Marquess of Yore, the pair of them preceded by a small headwaiter who continually turned toward them to bow as he directed their path to the table. The girl, though she had put aside her white veil, still wore the wedding dress of white satin and a white cap of the same material. She looked pale and sullen, but charming. Sir Layamon Brute wore the somewhat Germanic-looking gray dress uniform of the Royal Air Force, with embroidered silver wings on the breast, three equal stripes of a Wing Commander on each sleeve, and upon his head the dully gleaming helmet with its high, horsehair crest, under which his thin, ruddy, pleasant face with its small red mustache did not appear especially adequate. A saber in scabbard swung at his side. Amid applause from the many guests at the tables beside the pool the bridal couple were seated with their elders just as the March came to an end.

"Exactly like a chamber pot," said Sir Layamon of his helmet, which he took off now and placed in the center of the table.

"It does form a strange costume for an aviator," observed Mme. Mastaba. "I thought they wore something more *sportif*."

"I am afraid," said Mr. Aiken Drum, "that this war will not be much of a wedding present for you two." He shook his head seriously, and Felicia, who at seventeen remained very uncertain about the great world, considered for a moment the idea that her father had really arranged the war with the object of giving her pleasure, and that he now rather regretted having gone to all that trouble. Under the fleeting influence of this notion she smiled brightly at him, to show appreciation.

"It can't be helped, sir," said Sir Layamon quietly. "Felicia will stay with Mother at Yore. I shall pack off to my Group as soon as we get back." He looked tenderly at his bride. "Not much of a show for you, my dear," he said.

Felicia looked back with an appearance of equal tenderness and leaned over to whisper something in his ear. What she whispered was "You know what you can do with your stiff upper lip," but the others, unable to hear, interpreted the Marquess's sudden rigidity of expression as pleased surprise. After a moment he whispered back in her ear, pushing aside with his nose her brown hair, "I shall die in this war. You won't be troubled with me for very long." To which Felicia replied aloud, and with a slight smile, "We can't help that, can we?" It seemed to her that she was being unnecessarily cruel, but apart from having been both annoyed and fatigued by the long ceremony, she felt quite bewildered about the nature of the feelings that would henceforth, it seemed, be officially demanded of her. She had seen in the *Tatler* pictures of Yore, towering and ancient amid great trees, and it seemed to her that in order to live up to such a possession she would have to be somewhat haughty, inscrutable, full of cold, cryptic sentences and surprised at nothing, like a great lady in the movies. It was also true that she did not love her husband, but this was only because she did not know from any personal experience what love was, and also perhaps because he failed to frighten her, even when wearing the helmet with the horsehair crest.

A waiter brought more wine, the delicious, bitter wine from seaweed. Mr. le Mesurier turned on the radio again, and now an announcer was describing in a tense, professionally anxious voice the preparations for reprisal that were going on all over the world: the battleships and carriers getting up steam at Guam and Pearl and Scapa Flow; the huge aircraft engines beginning to turn on the runways at Reykjavik and Disco and Yell and distant Thule; vast, uneasy populations beginning to move through the Balkans, through Turkey, through India; the air of the world laced with radio messages; the President of the United States would speak to the Congress.

"The King of Thule," said Mme. Mastaba. "We used to sing that song at school. There was a golden cup, a silver cup?"

"This is the century of dreams come true, is it not?" Mr. le Mesurier with doubtful relevance observed.

London and Paris, the announcer said, were under attack from the air. There was no news from these places, there was radio silence from these places.

"What a strange phrase," said Felicia, "as though *radio silence* were more golden than other kinds."

"It is a technical term," said the Marquess.

"A technical term," said Mr. le Mesurier, "meaning silence."

"But look," said Mr. Aiken Drum, suddenly reaching out and turning off the radio, "the floor show is about to begin."

"Nów there is radio silence indeed," said Mme. Mastaba.

Across the water the orchestra had begun to play once again, a brilliant fanfare followed by a dreamy, muted tune.

"It can hardly be a *floor* show," said Felicia, "unless the performers walk on water, which I understand is not done even in the century of dreams come true."

"My dear girl," her father replied, "you do not know everything about the world as yet."

While he spoke the music became louder, and gradually the depths of the pool beside them began to glow increasingly with light. Soon the reflections of the moon, and the black surface itself, disappeared from view and were replaced by a softly brilliant fairyland of coral castles and coral foliage underwater. Small, brightly striped fish swam slowly about, and there was even the submerged hull of a ship, with broken masts and tattered rigging, half sunken in sand covered with waving green moss. It was altogether a beautiful and strange sight, which Felicia had certainly not been expecting, and it made her feel for a moment privileged to mystery.

"It is a floor show of the ocean floor," said Mme. Mastaba. "They have it only here, at the Beauldvoir. I have seen it many times. It is very beautiful."

3 —

Now through the softly radiant water, from the doorway of a distant castle, came swimming a dozen mermaids, naked and white as pearls. They moved effortlessly forward with sinuous twistings of their tails, and soon formed into a circle, around which they swam for some minutes.

"How do they stay under so long?" asked Felicia.

"They are said to be perfectly real mermaids," Mme. Mastaba replied, "imported from the Seychelles Islands. Only here do they have them. Nowhere else in the world."

"At the Beauldvoir you know you are getting the real thing, expensive as it is," said Mr. Aiken Drum.

"All the same," Mr. le Mesurier said, "I am inclined to think they are not real. Rather, the legs of those girls have been slipped into the hinder skins, the tails, you understand, of very large fish—glued there, you know."

"Ugh," said Felicia.

"But how, in that case, do they stay under for so long?" asked the Marquess. "Unless of course it is a trick," he added, anxious not to appear naïve.

"Ah," said Mr. le Mesurier, "that I cannot tell you."

"I will tell you," said Mme. Mastaba with a certain emphasis. "It is because they are real mermaids, imported." She frowned at Mr. Luc le Mesurier. "You men," she said disdainfully.

"But there are no such things as mermaids," said Felicia petulantly, feeling nevertheless as though she were betraying her whole sex for nothing more than a cheap rationalistic idea picked up at school.

"There are these mermaids," replied Mme. Mastaba.

"There are more things in heaven and earth, Horatio, than are dreamed of in your philosophy," said Mr. Aiken Drum.

"Horatio?" inquired Mme. Mastaba.

At this moment the music left off, and a galleonlike ship, manned in statuesque poses by a crew of perhaps a dozen men, moved slowly from behind the orchestra's island into the center of the pool; the spectators could see for an instant the outstretched hands of a number of waiters, porters and bellhops who must have given it a strong push. This ship came to a stop on the still water, its paper sails billowed out as though with a stiff breeze. One could see it wholly, down to the keel, seeming to hang in a medium scarcely existing, so clear and smooth the water; and down below the mermaids slowly swam about.

Now in the silence there broke forth the sound of a number of pianos dispersed around the place, a loud, confused rumbling and tinkling and clanging; and a blond young man climbed to the high poop of the vessel, placed one hand over his heart and, in the crook of the elbow thus formed, the golden crown he had been wearing. So poised, he began half to sing and half to declaim a long recitative interwoven with passages of balladry, to which the pianos formed a remote and intermittently allusive background. Because of those pianos and because of the fact that the young man did not sing extraordinarily well—he looked stupid, unhappy and rather helpless despite his breastplate, crown, scepter and golden hair —the group at the table did not easily distinguish at first what he was singing about; Felicia thought possibly he sung in German or some other foreign tongue. Presently, however, she got used to it, and it became clear that he was a prince "from an island beyond the foam" and that his wicked stepmother had prevailed with the king his father to have him exiled. Not only this, but because of his father's power no other nation would give him refuge, and in all the wide world he had only this ship for home, to sail the seas with till he died. His song was very lonely and sad even though he did not sing well, and presently the mermaids themselves rose to the surface and poked their heads through to listen. ("Ah," said the Marquess with satisfaction, as though he had been holding his own breath. "They are real nevertheless," said Mme. Mastaba.)

And now there came through the clear water from the coral castle in the distance a new mermaid. This one wore, like the young prince, a crown, and she too rose to the surface to hear his song. Upon seeing this creature the young man became more passionate in his declamation; nowhere in the world, on land or at sea, was there woman half so beautiful as she. He stretched forth his scepter, and in a burst of exalted and flourishing song declared that she alone must be his bride. The pianos rumbled loudly at this.

"He is quite Wagnerian, with his bare knees," said Mr. le Mesurier.

The mermaid princess now made her reply, singing in a voice cool and steady as a night wind off the water. She was indeed a beautiful woman, or mermaid, with very white skin and with long, black hair which even though wet curled in reptilian folds about her breasts and back. She would be his bride, she sang, but she could never leave the sea which was her home. She pitied his exile, but alas, they were doomed, the two of them, to eternal separation by the elements they breathed.

The young prince, hearing this, declared, still singing, that if he could not have her to wife the world held nothing more to please him—an exile and alone, condemned to sail forever across the seven seas. To have her love what might he better do than die, so be he died in her white arms? All this he sang in a voice which was evidently becoming somewhat distressed with fatigue.

The mermaid princess sternly yet perhaps a little coyly forbade him the death he so eloquently sought; while she sang she provocatively waved those white arms, making her breasts move just below the surface of the water. The hero, with an artificial vehemence and ferocity very convincing, insisted. She again imperiously denied. This went on, in the form of a duet, for some time.

"It is a little boring, *tout ce* Papageno-Papagena," said Mme. Mastaba, "but the spectacle is brilliant."

Felicia agreed. Charmed at first, she had very quickly become bored as the two lovers passed this theme back and forth between them, while the pianos went on like stones bouncing down a hill. The whole scene rapidly began to seem ridiculous, not least because the labored, healthy earnestness of the young man contrasted so unfavorably with the cool, queenly demeanor and effortless voice of the mermaid. Because she was bored, Felicia paid, finally, not much heed to the course of all these antics, and was in fact lighting a cigarette at just the moment when—with a theatrical scream of loving anguish and a somewhat awkward splash—the young prince cast away scepter and crown and leaped into the water, into the embrace of his mermaid sweetheart. And she? What did she do? Felicia was quite in time to see that she, her long white arms fixed firmly around her lover's middle, her silver tail flashing in one powerful turn and dive, dragged him away below. The audience, leaning over the edge of the pool, had a clear view of his silent writhings, kickings and strugglings, accompanied by chains of bubbles from the air in his clothing and one final chain of bubbles from the air in his lungs; after this—it had taken over a minute—he lay still at the entrance of the coral castle, until presently a cortege of mermaids swam down and carried him away, while on distant pianos empty octaves bounded angrily up and down their deserted, echoing stairwells. Then all was over, and the underwater light began to fade. It was oddly noticeable that scepter and crown, made of some light materials, still floated on the surface; but soon all was dark on the water, dark and opaque and resuming the reflection of the moonlight.

"So you see," said Mme. Mastaba, laughing, to the Marquess, "the mermaids were real, after all."

Felicia saw that her husband had got very red in the face. So he had not been expecting it either, she thought, and made herself smile as at some remote and secret thought.

"How did you like it, my dear?" inquired Mr. le Mesurier, putting his bony old hand upon hers. Felicia turned the smile in his direction.

"I thought it was quite sweet, really," she said, "but maybe just a little too long."

Mr. Aiken Drum coughed.

"It is doubtless on account of the expense," he said. "They prolong it deliberately, to make the most of the materials."

"I find it," said Mr. le Mesurier, "an ominously romantic conception. That is, after all, not the kind of world we live in today. It is more like—like this Valkyrie's headpiece," he added, indicating the Marquess's helmet with the horsehair crest.

"Ah, but there will always be romance," said Mme. Mastaba, profoundly sighing. "No matter what they do to the poor world, there will be romance."

"It is hard to believe," said Mr. Aiken Drum, "it is hard to believe that we are at war once again. Reality is harsh, after this fairyland." He gestured broadly toward the dark pool beside them.

"It cannot go on forever," said Mr. le Mesurier. "Before we know it we shall meet again, perhaps here in this very place."

"We are old," said Mme. Mastaba. "The world may never again be as we know it. But there will be romance for the young, will there not, Felicia?"

But Felicia had not heard. She sat very straight, with the smile of a great lady playing distantly upon her face, and was caught in a vision, wherein she saw her husband and herself, he wearing the helmet that lay there on the table, flying alone in the silent aircraft, high in the dark night, back to the stone towers and the stately trees of Yore. In her mind's eye, then, she saw herself walking endlessly through silent corridors hung with portraits, and down the sweeping curve of a grand staircase, all in the silence. The silence continued, it seemed for years.

"What are you thinking, my dear?" asked the Marquess.

Abruptly Felicia came to the surface of her dream. "I was thinking," she said with a laugh both grand and gay, "that if there's anything in the world I love, it's reality."

And though the Marquess seemed confused for a moment, the elders laughed indulgently. Then they all had more of the bitter wine from seaweed.

A Secret Society

SLOWLY, beneath the white ceiling, the four-bladed fan swung round and round, making no perceptible difference to the heat, which was intense, though by no means so bad here as outside. Beneath the fan, the dentist's lamp seemed to crane its neck like a small dinosaur's, and to peer down Mr. Paley's throat, into his eyes; blinding from one angle, bland from any other. Beyond his feet, through the window where "A. M. Harris, Dentist" was written backward in an arc of gold letters, Mr. Paley could see the sidewalk and buildings opposite. At the door of the newspaper office a small crowd stood around something which he could not make out, but he recalled the announcement in the paper that if the heat wave continued someone was going to attempt to fry an egg on the sidewalk, and that no doubt was what was going on at the moment.

Judson Paley was blessedly being left alone in the chair for a few minutes while the novocain took effect, stiffening his jaw, numbing his palate, making, it seemed, a kind of cold hollow deep in his mouth, so that his words, if occasion required any, would probably come out sounding odd. He tentatively took between his teeth the loose flesh at the inside of his lower lip, and squeezed rather than bit, savoring the fine distinction of feeling—that is, he could feel himself doing this but could no longer feel what it properly felt like. Something like that, he decided, constituted also his relation to the whole of life, which he received by intelligence without quite ever sensing its just weight or pressure.

In the belief that he was now more relaxed than he had been, Mr. Paley sighed and moved a little bit, discovering that no matter what he believed he had all this time had his toes cramped up inside his shoes and his head not quite touching the headrest of that chair, which seemed made, in his opinion, for tension rather than ease. There was something childlike about his position—left there, while the adults, so to say, the dentist and hygienist, went invisibly about their business—and he would have liked to turn on one side and nap for a few minutes, but this the chair stiffly prevented, so he merely sat there, with his mouth hung receptively open. He was relieved to have the anesthetic, but somewhat annoyed with himself for accepting it against the doctor's somewhat grudging offer.

"It would be better to do without," Dr. Harris had said after the first vicious bout with the drill. "We are working very near the root in there, and I can go on more comfortably as long as I know it's hurting a little bit. If it stopped hurting, you see," he explained, "then I'd know we were in trouble."

But Judson Paley's nerves, after a moment more, rejected this arrangement, and despite himself he began to tense up and all but close his mouth as the drill approached.

"Just a little decay in there, still," Dr. Harris said persuasively. "A minute more."

"I guess it's the heat, Doctor," said Judson Paley. "I'm all on edge. Maybe I'd better have the shot."

The shot was given, though Paley thought he heard in the doctor's voice as he consented something like irritation. I am wasting his time, he thought. He feels he is being cheated of five dollars for the extra fifteen minutes this might take. Might he properly offer to make this up in the fee? But that would be embarrassing. Besides, a dentist was a servant of humanity, and not in there to make money hand over fist—oh, hardly. Mr. Paley wondered how one became a dentist, or, rather, why, and decided that probably some streak of native cruelty, a delight in hurting people, particularly if this could be made out to be for their own good, lay at the back of it all. Besides, he said to himself, it's a living, like anything else.

"Now I guess we can get to work again," Dr. Harris said, bringing the drill down without a wasted motion. For a few moments Judson Paley's view of the world consisted of utter extremes of closeness and remoteness: the drill, and Doctor Harris's strong yet soft hand, so close they blurred, while everything else, even his own thoughts, seemed to blur with distance. The novocain had the odd effect on him of removing pain without removing his anticipations of it, so that he was still tense and began to sweat all over. Besides that, the force of the doctor's argument against the drug preoccupied him; the nerve of the tooth might be destroyed already.

"Just one more little soft spot in there," Dr. Harris said, his voice soothing but the lips through which it came entirely grim with concentration.

There followed presently the business of filling the cavity, which entailed all sorts of preparations with equipment, some of which looked very medieval, the little blue-gas flame at the edge of the tray particularly. Dr. Harris, more relaxed now, loaded Mr. Paley's insentient mouth with cotton cylinders, clamps and a suction tube for draining away the saliva; moreover, he kept his mirror in there with one hand even when he turned away to see about the cement which his nurse was mixing.

"Important to keep it dry," he said, adding pleasantly, "Do you think there will be a war over this business in the Pacific?"

It was a subject upon which Judson Paley had opinions of a pronounced but somewhat complicated kind; indeed, as a reflective person, he but rarely found questions which he could answer with a yes or a no. In consequence he gagged somewhat metallically, all in vowels, and Dr. Harris nodded.

"Yes, there's something in what you say. These things usually pass off, though, in my experience."

Then Mr. Paley had to sit with his mouth clamped tightly shut, under all the pressure he could bring to the job, while the filling dried. His brain raced helplessly, out of gear, with the subtle analysis of the world situation which he was quite unable to deliver, and Dr. Harris said, "Miss Mantes can take you this morning," and added, as Mr. Paley's eyeballs seemed to bulge with impatient negation, "then you wouldn't have to come in again. You could get everything done with at once."

Despite his immediate sense that the overheated world would explode if he did not get out of the dentist's chair and office in five minutes, the argument appealed to Mr. Paley's reason. There would indeed be an advantage to having all dental work out of the way for another six months; another half hour, he thought, and his freedom, for that time at least, was absolute. So when he was able to speak he tried one last feeble gambit by suggesting that perhaps his teeth did not need cleaning; at which Dr. Harris smiled merely; and then consented to get out of the one chair and into the one next door, where Miss Mantes, buxom, powerful, leaned against him in a horrid way suggestive of intimacy while she pried and scraped and chipped and, finally, brushed until Judson Paley's mouth foamed coldly with blood and cream.

Again he felt like a child. Daddy is through, and now it's Mommy's turn, was the way he thought of it as Miss Mantes' starched white breast squeezed against his shoulder impersonally.

"Your teeth are quite green," said this woman once, in her plain-spoken and severe way. "The gums have receded since last time, even, and they bleed very easily. How often do you brush your teeth?"

Mr. Paley pretended his mouth hurt too much to allow of an answer. It's time to go, it's time to go, I'll come back later, another time, next year—these thoughts went around in his head. His muscles stiffened, his behind itched, his eyes filled with the tears of impatience and generous self-pity; but at last it was over, and out he went, his mouth numb with novocain which did not prevent his teeth from feeling suddenly naked.

2 —

The heat really was intolerable, and it was only eleven. Mr. Paley crossed the street to see whether someone had fried an egg and ascertained that they must have, for some yellowish goo and bits of white, blackened by someone's heel, stained the sidewalk.

He stood there in the blazing sunlight for several minutes, not wanting to go home. It seemed to him that he deserved some sort of special reward for the torment of the chair; he might, for example, treat himself to lunch at the Prince's Grill. But it was still barely eleven. He would have to fill in another hour at least.

As he stood debating the possibilities in his mind, he became aware that the object of such external attention as he had left over was a large policeman standing on the curb looking intently at a parking meter; thereupon Mr. Paley's thoughts took a very strange turn.

His eyes took in the policeman's stout, hard form, the sweaty shirt, the heavy whipcord trousers, the high, peaked cap, and most of all the huge black revolver which sagged heavily in its holster against this man's thigh and flapped a little with his every move.

Judson Paley thought, I am a respectable and well-known citizen of this town. I have lived here all my life. I have even said hello to that policeman now and then, and know that he is called Louie. Yet I might go up to him and hit him in the face, and he would put me in jail.

The image of a jail (where he had never been) irrelevantly presented itself to his mind as dark and cool, a deep hole with earthen walls and some kind of concrete structure overhead.

Or I might sneak up behind him, grab out his gun, and threaten him with it; he would get it back and shoot me. Or perhaps I would shoot him. There would be a struggle, anyhow, and the chances are I would finish up hurt, imprisoned, my reputation ruined, big scandal, picture in the papers—Court Finds Insane. . . .

These thoughts went through Mr. Paley's head rapidly and not in sequence or order; more as images than as thoughts. There was an odd fascination in them, and in a few seconds he saw the whole affair taking place not once but several times. Meanwhile he took a step or two closer to the policeman's bland back. He was now nearly close enough to reach out and grab the black, ridged butt of the gun, which he now noticed, however, was attached not only to the holster but also to the policeman himself, by means of a silver chain set in an eye in the butt; the other end of this chain seemed to be tucked into the whipcord trousers at the waist.

So they've thought of that as well, Mr. Paley mused.

The policeman suddenly turned to face him at a distance of two or three feet, no more, his hand vaguely nearing the gun as he came around. The meaty face, set in impersonal and random anger, relaxed into a smile.

"Mr. Paley," he said civilly, touching his cap. "Morning, sir."

"Hi, there," said Judson Paley. "Hot enough for you?"

"You bet," the policeman said, and turned his back again. Mr. Paley slowly walked off down the street.

One or two doors away there was sitting on the step what could only be called a bum: an old man, his seamed face unshaven and bristling white, his eyes on Mr. Paley. Clearly he had taken in the little episode just passed, and it seemed possible to Paley that he had taken in also the dreamy episode which the real one had replaced, only just in time. Paley thought there was a sneer of knowledge, perhaps of complicity, on this man's face, and, averting his eyes, pretending to be interested in something across the street, he went rapidly on.

3 –

After wandering about for only a few minutes more, Mr. Paley took himself in hand. On the principle that it was best to get everything done in one day, and as he had an hour to pass before lunch, he went for a haircut, an experience which had always seemed to him among life's most disagreeable necessities.

The barber, old Mr. Bill, whom most people called Billy Boy, was not busy, though his shop was crowded, typically, with the sort of riffraff that came in every day to read magazines and talk. Mr. Paley felt like a sacrificial animal as he climbed into yet another leather chair, his third of the morning, and all those men stopped talking for a moment while they took a remote interest in the back of his head.

Old Mr. Bill had been cutting Judson Paley's hair for many years; Paley could remember, though he did not care to, how his father used to bring him down here when he was of such a size that he had to sit on a board across the arms of the chair. His hair had been golden and curly at that time, though it darkened while he was still a boy, and he had used to cry, throw tantrums, and wriggle desperately, hating Mr. Bill throughout the performance, which took place monthly. Mr. Bill must have been a young man then, for Paley was now near forty years old himself, but it did not seem as though the barber had changed much in appearance over the years; his hand must have been steadier then, but Paley did not really remember that this was so; he simply assumed it.

He had been in the chair for only a few minutes when he began to feel the idea of having a haircut was a bad mistake. It was hot in the barbershop, there were flies buzzing around everywhere, there was unswept hair all over the floor; worst of all, his own impatience now made him break into a sweat, and the sweat caused his own hair, as it was cut, to stick to his face in falling, where it tickled and itched horribly. Nor was it much help that Billy Boy, gray and mincing as he went about, knew that he did not like to talk, for that merely meant that the barber continued his widely ranging conversation with his lounging clientele, often stopping right behind Mr. Paley's ear to deliver himself of remarks which needed to be accompanied by gestures.

Experimentally, to see if his mouth were still numb, Paley bit his lower lip, inside. There was as yet no sensation, and because he was exasperated at having his hair cut, at having to sit still and sweat thus, he bit his lip again, and began to chew on it. There was no taste, only perhaps a suspicion of salt, but the flesh felt pleasantly rubbery, resilient, under the pressure of his teeth.

"I've been over to do for Peter Harding this morning," Billy Boy said, flashing the scissors next to Mr. Paley's ear.

"He's lucky to be out of this heat," someone said, and there was a laugh which the barber quickly suppressed.

"You wouldn't want people to talk of you that way," he said; "well, don't talk of others that way. They say he suffered real bad; it was a mercy to him he finally went. His face, I tell you, when I went to shave it, it was all screwed up in agony. A cancer, he had."

"You old bastard, there's no way you wouldn't make a buck, is there?" Thus one voice, and another, "What do you get for doing a corpse?"

Billy Boy twitched the scissors nervously, and said in a voice of evident delight, "Well, boys, it's a special occasion, after all, and not a job everyone'd like to take on—people are usually glad enough to give me five dollars just to see it over and done with."

"Five dollars!"

"Remind me, when my time comes, to come down and get shaved the day before I go."

"Be glad to do you—any time," Billy Boy said.

Judson Paley, through all this, chewed sullenly on his lip and, when possible, looked straight into the mirror before him. This mirror seemed to render him an oddly remote and atomistic account of things: he was able to stare at himself and see a stranger whose impassivity contrasted with his own intense, inward discomfort. He began to think how the same mirror had contained his image over so many years, and this led him to consider how the same hands, Billy Boy's, had professionally touched and smoothed and turned the head of boy and man—these hands, now touching him, which had so lately touched the face of the dead. This thought did not bother him; on the contrary, it gave him a kind of patience to put up with the heat, flies, hair, the inane conversation and laughter, the terribly slow passage of time—he was literally sweating it out—and, worse perhaps than any of these, the way the barber had of leaning his body up against Mr. Paley's arm on the arm of the chair, an apparently professional or at least unconscious intimacy which Paley filled so full of frightful suggestion that he was too embarrassed to move his arm away.

When at last the haircut was finished, and he could stand face to face with Billy Boy and give him a dollar, Paley felt better; his head seemed naked and cool, and his ears felt as though they stood out comfortably. At the same time, there was loose hair on his neck and some down his collar.

"Good day, Mr. Bill," he said in a pleasantly offhanded way.

"Come again, Mr. Paley," said the barber, whose smile vanished, however, as Mr. Paley went through the screen door and down the steps.

"There's a proud little son of a bitch," he said to the company.

So they kicked that around for a while.

4 —

Judson Paley lived high on the Hill, in the old, prerevolutionary part of town, in a house which looked down on the valley which contained the results of both the American and the Industrial revolutions. From his front window he could see the factory his grandfather built: a dark-red, brick fortress with a green copper roof, surrounded by wooden sheds also red in color. This factory was empty, Judson's father having sold out to a corporation which subsequently moved to the South; on the judiciously invested proceeds of this sale, with other family properties, Judson and his sister had lived for many years, and could live for a good many more, in a respectable state which while it was no longer wealth was not poverty either, or even near it. The house might have been thought much too large for them, and in fact they had closed down parts of it for economy's sake, but they liked it too well ever to move, for they were both of rather settled habits.

It is sad to consider the end of a style, even one not particularly lovable at its flower. Judson and his sister Alice lived the end of theirs rather dramatically, if drama consists not in loud display but in a full consciousness of what is appropriate to a given situation. They were inheritors, that was their role in life, to stand in dignified and lonely separation (not protest) from a world which, as it must, was going on to other things; this attitude suited something naturally conventual in their dispositions. They saw themselves, in a quiet, sometimes slightly humorously amazed way, as a part of history, the representatives of subtle dooms brought on only by time; their teeth fastidiously set on edge by the sour grapes which the fathers had eaten. Sometimes they would see themselves as "an old provincial family"; the English or European idea of "a provincial town" pleased them, and filled them with a sense of the mellowing, autumnal peace which they found also in some novels of Trollope, a favorite whom they would sometimes read aloud.

There was yet some bitterness in all this, though they scarcely spoke of it even to each other, and would in no case, either of them, have discussed it with anyone else had there been anyone else. They had gone to Harvard and Radcliffe, had lived afterward in France for a year, then they had gone separate ways, he to New York, she to Boston—until, only a year after, the death of the father. In those early years Judson had the intention of being a painter, while Alice wrote poetry —the idea of their professionally pursuing those arts had been regarded in the family as too ridiculous to be dignified with the name of revolt. But in any case the sale of the family business, the death of the father, finally, in another five years, the mother's death, made even the idea of such a revolt unnecessary. They might now do as they pleased, but fifteen years or more of doing as they pleased had made it seem that freedom itself was the revenge which a dying family had taken upon its somewhat weakened and last members.

How silently and quickly, in retrospect, those years seemed to have gone by. How empty they were to look back upon. How dull! an outsider might say. But they had not seemed so, and Judson at present did not think they had been so. He dearly loved his sister, as he always had, and sometimes even thought he might presume she returned this calm affection so strongly, quietly, tenderly, that it was on his account alone that she had not married. For she might have married well, being not at all an uncomely girl, though perhaps rather strong and decent than actually beautiful, with something always a trifle mournful about her face, which was maybe a bit too long.

At all events, he now thought, it had been—it was—a life which suited him and suited her, especially in being old-fashioned and out of date, constructed upon a model, or the memory of a model, quite lost. They were, he would say without either false pride or false modesty, *gentlefolk*. They did not despise others for not being, but they themselves could not be otherwise, and took a bittersweet pleasure in keeping to themselves on that account. Even the failure of their youthful ambitions had been so slow, so gradual, that it did not seem to be failure; those things had merely relapsed gently into oblivion, until they became "things we used to do"; there were a great many more of these, as well. They had studied local history, looking up old documents, driving deep into the country roundabout to identify this place and that; they had become bird-watchers and collectors of flowers; they had briefly taken up science, or, as they preferred to call it, Nature Study; there had earlier on been a bridge-playing period, then a period of chess—which they agreed to drop after only a short while because it was too serious and tended to make them angry—while nowadays they played various forms of rummy. Once in a while the arts reappeared; they would take up with much spirit the children's verses which Alice was to write and Judson to illustrate; they had even got an enthusiastic letter of encouragement from a publisher in New York; but nothing ever really got done, and neither of them, in Judson's belief, really had ever cared.

In the Prince's Grill, so-called because the proprietor was named Prince, Judson ordered a martini and enjoyed it so well that he had another after it before ordering lunch. The restaurant was dark, with paneled walls and dark, coppery mirrors which held what seemed endless repetitions of white tablecloths, shiny silver, people eating; it was hard even to identify oneself in the maze of reflections, or to be certain how one's image could ever have got to walls seemingly so far removed and at such odd angles. The place was air-cooled as well, so that Judson shivered for a few minutes when he first came inside; the cold air and the icy drink, served in a long-stemmed glass whose elegance pleased him even if it was a tawdry imitation of the old stemware, formed a delicious element in which he felt happy for the first time that morning. Somehow the continued numbness inside his mouth entered into and increased his pleasure; until his food came he chewed steadily on the inside of his lip, which had developed a large, hard bump from which tiny rags of flesh seemed to hang.

The waitress, too, was pleasing in his eyes. A soft young girl with honey hair and a friendly smile, she seemed, he thought, really interested in taking his order—not like so many of these people with their grudging frowns and air of being overworked—so that he kept her there by his table for a couple of minutes by a coy pretense of being unable to decide between the swordfish and the mixed grill. He liked the starched black uniform she wore, with its petite white apron and frills; he liked especially the way in which it seemed to stand stiffly away from her body, with an impression of warm space existing within; and her arms were so softly rounded as she reached in front of him on various errands that Judson had to smile tolerantly at his immediate impulse to bite that smooth, sweet flesh so near his mouth—how surprised the little girl would be!

Surprised indeed, he thought. Then there would be screams and commotions, the manager would come up, all the other waitresses as well, the police would be brought in, reporters would rush up in two minutes. It seemed to him both horrifying and fascinating that this little impulse, from whose fulfillment in action, after all, he was separated by what? could change his life in a moment. One did not of course *do* such things; but why did one not?

Morality had nothing to do with it. Oddly enough, a girl like this, who would scream blue murder if one bit her arm in a public place, would probably have no objection whatever to becoming one's mistress under the proper circumstances. Indeed, he had sometimes wondered if this particular restaurant did not have a secret second existence as a house of prostitution; the waitresses seemed to be new ones whenever he came in, and they most of them had an identifiable air of rather careless, weary charm. Judson had never pursued this suspicion, but this waitress today was so altogether cute and pretty and friendly that he momentarily fancied himself standing before some secret door upstairs and saying easily that he wanted "the little blond one, I don't know her name."

This was a sort of thought which came only rarely to Judson Paley, and surprised without really bothering him; he had never been much of a one for women—nor men either, he felt it necessary to add even in the privacy of his own mind—and, in fact, the entire realm of sexuality was one which he thought himself lucky to have been able to dismiss from his life after a very few youthful experiments. Fashionable as it was these days to regard that particular itch as intolerable, incessant, precisely by reason of one's masculinity, one's inalienable nature, he had discovered that it simply did not bother him; and accepted that disability, if it was one, as a fact.

Even now, his real feeling for the waitress had perhaps little enough to do, even prospectively, with lust; it was more nearly a wistful tenderness, as if she were already, in his eyes, someone he had known a long time ago. Still, he felt a wish to know her better, and when she brought his check to the table he kept her there for a few moments, first by asking her name.

"Janice," she said, with the easy assumption that her first name alone would interest him.

"Have you been working here long?"

"A few weeks."

"Do you like it? You seem to."

"It's all right, I guess," the girl said tentatively, as if showing a willingness to be drawn out.

"What time do you get through this afternoon?" Mr. Paley asked, surprising himself.

"Oh, at four, about," she replied carelessly, pretending not to recognize the drift of all this.

"I'd like to take you out for dinner, then," said Mr. Paley, blushing, and smiling, and drawing upon everything in the way of boyish charm which he could put his hands on at the moment. "We could drive up into the hills to Hartland, maybe."

"Ah, I couldn't do that," she said, appearing nevertheless to consider it seriously. "My boy friend wouldn't like it."

"You're going to meet him?"

"Well, I usually do, after work. We're engaged." She showed her hand, with a ring.

"Congratulations, Janice," said Mr. Paley. "I'm sorry if I've bothered you."

"Oh, that's all right, sir," the girl said as she left him.

Judson Paley's feelings about this little episode were somewhat confused. First, apart from a dismayed embarrassment, a sense that he had been ridiculous—the one thing one ought never to be—and that the girl was telling the other waitresses about him, he also had a suspicion that she was lying about that boy friend. It was as though, standing before a door (the secret one upstairs?) he had been denied entry on no particular moral principle but only because there was some secret password to common humanity, which he did not possess. At the same time, he felt relieved at having been turned down, and imagined how, had things gone otherwise, that boy friend (who conveniently leaped into existence now on a large scale) might have been waiting for him on the street at four when he came to call for the waitress.

Under the influence of these considerations he left the girl a larger tip than he would ordinarily have done, paid his check, and wandered out, to be stricken at once by the blasting heat, which he had forgotten. A trifle dizzy with drink and food, his heart still thudding heavily under the influence of embarrassment about the waitress, he stood out on the sidewalk in the sun, wondering if there were anything else to be done about the day, and finding his only pleasure in rolling between his teeth the hardened lump in his lower lip. Surely the novocain ought to be wearing off about now? But he could feel nothing.

Standing there thus, Paley had a sad, desperate vision in

which this day became the image of all his days. He had spent the morning being ministered to by professional hands, which fed him, cleaned him, saw to his health, made him presentable; and in all this he could find nothing human, nothing of interest, nothing that embodied any recognition of himself as a person. He had suddenly a strong sense of his own flesh, his bodily being, naked inside his clothing; and of the darkness, liquid and mysterious, within the flesh; and could imagine the hands even of the undertaker busied at last, professionally, over his cooling, silent, everlastingly isolated self. What did it mean? What did it amount to?

Heavy trucks roared through Main Street, rattling windows, shaking (it seemed) the sidewalk. The air, filled with fumes of gas, trembled visibly in the heat. People pushed by this way and that; everyone was going somewhere, but where were they going? Why? And what would they do when they arrived? Who were they? It was as though civilization altogether was formed of secret societies, guilds, brotherhoods, sects, factions, from whose crossing multifarious memberships he alone was excluded. For an instant he saw a symbol of his separation, a gesture of definition, in the idea of throwing himself under a truck just now passing; it was as if the sidewalk were the bank of a river, and death itself flooded rapidly down the street: the final solution, available always and everywhere, like any other mass-produced convenience, like any door people were seen to enter but never seen to leave. The police station, the hospital, the asylum, all those doors past which the citizen, as on some vast pinball machine, threaded his endangered and helpless way. And there was no escape from death except by dying; no graceful resignation no matter what one gave up or professed one's readiness to give up; the clock of one's own infernal machine continued to tick.

He should go home; there was nothing for him to do here,

in this heated hive overgrown with shops and movies and banks—which was, however, his home town. He was reminded, on this, that he ought to go to his bank, just up the street, and draw out some money for Alice, since she preferred to pay cash for things.

The bank was a pretentious marble building at the next corner. It resembled a tomb, Judson thought, in having that ornate, ambiguous solidity as to which one could not tell, of keeping in and keeping out, which imperative was the more important; this very strength, in his opinion, testified also to the existence of death, existence of evil, here on Main Street in the sunshine. Chewing with bitter industry upon the cud of his own flesh, which did not cry out, he entered the building.

The bank was crowded, and not air-cooled; the marble resonance inside gave a momentary impression of chill, rapidly transformed into a feeling that one would stifle. Nonetheless people seemed very good-natured and easygoing about standing in line before the barred windows. All, that is, except Judson Paley, who quickly felt himself as it were taken by the throat by his impatience at two women directly in front of him, whom he would have liked to shove roughly out of the way. He looked around him in a rising panic, as though to say that there must be some alternative, somewhere, to a situation of this kind.

The bank guard strolled past and took up a stance quite near by; that fatuous stance of authority assured of security by nothing more than eternal boredom. The handle of this man's revolver stuck out of the holster a foot or two from Judson's hand and unattached, he saw, by any silver chain. Judson grabbed at it and the weapon came up in his hand.

The guard, an old, even superannuated person known to Judson only as Alfred over the years, swung around bearing an expression of absurd amazement as he reached for the empty holster.

"Now, Mr. Paley, sir," he said pleadingly, uncertain whether to be terrified or to smile, and finally combining both expressions ineffectually.

Judson backed a step or two away. Other people in the bank, it seemed, had not even noticed his action, and he cried out sharply, "Hey!" It brought on a silence which lasted and lasted; then there began to be screams, shrieks, whispers, and a wide space appeared between Judson and everyone else; in this space, which went with him as he moved, he backed to the wall.

"Mr. Paley," the guard cried in a sort of reasonable tone rising to a scream, "what do you want with that gun?"

And when it came down to it, Judson did not know. He saw that he held in his hand—in both hands, as a matter of fact—the absolute upon which everything was founded, the black imperative whose existence made conditional the exist-ence of everything else, the banks, schools, stores, theaters; waitresses, barbers, dentists and hygienists too, for that matter; himself as well, come to that; and shamed and made hypo-crites of all. This absolute he was unable to use in a proper manner, and, while everyone watched in silent horror, he turned it to his mouth and awkwardly, with both thumbs, pushed on the trigger.

He fell fainting to the ground, quite without becoming aware that nothing had happened, his general innocence of the truth of civilization covering also a specific innocence about the device of the safety catch.

Once the danger was over, everyone was indignant and relieved, but much inclined to leave Mr. Paley to the proper authorities, who in this instance acted quickly to suppress all needless publicity and outcry. The physician, rather than the policeman, was called for and got. Mr. Paley was taken into the president's office and stretched there on a leather couch, examined, pronounced to be suffering, in the first instance, from shock; though doubtless from other things as well.

"The heat, maybe?" said the bank president doubtfully. He did not want to press charges, because, no matter what was right and true and just, such things never worked out well for banks, never half so well as the great remedy of silence. He had decided already that Mr. Paley had had a stroke. People might talk all they wished about a gun in his hand; the gun had not been fired, no damage had been done; people might talk, but people constantly talked.

At last the president himself drove Mr. Paley up the hill to his house and delivered him, white and weak, into the hands of his sister Alice. In the course of the drive the two men spoke very little except that the president asked, "What did it feel like? I mean, what made you want to do that?"

"Don't you know?" asked Mr. Paley.

The president took his eyes off the road very briefly to look into Mr. Paley's eyes.

"Yes," he said. "I have thought of it."

Alice, who heard nothing of the episode of the gun but only that her brother had fainted, put him to bed at once and made weak tea. She brought up a little whisky with it. Judson was sitting up in the bed, and smiling.

"Do you remember when we were little?" he asked. "We used to go to bed in the daytime like this, and the sheets were so white and cool, and the birds would begin to sing in the tree outside?"

"Yes, my dear, I remember. Now you should drink this while it's still hot."

"Ouch!" cried Mr. Paley at the first sip of tea. The novocain had worn off, and his mouth was raw and bloody inside, the lacerated flesh hanging down in tiny strips and flashing with sharp and pinpointed pain. It felt strangely pleasant, though; lively, he would call it. And he said to his sister, with a feeble but boyishly open smile, that he thought people really loved one another and were kind, after all.

"I'm sure they are," said Alice.

And in a few minutes more he fell fast asleep.

The Guilty Shall Be Found Out and Punished

For maybe as much as the past two weeks I have noticed on and off a slight itch under the heel of my right foot, but not until this morning did I become concerned enough to try to do something about it. Not even an itch, really, but only a slight, distant tickling sensation, as though once in a while a feather were brushing across the sole of the foot, or as though a fly had landed there. Even less than that: as though I had just realized that a fly had been sitting there all the while. Of course, as I was wearing shoes, none of these could be an explanation, but I want to show you if I can just how slight an irritation it is—and how irritating.

When I really noticed it, this morning, just after reaching the office and sitting down to read through the paper, my first thought was, Yes, there it is again. *Again*, you see. So I had felt it before, obviously, but not until this time had it seemed important enough to bother about. Had it increased, then? No, I could not honestly say it had increased. But somehow it had managed to get my attention, that more or less absent-minded attention with which we see, or feel, that something on the desk is out of place, say, and which will not let us rest or go on reading until we have straightened it up, whatever it is. I tentatively rubbed my foot up and down in the shoe, the shoe up and down on the carpet.

There was very little give as between the foot and the shoe, and in what there was my foot slid all too smoothly; if only my socks had been of some rougher, more prickly material, I felt, even this slight motion would have given relief, but against silk or nylon I could get no friction at all. I rubbed my foot up and down a little harder, but without result.

Well, then, never mind. Don't think of it and it will go away.

I always get two morning papers, the *Times* and the *Mirror*, and it must be that I feel a bit ashamed of this duplicity, for when I come into the office and pass Miss Moss I always have the *Mirror* tucked away inside the *Times*, as though it would not do for a person in my position to be seen carrying the *Daily Mirror*. That is nonsense, of course, for in a number of ways the *Mirror* is the more interesting paper—and anyway Miss Moss has ample opportunity during the day to see that I do in fact read it—but I still carry it hidden within the *Times*.

On the morning I am telling you of, I scarcely bothered with the *Times* at all, perhaps out of a feeling that I must be distracted from my little itch or tickle by stronger medicine. On the front of the *Mirror* there was the picture of a pale, dark-eyed young girl who looked at the camera (and at me) with an earnest, rather questioning expression—very serious, and yet as though she were just about to break into a smile. According to the caption beneath this photo, the young woman had been arrested "in connection with a city-wide probe of high-price vice." It seemed a shame for such a sweet-looking girl to be involved in anything so sordid; one look at her, and you would have the certain feeling that there must have been a mistake. Those dark, serious eyes . . . I felt a fatherly tenderness toward this person whom I had never met, and for one absurd moment actually considered coming forward and offering myself as a character witness.

"Your Honor, I have known the defendant since she was a child in the cradle. . . ."

I could not fail to notice that my foot was tickling rather badly, and without ceasing to read I ground my heel angrily down and around in the shoe, but without much effect.

Of course, I am no innocent, and I know that prostitution does exist. It must, I say, and always will. People should be realistic about these things. In our business, when we entertain visitors from other cities, we often include an introduction to some young lady, a model perhaps, and if anything out of the way should take place, why, that is not our business—or in another sense that is exactly what it is, our *business!* But at the same time, one could not help feeling pity for those poor girls. Theirs is a sordid trade.

I stamped my heel up and down a few times. The irritation seemed to fade away, but as soon as I stopped it came back again. I began to get a little angry. It was a very unreasonable sensation.

There were also two pictures of a young man "shot to death by police in accident," and it appeared from the accompanying story that this poor fellow met his end while chasing an armed robber who had held up his father's place of business; the police, joining in late, had mistaken him for the man he was after, and here he was, dead. One picture showed a white-sheeted bundle lying on a rainy road near a street lamp, with white faces of policemen grouped above, in the darkness; the other showed a smiling young man in cap and gown holding a diploma. How dreadful! That it had happened by mistake, and that even the stern policemen would have apologized if they could, made it so much worse.

But by now the sensation under my heel would not be denied. Not that it had got worse; no, it was the very gentleness and subtle constancy of its suggestion that began to get badly on my nerves and prevented me from concentrating further on the news.

I began to think seriously what I might do. If I could have thrown myself vigorously into some difficult work there is no doubt I should not have noticed my little trouble for the rest of the morning; it was after all so slight an inconvenience, it did not have even the ominous suggestion that it might be the first symptom of something else, something much worse. Not even a pain, merely a nuisance.

But—it was perhaps the penalty of my position—no work offered itself to be done. My habit was to read the papers until Miss Moss brought in the letters typed from yesterday afternoon's dictation, and these I would then sign. After that I would confer with the heads of several departments, make a brief tour of inspection through the building, and by then it would be time for lunch.

I concluded that I had better take off my shoe and sock and make an investigation. Perhaps there would be some little abrasion, perhaps a splinter—it might be nothing more than a piece of foreign matter in the heel of the shoe itself, and really not at all to do with my foot.

It seemed to me that I was extraordinarily naked, sitting there in the office alone with my bare, white foot. An office is so much the place for being fully clothed and in your right mind, so much *not* the place—my office, anyhow—for any sort of disrobing and informality, that I really felt rather foolish. And my empty shoe, too, gaped at me from the floor with its open mouth and the smiling crack across the toes. This was disturbing, and I recalled that in my boyhood, getting up and out of bed on a school morning, the first thing I used to see would be my shoes, which seemed to stare at me like idiots from the floor beside the bed. How that used to enrage me! But of course there was never anything I could do about it.

There was also, I now noticed, a slight, cold draft at the floor level, though the rest of the room was if anything too warm.

It is always an odd and disturbing sensation one has when forced to observe closely a part of one's own body which one does not usually see—which one cannot, say, see directly, at least not without considerable inconvenience, and which one does not as a rule confront in the mirror. It is something of a shock, I find, to have to acknowledge the real presence of such a part, which is coarser and uglier than any ideal impression we may carelessly have formed of it. So now with the sole of my foot.

It was difficult enough, in the first place, to get a good look at the spot I wanted. Finally I had to crook my knee up so that I could rest the heel on the glass top of the desk, and then force the toes rather painfully down to bring the surface of the heel to such an angle that by leaning forward and to the left side I could inspect it closely. Even so, I was still looking rather along the surface than at it.

The flesh there was at once hard and resilient, rubbery; mingled with its healthy pink was a disagreeable yellowish tinge. When I probed with my fingers, however, both colors fled away, leaving the skin very white, only to flood back in something revoltingly like a blush when I released the pressure.

I could readily enough locate the focal point of the sensation, the tickling. But I could not for the life of me see anything there that accounted for it. There was no bump, no swelling, no pimple, no particular sign of irritation or bruising, no cut. Something like a little splinter lay perhaps half an inch or so away from the spot, and thinking that I had located the source of the bother, I happily managed to tease it out by means of my tie pin; but the little itch remained unaffected by this surgery. Now I pressed the place itself with the sharp point of the pin, and this gave some relief, though the tickling began again as soon as I let go.

I was unwilling to probe more deeply with the pin out of a feeling that, hard as was the surface flesh of the foot, hardened by a life of walking, by so much would the under layers be soft and tender, and I did not know how deep or shallow the surface layer might be. Besides, there was the danger of infection; before going any deeper I would be well advised to sterilize the tie pin by holding it in a match flame, and I considered that was making altogether too much of the matter.

At the same time, the thought flashed through my mind that there would be something vastly relieving if I were to plunge the pin right to the hilt in my flesh, there at the spot from which this insane tickling emanated. The violence of this idea made me shudder slightly, half horrified and half pleasurably attracted.

There was a perfunctory knock on the door and Miss Moss entered.

Everything happened so rapidly, so much of a piece and in the one moment, that it is all but impossible to say whether I succeeded in getting my foot down and behind the desk before she saw it. Probably I did, and yet it is likely too that there remained with Miss Moss the clear, fleeting and ridiculous retinal impression of her employer's naked foot on the desk as she walked in. There it was, and then there it was not; her consciousness, I think, could have taken in this piece of news only to reject it as an extravagance, the remainder—for it was still early in the day—of last night's dreaming.

We looked at each other, nonetheless, with some suspicion, Miss Moss and I. My feeling was that of the guilty child who thinks he has concealed the evidence of whatever crime he has just been up to, but who, as the room is keenly swept by adult eyes, dreads that every piece of furniture, and particularly anything the least bit out of place, is speaking against him. The *Daily Mirror*, for example, lay spread over the *Times* on the desk, near where my foot had been a moment before.

This Miss Moss had not been with us long, and I had not yet made any attempt to get to know her better than would serve our working purposes. In that connection, at any rate, she seemed a sweet-natured and capable girl, rather more reserved than most, perhaps even a little cold in temperament, and quite handsome. A girl of breeding, was my impression, and one would not want to rush things or make any coarse overture to this kind. I admired the air she had, of chaste young pride, even of a certain primness, yet I thought also that there must be a violence under that surface, and hoped to find out about it in time. With her, as with the girl pictured that morning in the *Mirror*, there would be more than met the eye. A secret, there was always a secret. The flesh of my foot continued to tickle as I met her look, and surreptitiously I rubbed my naked heel up and down against the carpet, which was however too soft to afford me any alleviation.

Miss Moss remained standing there while I signed the letters she had brought. It seemed to me that the cold, secret nakedness of my foot beneath the desk, hidden from her awareness but so present to mine, made a slight bond of intimacy between us. If you only knew, my dear, was my thought—though what her knowing this would have meant to our relations it is really difficult to say, as it is difficult to say why this absurd thought should have stayed in my head, as insistent as the tickle in my foot, all the time she stood in the room before my desk.

As soon as she had gone I placed my foot back on the desk

and resumed the examination, but with no better success than before; my foot refused to give up its secret. I would by now willingly have accepted a cure even without a diagnosis, and I began to scratch the place. Whereon I made the awkward discovery that I could not scratch hard enough to make any effect whatever, because of the ridiculous relation of the foot to the rest of the body, which made it impossible for me to exert any real pressure, especially with the left hand. I was in the position of that ancient Greek, whose picture I remember from the schoolbooks, who discovered the principle of the lever and announced that he could move the world if you gave him a place to stand.

I did not want to move the world but only to scratch, in a serious and effective manner, the heel of my foot—yet I too had to have a place to stand. I quickly ran my wheeled swivel chair over to the window and began rubbing my heel against the radiator grill. This might have been just what was required, except that when I put the pressure on the chair simply slipped away backward under me.

Then—and by this time I was really quite angry—I stood up and rubbed my naked foot back and forth in the carpet, heavily and for a long time, until the heat generated by friction became recognizable as pain. But I now discovered that this painful blistering effect, which ought to have overlaid the tickling and driven it out, or at any rate suppressed the consciousness of it, did no such thing. I could now feel, at once and separately, the pain and the tickling, neither one having any effect on the other. As soon as I realized this, of course, I stopped, but I had already badly blistered my foot; there was a raw, red place about the size of a half dollar, where I had rubbed right through the skin.

I put my shoe and sock back on. It was really ridiculous, I told myself, for a grown man to be behaving in this way. For what I had just done bore a very real resemblance to what a child might do in a rage, an ungovernable tantrum.

"Here the world is so full of suffering," I said, "and you cannot show the courage to disregard a little tickling sensation in your foot."

But I will not detail the way in which I got through the rest of the morning. I have said enough. All during lunch, which I took with three of my associates, my foot continued to bother me, so that I really paid little attention to what was being said. The one thing I did both hear and heed—it is odd how, under conditions that make us withdraw into a private world where we attend only to our own necessities and regard all else as a meaningless distraction, we are likely to be aware precisely of those remarks which are not innocent and have a bearing on our situation—was a brief exchange about a man whom I too remotely knew, who was now, they said, dying of cancer in the Harkness Pavilion. Three weeks ago, they said, he had been in health, or had seemed to be.

Now I did not, on hearing this news, fly into a panic and believe that the little sensation in my foot was the beginning of a cancer. But I began to think, after all, that at my age it paid to be careful, and the story of the man in the Harkness Pavilion—a name which presented to my mind the odd image of a tent on the desert, with blue and white banners waving over it and the sick man lying inside—offered me a kind of justification for taking myself and my ridiculous foot off to the doctor that afternoon. It was queer how I did not in the least believe my little complaint had anything to do with cancer, or with any reckonable illness, and how I yet, without that story, would have felt too ashamed to go before a doctor and have the matter looked into. But trivial as it all undoubtedly was, and therefore even a bit shameful, my foot nevertheless was beginning to impair my business efficiency, so that I owed it not only to myself but also to the corporation of which I was a member, to have it attended to. So after thinking it over in the office for a lonely hour after lunch, I announced to Miss Moss that I was leaving early.

"I hope you haven't hurt yourself," she said. "I see you are limping a little."

I looked at her strictly for an instant, to see if by chance this remark carried any sarcastic implication that she had after all caught me that morning with my foot up; but her blue eyes looked very guileless.

"It's nothing, thank you, Miss Moss," I said coolly as I left. Indeed, not on account of the affliction, which was not physically disabling, but on account of my savage attempt at a cure, my foot hurt very badly where the skin was stripped off—it stuck to my sock—and I had to favor it as I walked. But the tickling sensation remained perceptible right through the pain.

2 –

I have gone to Doctor Garvey for a number of years now, whenever illness has hit me, and I believe him to be thoroughly competent. He is, though, a rather crusty old gentleman—the vanishing type, almost, of the country practitioner, very oddly at home on Park Avenue—and I have sometimes felt he regards at least my minor ailments with contempt, as though they were moral questions. He is a rigid disciplinarian; when you put yourself in Garvey's hands you must expect to be told a few things, in an elevated tone, about the duty of keeping yourself fit; and you must expect also to do what you are told.

Bearing this in mind, I wondered whether I would not be better off with a specialist—whether one of those high-priced individuals would not very likely be more sympathetic to so niggling and altogether obscure a "disease." But I could not decide whether I wanted a foot specialist or a skin specialist—

and besides, was this not really coddling myself too much? I had better, I thought at last, go to Garvey and take my medicine.

In Garvey's waiting room I had time to look through a news magazine or so. But my heel was tickling me by now so very much—as though impatiently conscious of imminent relief, or I was regarding it in my mind so constantly—that I scarcely paid much attention to what I read. Painful as it was, I could not resist rubbing my foot, though very gently, up and down on the carpet, and this seemed greatly to annoy a fierce, white-haired gentleman with his arm in a sling who came in after me and sat in a chair opposite, whence he directed steadily on my foot a glare of displeasure. I resented this, though of course I could not say so, and also began to pity myself somewhat. Your injury—I turned my thoughts on the old gentleman—is superficially serious, it makes a good appearance, it is a real, recognizable hurt, a broken arm, which everyone would acknowledge and sympathize with. Yet it is really nothing. It may be, after all, that my trivial and invisible tickling is far more serious, more deeply serious— even though you, sir, would doubtless laugh were I to mention it. And I was extremely pleased that the nurse called me into the consulting room ahead of him; I felt I had scored a small victory.

Garvey sat there with his hands folded on the desk: big, powerful hands, very white but with thick dark hair on the backs of the fingers. He regarded me intently out of his keen blue eyes while I, with a sheepish and diffident attitude, told him my trouble.

"Well, let's have a look at it," he said in an indifferent, bored voice when I had done. "Come on now, off with the shoe and sock."

He was speaking to me, I noticed, as he might to a child who had already shown resistance to his care. A professionally wheedling tone, ready to become severe. I obeyed, and he knelt down to take my foot between his hands. He reached up and directed the desk lamp to the spot.

"This what you mean?" touching the blister.

I winced. "No," I replied. "I'm afraid I did that myself, trying to get rid of the tickle."

He looked up at me earnestly for a moment with his blue, expressionless eyes, as though trying to penetrate my thought.

"But it tickles right here," he insisted, putting his finger, indeed, on the exact place. "That is the spot?"

"Yes."

"There was no swelling, no mark, a blister or anything like that? I mean, before you rubbed the skin off?"

"No, Doctor, there was not."

"Umph." He got to his feet and sat down again behind the desk. My foot stood alone and white on the floor.

"I'll give you something to take away the pain," he said. "It will heal that blistering in a few days. As for the other, the tickling, as you call it—I don't see anything there, of course. You've rubbed off the skin. Probably some slight inflammation of the epidermis there. The flesh on the palm of the foot is quite tough, indurated, you know, and you'd feel as mere tickling there what would be a pain on another part of the body. It will probably go away of its own accord when the blister heals, if not before."

"Then it's your opinion I've nothing to worry about?"

"Worry about? Worry about?" There was a pause. "Worry about it all you like," Dr. Garvey added cryptically.

"But it's not serious, then?" I insisted on having an explicit statement.

"I imagine you had decided it was cancer," he said with a broad smile. I smiled too.

"Of course I knew it was silly," I replied, "but one can't be too careful."

"All you people are frightened to death of it these days, aren't you?" he said, still smiling steadily.

I could not imagine what he meant: all what people?

"You can put on your shoe and sock again," he said. "I'll give you an ointment that you can apply as soon as you get home. There is a great deal of propaganda about cancer these days, isn't there? It's the disease in fashion, I suppose—a few generations ago it was TB; now it's cancer. We get what we ask for. But I shouldn't worry about it just now if I were you. When it hits you, if it does, you won't have any trouble recognizing it."

Going to his cabinet, he got out a tin of salve and wrote a few instructions on the cover before giving it to me. Plainly he regarded the whole business as so trivial that he would not soil his hands by dressing my blister himself.

"Well, then, off with you," he said jovially, not offering to shake hands. "Cancer. Ha. Don't be ridiculous."

And so I was dismissed. The old man from the waiting room passed me in the hall with a glance of strange anger, as though I had purposely taken up time belonging to him.

Now I had the salve in my overcoat pocket, and in my mind the assurance that I was not really ill. On the way home I bought a couple of evening papers and felt rather relieved. And not until I was settled down in my armchair with the news, having first applied the ointment according to directions and put my foot up on the hassock and made myself quite comfortable, did I realize that the one thing Garvey had not done—had not indeed paid any real attention to—was rid me of that tickling sensation. It was still there, even through the blister and even through the ointment, and if it had got no worse neither had it got any better.

Then it was that I began to feel very bad, very blue. I tried to read the papers, but I could not concentrate on anything except the tickling in my heel. There was another picture of the young prostitute, but it had been taken from a different angle, or in a different light, and she looked not so young or so innocent now. I thought without pleasure of Miss Moss, and it seemed to me I knew, whatever ideas I had entertained on the subject, that Miss Moss would never in fact enter this comfortable bachelor establishment of mine, and that I would never get to know what sexual frenzy and bitter, lecherous violence lay behind that cool, clear forehead and in the depths of those cool eyes. I lived alone by choice, of course, but it had never struck me till now how there was really very little choice about it. My heel, my absurd heel of Achilles, would go on tickling until—why, until it stopped, of course. What more could be said? See a doctor? I had already done so. My ailment was so slight, it seemed, as to be beneath medicine. When I asked myself—assuming this thing continued, as it seemed likely to do—what I would do about it, what I could do about it, the answer came back very simply: nothing; you can do nothing. Suffer. That is all. It is something you have to live with. Forget about it when you can, and when you cannot, think about it. Perhaps, even, you will be unable to sleep, or if you do get to sleep the little tickle will develop itself night long in fantastic flowering shapes through your dreams, so that your sleep will not in any sense rest or refresh you but will be merely a different experience of the tickle, or itch. But very probably you will not be able to sleep at all, and will die of a white fatigue and inanition and draining away of blood.

Probably something like that is what Garvey meant when he said, "Worry about it all you like."

A Commodity of Dreams

IN A LITTLE BLACK HOUSE in the woods the dreamer lived; and I met him when I was lost, hungry and ill tempered. But I still had wit enough about me to realize, as I rushed forward to ask directions, how odd it was that there should stand, before a little black cottage in the woods, a uniformed and armed personage,whose appearance suggested some combination of beadle, commissionaire and constable; he wore a black greatcoat with golden buttons, a leather belt from which hung, on one side, a great pistol, and on his head, incongruously, was a silk hat. He stood at ease, and did not actually change his posture as I came up, but seemed to grow slightly more tense and to take, with rapidly flickering eyes, a kind of professional survey of me, which finally fixed on the binoculars slung about my neck.

"Bird-watching," I said in explanation. "I've got lost. Perhaps you could direct me to the road." There was a silence, which lasted a few seconds until I got nervous enough to add,

"Any road, of course," and to realize, as the silence settled back, how silly this must sound.

"Ah," he said finally, and, following with my eyes the slight turn of his head, I saw, a few yards off to the side of the cottage, a modern building of brick and concrete mostly sunken in the earth, like a hurricane cellar, or a bomb shelter. It occurred to me that I had come across some highly secret military installation or experimental center.

"Maybe," said the guard, who looked in the fading light to be an old, probably feeble man and had drooping white mustaches which made a pathetic assertion at the front of his somewhat shrunken face. "But you'd best come see the Master, all the same."

"Oh, that's not necessary at all," I said politely, struggling with a slight feeling of annoyance. "I'm sorry to have to bother you—" But I was talking to the empty doorway; he had gone inside. In a moment a lantern appeared in his place, and behind it, lighted from below, a little, sandy man—not only with sandy hair, that is, but of a very light, pebble-grained appearance, washed out, desiccated, leached away by some receding torrent and left, it appeared, to crumble at his leisure. A scientist, certainly, was my thought, and this is some government work he has been put away here to do secretly.

"Come in, won't you," he said, and this phrase of peremptory hospitality left me no choice, for he turned away at once. As we went within, the old guardian of the place slipped by me and resumed his post.

"You'll have tea, of course," said the sandy man, leading the way with the lantern into a room otherwise lighted only by firelight. "I'll get another cup." And he vanished into some shadowy, low-ceilinged area beyond the fireplace.

"I've only come to ask my way," I called after him, but this explanation, and even the voice in which I offered it, sounded curiously weak in the silence and the gloom.

"We'll soon set you straight," came the reply out of the darkness. "I have to be careful, though, of course."

Careful? Of what? And yet, surely a military or government man would have said, as they always do, *we*—"*We* have to be careful."

My host now returned, carrying a cup and saucer of very delicate china, through which the firelight shone. We stood for a moment, then, as there seemed little else for it, sat down in opposed chairs, and regarded each other in the fire's light.

"Sugar? You're an American, you very likely don't take milk? Perhaps you don't even care for tea?"

"A cup of tea would be fine," I said. Looking more closely at the man, I found, in addition to his sandy quality of failure and debilitation, some effect of sharp cunning, of pertinaciousness, in his small, close-set features: little eyes, of an indistinguishable color, a small, pointy nose. "It's nice of you to take the trouble," I added, "but I've really got to be getting on right away."

As Englishmen so often do, he took no notice of what I said, but went right along on his own line with another question which was not a question but an assertion.

"You'll have been up seeing the waxwings. Pretty little things; I often watch them myself." And he handed me across a plate of little cakes.

"It'd be very strange, waxwings in March," I said with a smile. How shrewd the little man was. Doubly shrewd to choose waxwings; though they don't winter in Britain they should have sounded plausible to an American because they do winter far north in the United States. And triply shrewd to pass the cake at the same moment, as a distraction. And yet, since I had seen through it, by luck and an odd shred of information, it all looked pretty silly, too.

"And the mustached warbler," he went on, without returning my smile.

"Look," I said, "I am obviously a bona-fide bird-watcher, or I wouldn't have known about the waxwings. And now you've put me on my guard I am certainly not going to consent to any mustached warbler other than the one who stands outside your door. I don't know what it is you do up here, and I've no idea of pushing my way in to find out—in fact, though it is good of you to give me tea, I ask nothing better than to be shown off your property and on to a public highway just as soon as it can be arranged."

"That's all very well," he said in a kind of mean and aggrieved way. "We welcome legitimate visitors, you know, at the proper hours. There was no need to come up out of the woods at nightfall."

I repeated, tersely, to all this, that I had got lost, that I had explained myself once, twice and again. "And that should be enough," I concluded.

"Yes, I suppose so," he said, strangely disconsolate. And we sat there for a few minutes not knowing exactly what to say. I wanted to go, and I felt I ought to go; but there was no point in going without directions. Also I was tired, and the tea was welcome, and whatever the spirit might say the body was very unwilling to stir itself. For his part, he seemed to be going through some intricate calculation about me, outwardly signified by keen stares, shakings of the head, even slight mumblings into the teacup, until I decided he was simply wrong in the head.

"You Americans are very self-centered people, aren't you?" he finally came forth. "Egotistical, not very interested in others?"

"I am not very interested," I said, "in sentences beginning *You Americans.*"

"You haven't even asked me what sort of place this is."

"If I had, you would most likely have said, 'You Americans are always sticking your noses in other people's business.' I assume," I added, "that whatever you've got in that bomb shelter outside is a military secret."

This seemed to please him, for he laughed. At least he tittered for such a time, and at so high a pitch, that it got on my nerves, and I said, "It must be depressing to have a military secret so ineffably dull that you can't persuade people to ask what it is." This stopped the tittering, all right. He looked very sad all of a sudden, and said, "Yes."

That *yes*, dull as it was, put a stop to conversation for the time being, except for his presently adding, "Not military, though," after which the silence again closed in. But it was enough, with the tea and the mystery, to get my attention; for if military secrets interested me not at all, civilian ones vastly did. I began to see that this middle-aged, dried-up, not superficially attractive person had a secret, whatever it was, for the one purpose only of revelation—what else are secrets good for?—and that, hidden away (for secrecy's sake!) up here in the forest, he must have but small audience, occasional and stray, whose want of curiosity would appear to him as a major disaster.

"I am, you see, a dreamer," he said at last, with a curious mixture in his tone of pride, apology and the most awful humiliation. "A dreamer," he repeated, somewhat more aggressively.

Did he mean a poet? an inventor? a mystic, hermit? Would he, when he led me (as he surely meant to do) into his brick workshop, show me an epic, a new cosmogony, the first flying machine, a plan to establish universal peace or predict the future?

"There's no reason why I shouldn't show you around," he said, and with evident effort brought himself to add, "If you like, that is."

"Oh, I really can't stay," I said, rising, for I was still

annoyed at his absurdity and determined to show no interest whatever.

"It wouldn't take you but a few minutes," he said with a sad petulance, "but I suppose you're very busy . . ."

This attitude made me a little ashamed; I saw also something pleasingly silly in the spectacle of two grown men in a cottage in the woods at nightfall, one saying to the other, "I suppose you're very busy."

"It's not that I'm not interested," said I. "For a few minutes, maybe. It's really very kind of you."

He led, and I followed his lantern out the front door, where the old gentleman in the silk hat immovably stood. It was by now quite dark. The lantern stopped and swung about suddenly, and I bumped into my host, who merely said, "I'm sor—sorry, Mr. Uh?" while the lantern bobbed down and up as if he were bowing. So we exchanged names there in the dark; his was Captain Lastwyn. He even gave me his card, which I put in my pocket. When he turned again and held up the lantern, I saw, beside the doorway of the brick building, a black sign with gold letters which read:

Museum & Library
of
Dreams
WEEKDAYS 10-4 CLOSED SUNDAYS
ADMISSION 6D.

"It's all a trifle irregular, in your case," he said, "so we'll not trouble about the sixpence."

"Oh, no," I said, determined by now that every form of our little farce should be gone through with. "I insist on paying in the usual manner."

"Well, sir, you are very kind," he said, with embarrassing deference, in accepting the coin. The exchange of money, however, seemed to put us in a different, more manageable relation, and by the time he had opened the door of his cellar and we had descended into it, by the time he had switched on the light—there was electricity laid on here, though none had been evident in the cottage—and turned to address me, he had a new authority in his manner.

"Perhaps you'd care to sign the guest book?" leading me to a register on a deal table to one side. I signed, noting the last entry before mine to be dated three weeks before. It was, certainly, an odd spot for a museum.

"How very interesting," I said, insincerely, and for want of something to say. For so far as I could see, except for some pictures on the walls, two reading tables with chairs, and a long glass cabinet in the center of the room, the entire establishment consisted of filing cabinets, which neatly lined the walls and here and there jutted out into the room to form alcoves.

"Ah, well," he said, correctly interpreting the falsity in my tone, "it reveals itself, the museum does, only rather slowly. You'll scarcely have time to form an impression." Again he made me feel a little ashamed, for being caught sneering at his pathetic exhibition. "Perhaps you'd best start by having a look over here," he said, indicating the glass cabinet.

I went over and looked in. At the center was a neat type-written card which read: "Objects and Facsimiles of Objects of Frequent or Striking Appearance in the Dreams of Capt. Frank Lastwyn, R.A. (ret.)." To both sides the "objects" were neatly mounted with pins and glue on a kind of gray cloth, very professional and museumlike in style. There was, for example, a little silver cup, rather bent, such as is given to parents at the birth of a child; there was a gull's feather; a snuffbox; a tiny crucifix on a golden chain; a woman's hat, very old and dirty; a horse's hoof; a table napkin comically knotted to resemble a rabbit; a schoolbook, a battered Greek primer open at a line drawing of two naked wrestlers; a stuffed woodcock with the beak missing. I moved around to the other side, and there were more objects: the cover of a golf ball, a dinner plate with a red, open-mouthed fish painted on it; a pair of gold spectacle rims with the glass broken out; a piece of rough rock and masonry with a hole in it; and a number of other things I can't remember.

"You've no idea the trouble I was put to getting some of these things," said my guide, who followed at my shoulder while I inspected the things. "That crucifix, there, belonged to a young lady—in my youth, you know. She died. And by the time I knew I needed that piece, of course, you know how it is—her family had moved, her brother was dead too, no one seemed to know where her younger sister had moved to or even what her name was—she had married, you see. But I persisted, and as it turned out she had the crucifix, was glad to have someone who remembered to give it up to. We had a cry over it.

"That hat, now—took me four years, from the time I first dreamed of that hat, till I remembered it was hers, my young lady's. Just came to me, one afternoon. *That* one—" pointing at the hat in the cabinet—"that one's a facsimile, of course; no one would have saved a thing like that. But it's an exact likeness; it was on a market day in Bedford I saw it, recognized it straight off, and bought it up.

"The rock and masonry piece, here, doesn't exactly belong. It's from the Roman Wall over yonder, that they dug up in thirty-nine. Not that I didn't dream of the Wall, and often, mind you, but I never dreamed that exact piece." He smiled rather confidingly at me, and added poetically that he kept it because remembering one's dreams was, after all, something like "digging up a Roman Wall, especially a piece with a hole in it."

"Yes," I said, turning to face him. "So you really are a

dreamer, after all? I thought you meant you were some kind of inventor, or possibly an artist—you know, impractical."

"Oh, no. I never had any talents along those lines, sir," he gravely replied.

"And these, I take it, are the dreams?" I gestured at the line of filing cabinets. "What a vast lot of them there must be."

"It is not, actually, that there are so many dreams," he said. "It is the cross-filing that takes up the space. Of actual dreams there are, I should say, only slightly more than three thousand at this moment. But it did, one day, occur to me that if the collection were to be of any real use it had to be articulated, indexed, catalogued for ready reference." He smiled at me once again, a rather touching smile. "There was trouble, if you like—and cost, as well. The typing alone—I had to give up recording new dreams, as a regular thing, for several months, while I made copies of the old ones. But it was all most instructive. I had the town librarian in, for the filing. A nice woman, but she could make nothing of it; she would have stuck things away under the headings she was accustomed to—dreams of economics, philosophical dreams, religious dreams, dreams of domestic science, poetry, fiction . . . She was an odd one. At last I lost my patience with her. 'My dear lady,' I said—but there's no point in my telling you all this, is there? Perhaps, instead, you'll examine a sample of the kind of things we did?"

Captain Lastwyn opened a drawer, hunted swiftly through the folders neatly ranged there, pitched decisively on one and brought it out to the nearest table, where he spread it out, continuing meanwhile to talk about filing.

"I got, finally, a very nice girl, university trained, who had done inventories for one of the big shops—Harrod's, I think. She understood right away what I was about, and we worked it out together. Have a look here."

At his direction I sat down before the open folder, which contained, in typescript, with a date, the following record:

> I am in the hallway of a strange house, with stone flagging on the floor. My feet are bare. At the end of the hallway I see daylight, and the surf of the sea breaking up on the flags. Mrs. Page, whom I cannot see clearly, says in a loud voice, "Time to trump the geese." I wake up, very fearful.

"Yes," I said. "I see—" conscious in a bemused way that there was so much I did not see at all.

"That is the reading copy," he said, turning the page. "Now here is what I like to call my Variorum edition."

On the next page the dream appeared again, but here heavily annotated. Captain Lastwyn ran his finger down the margin.

"The stone flagging, you see, occurs in numerous dreams of this period; their index numbers and dates are given here; so also with Mrs. Page. Here, in red ink, we refer to dreams in which Mrs. Page appears in combination with some other person. Dreams of the sea are catalogued so; and here is a list of references to other dreams which end with my waking in fright.

"Completeness, you see," he said, drawing himself up and walking a few paces away. "Completeness at all times, and absolute control over the materials. That is the object. And that, too," he added, relaxing, "is what takes up so much space."

"What a fascinating hobby," I murmured, continuing to look at the page because I did not just then wish to meet his eyes.

"Of course, if you like to look at it that way," he said, in a resumption of his former grumpy tone.

"I didn't mean *hobby* as a reflection on it," I said.

"It takes up all my time," said he simply.

"I'm certain, in fact, that it is a work of great potential value."

"Ah, as to that, only the future can tell." He rummaged in a filing cabinet at some distance and brought over three or four more folders.

"These are very recent," he announced in a tone of some little artistic vanity. I dutifully read through them all, admired the cross-indexing, the cataloguing—the completeness and control. When I used these words, Captain Lastwyn evidently became quite pleased with me.

"You've been, I gather, psychoanalyzed?" I said at last.

At this he looked not quite offended but rather blank.

"No," he said. "I never saw the need." Then, as though feeling the incompleteness of this, he added, "It would rather spoil the beauty of the dreams themselves, I've always thought."

"Do you have many visitors," I asked, "to your museum?"

"No, not a great many," he confessed. "A few stray walkers, like yourself. And on Saturday afternoons, in fine weather, a number of people from the town come out. But they haven't," he added hesitantly, "the serious view. Want me to read palms, and so forth."

"Well, you are rather off the beaten track here, aren't you? Still," I said, "I should think, when the word got around a bit, there'd be clusters of psychiatrists and such out here, and maybe a few novelists and poets—sort of picking up images where they could, you know. You'd become a fad."

"There's the danger," said Captain Lastwyn seriously.

"Danger?" I echoed. "But surely you want people to know? You *seem* to want people to know."

"Well, sir," he said, walking nervously up and down behind me, "I do, and I don't."

As I had nothing to say to this I sat still, idly turning the pages of one of his folders, then of another, reading a sentence here and there: "I am at school again . . ." "I wake in a mood of deep despair . . ." " 'You must eat until you see the fish on the plate,' says my mother . . ." Ah, you strange, strange man, I thought, you strange little sandy sandman, you are about to tell me something, you are pacing up and down and up and down, but soon you will decide.

There was the scrape of a chair across the tile floor; in a single motion Captain Lastwyn placed it before me, across the table, and straddled it. His chin rested on the back, his wishy-washy eyes looked into mine, I noticed for the first time that he had a thin, sandy mustache, and he said, "I haven't had much of a life, you know, in the ordinary sense."

Oh, dear, was my thought at this inauspicious beginning.

"But then," he continued, "who has? I mean, what is it all about, what does it leave you with, after the shouting, what do you remember of it?"

These questions clearly required no answer from me.

"I lost my wife quite early on; we had one child, a boy, who was killed in the desert in forty-three. I was shot up early in the war myself, and invalided out. My being a professional soldier in the first place was accident; I'm not really the type, you can see that—or if not accident, then just the way such things are arranged . . . or were." He paused. "We were what used to be called a good family," he added, "and we always had one son in the army. It was natural, you see."

"Yes," I said, to help him over this point, where he seemed to want to stick.

"Funny—" he took it up in a new tone—"how you're brought up well, on such and such an amount of money; you become used to living in a certain way—but because there are, all that time, five of you, brothers and sisters, each one, at last, can have only at most one fifth of that. *And* things getting dearer every day, *and* at the same time meaner. Funny."

"Things are getting harder everywhere," said I.

"Ah, it's not that, not that alone," he quickly said. "They know what they're doing, of course." *They* being, presumably, the Government. "It's that all our lives it's the same way; we're cut down and down and down.

"When I came back here—that was the keeper's cottage, the one I live in now—when I came back, I thought about such things a great deal. Oh, yes, a great deal. But thought did nothing; thought is like everything else, a cheat. I began to dream."

"You began to dream," I affirmed, like a chorus in *The Mikado*.

"I wanted, do you see, to save something out of it all." He put this with peculiar vigor, as though such an idea could be got across by brute strength alone. "I know, I know, dreams can't make us immortal—but can't they double our lives, our experiences—triple them, multiply them by, who knows, an indefinite factor?"

I said, truly, that I had never thought of this before.

"*If*—" and he raised an emphatic finger—"*if* we truly possess them."

"Ay, there's the rub," I said.

"Think, then," went on Captain Lastwyn, seeming actually to glitter with a kind of dry, sandy light of exaltation suitable to his nature, "if we do not forget, do not let go, but hang on—" he clenched his fist in midair—"hang on to the end!"

"What then?"

"Why, we've had," and he seemed to look for a sufficient expression, hesitated, lost it, and concluded simply, "we've had so much *more*."

"More what?"

"Life."

"Ah."

"I began to dream." He returned to the attack. "I taught myself, by practice, to remember. I kept a pad and pencil by the bed, and in the morning I would copy out what happened there—" and he waved back over his shoulder as though to some definite place. "It was quite easy, after a while, though now and then, I find something in me doesn't want to remember."

"How did you overcome that?" I asked, thinking of all that psychiatry had to say about *resistances*, and glad to have, for a change, some constructive question.

"Ordinary strength, sir," he said in a modest yet perceptibly military way. His shoulders straightened slightly. "All things yield in time, one learns that in the service, though the mind doctors," he added, exactly catching my thought, "won't allow it." And now he leaned forward to me, to say quietly, with intensity, "I have seen it all—again."

"Again?"

"The little boys and girls, my home, the way we used to live, the little things which happened that one doesn't remember. I've had them all back, I have them all back."

"Here?" I asked, indicating the files.

"Here, and inside me." He bowed his head a little, and added, "I have seen my father smile again, and spoken to my mother—though we said only silly things." As he raised his head I was not surprised to see tears in his eyes. "It was all out of control," he added, "and jumbled up. But it was there, and I saw it.

"You can understand," he added in a firmer voice, "why I'd not be interested in psychoanalysis. It is my dreams I want, and I want them for themselves."

"Yes, I understand," said I, hovering for a moment, a little insanely myself, between criticism and sympathy.

"I can dream at any time I want, now," he said brightly. "I can drop off in the middle of the day. In a few seconds I can spend hours elsewhere."

"It is a marvelous power," I said, and we sat in silence for a few moments until I added, "But what about all this?" meaning, generally, the museum and library.

"Yes, all this," he agreed glumly. "It started simply enough. I wanted to have a record, you see. After all, the idea was not to lose it once one had got it back. And it is history, isn't it, like anything else?" He pronounced the word *history* with a certain reverence.

I had, on this, a brief, confused impression of pyramids, battles of Marathon, Yankee Stadium, long rows of thick volumes, lonely stacks of documents . . . "Yes," I said, "that it is."

Captain Lastwyn seemed pleased at this but sank back after a moment into his gloom, and said somberly, "But it costs money, it takes time, one can't simply let things go, they must be kept up in order, mustn't they?"

"Completion and control," said I.

"And then there's the danger of theft," he said. "Which is why I keep Rennett with me—" gesturing toward the cottage —"he used to live here, in the old days. He was the head keeper when my father lived."

"Insurance—" I began.

"What could replace it?" he asked mildly. "It's not worth anything that money can pay for."

"But just in case," I insisted. "If it burned down, for instance . . . "

"If it went," he said, "I should go too." He looked at me keenly, as keenly as those faded eyes could, and said, "I have terrible fears about it, you know."

"I know," said I.

"I'm proud of it and want people to see it. It is something to have done in this world, isn't it? Not much, but something

—a man with his history, complete, like this? And yet, I have the most dreadful fears."

"That people may steal it?" I asked, smiling.

"That people are stealing it, with every look they give. That I have somehow, very painfully, thrown myself open to the world."

"At sixpence a throw," I reminded him.

"But I must, don't you see," he said half apologetically and yet with a certain quick effect of anger. "I can't support it all on my own."

"But you admit you don't take in many sixpences. It couldn't be much support."

"No."

"So that the whole enterprise is more or less going to pieces at this moment?"

"Yes."

"And you won't advertise it a bit, to scholars and such?"

"No," he said stubbornly, and though his head was bowed I had the idea he was again crying, or nearly. "I don't want—scholars. I shall carry on while I am able. And after that—" He let it go here, and stood up. "I've kept you rather long," he said. "Didn't mean to bore you with my woes. Sometimes, you know, one wants to talk."

"I know," said I, also getting up. "I suppose you have a fund for maintenance? If someone should make a donation?"

"No, I haven't," he said, watching me closely while I got out my wallet.

"You should have," I said. "Let me begin it." I held out a pound note. "I am interested in the work and would like to see it go on."

"Well, sir, you are very kind," he said again, and took the money. Again it seemed that our relation had changed, and we stood in a silence very constrained.

"I'll show you to your bus stop," he finally offered, and I

agreed that it was time I went. I took one last look at the Museum & Library of Dreams before he turned off the light, and then we set off down a crooked path through the woods, he leading the way with the lantern held high, and I following.

It was a short walk; evidently I had first approached his house from the other side, the road being only over the hill. But in the darkness of the country night I somehow felt more deeply than I had inside the poignant oddity of Captain Lastwyn's life, its desperate and compromised endeavor to salvage the ruins and hulks of time, keep them somehow safe, and exhibit them for sixpence.

We came out at a bus stop in a little lane arched over with branches. Beside the bus signal was a replica of the sign at the museum door. Captain Lastwyn shifted the lantern to his left hand, evidently with some idea of shaking hands. But he seemed to think better of it, and we stood there.

"You'll get your bus here all right," he assured me. I thanked him, and said he need not wait with me. But he seemed unwilling to leave and, finally, after some pawing of the ground, asked me if I thought he was a happy man. "As much, I mean, as any of us can be said to be? In your opinion?"

"Why, yes," I said after a pause intended to look like deep consideration. "You have, as you said, your history, complete, and that's more than most of us can say."

"Yes," he said gravely. And we stood there some more, until after a few minutes we saw the lights of the bus approaching.

"When I die," Captain Lastwyn said to me by way of farewell, "I have arranged to leave it all to the British Museum."

"Indeed?" I asked, as the bus drew to a stop. And as I stood on the step and the bus began to move he grinned broadly all

of a sudden and called after me, with his first and last show of
humor.

"What'll they make of it, those poor beggars, do you
think?"

"I've no idea," I shouted back, turning away.

The inside of the bus was crowded, so I went up on top,
where I was able to settle into a front seat and watch the deep
lanes unroll in the headlights.

The British Museum, I thought. That was probably the
place for it; they must have stranger things even than dreams
stored away in that great marble and granite barn, among the
plundered and boughten confusion of empires. They would,
at the British Museum, look at it all twice, and imperturbably
file it away under *Dreams* . . . which was probably where
everything, after all, belonged. We were all, I thought sleep-
ily, going down in history, whether as Tamerlane or Genghis
Khan, Beethoven, St. Francis or Nesselrode who invented the
pudding. Or as Capt. Frank Lastwyn, R.A. (ret.), or as
anonymous nobodies, such as myself. And ho-hum to it all.

The conductress appeared, and when I stated my destina-
tion, said; "Yer on the wrong bus."

"Wrong bus?"

"Going the wrong way. You should have crossed the
street." She was very kind about all this, but clearly she
doubted my ability to cross the street unaided.

"Where does this bus go, then?"

"The other way. Ampthill."

I considered this, being very sleepy and under no necessity
of going back to my hotel this night.

"I could, I guess, get a meal and a room at Ampthill?"

"You could," she said doubtfully, for now I was behaving
queerly, like a foreigner.

"Very well, to Ampthill, then," I said, and gave her a note
to change. While she counted out the money I thought again

of Captain Lastwyn. How typical that his final effect on my destiny should be to put me on the wrong road; or on the right road but going the wrong way. Then I remembered that I had never, after all, told him where I was going, but foolishly got on the first bus which presented itself.

"Yer change," the conductress said, a little nastily.

"Oh, yes, thanks," I said, taking the money and looking into her face, a very pretty but very tired face framed in terribly peroxided hair, and with clear blue eyes. Behind it, clearly, was a thought which began, These Americans . . . ! while on my side I was thinking, These dreamers . . . ! And the huge bus blundered along among the branches of the leafy lane.

The Web of Life

IT SEEMED AT ONE TIME that my great-uncle Magus might achieve immortality. I do not mean that immortality, so unctuously offered by religion, of the incorporeal part; nor that of Plato's souls flapping on some huge clothesline strung across the sunlit void; nor yet that slender immortality of fame that the poets speak of: but the immortality of flesh itself, the feeble, final, blotchy-skinned and cantankerous immunity from time, the disaster of the Struldbrugs. It is an interesting speculation—though out of place here—that there may be immortals among us. One daydreams of them sometimes that they take their slow, nitwitted way across the world, forging their passports, collecting surreptitiously the odd and complicated proofs of their identity . . . and bowing with a horrible smirk of recognition on meeting one of their kind.

Of course in this particular instance it was an illusion, one to which the example of my great-uncle makes it appear the very old are much subject, of having emerged from the long tunnel of the years into a broad meadow where but for the electric buzzing of the sun silence is complete, where nothing of consequence is any longer likely to happen.

But then, Great-uncle Magus was not so old as all that. I was unduly impressed because I had lived with him thirty years since being orphaned at the age of five, and during all that time could not remember him to have changed—as what change would there be, to a young man's eyes, between the sixties and the nineties? His white bushy hair and eyebrows, the many-diamonded pattern of the back of his hand, the little muscles working in his jaw as with his mouth regrettably open he ruminated four times a day the characterless mash he immemorially had fed upon—none of these had changed. Nor was he above nourishing in his small grand-nephew the impression of his implacable permanence: he lied, and lied fantastically, about the great men of his acquaintance: Mr. Lincoln, Mr. Jackson, even the Father of our Country. ("I was a young man then," he said apologetically to the stupid little boy at his knee.) As I grew up I did not outgrow the lies. They became a mythology, and he an American Kronos, and I invited friends home from college to meet him and be impressed: "a fabulous old gentleman," I would earnestly say, showing off my only wonder.

Regarded objectively, my great-uncle Magus was a peevish, disagreeable creature as avaricious as wealthy, and he stank. I do not wish to mitigate the effect of that last by a euphemism, for the old gentleman unfortunately exuded corruption like a civet and was rather proud of it. But one becomes used to all things in time, and I was not in a position to regard him objectively: had he not given me so much? And would he not in the fullness of time give me so much more?

"It will all be yours," he would say, having no objection whatever to discussing the improbable event of his death. "I am leaving it all to you and your dear Audrey." My dear Audrey.

For among the many things Great-uncle had given me was, when I attained the suitable age of thirty, a wife. It is difficult to imagine, in retrospect, how Audrey was passed off on me as my distant and southern and poverty-ridden cousin, the last of some collateral line, for I had been brought up with all the suspiciousness of the very naïve. At any rate it was managed (to use the exact word) with a kind of cynical grace by Great-uncle, who brought us together as he might have coupled spaniels, by letting nature do the work.

"This is your cousin Audrey." A tall, dark young woman, slender and nervous, with eyes as brilliant as little marbles burning fiercely in her pallid face. She was given—in that palatial establishment so empty she might have had a wing to herself—the room next to mine. Life became mysterious, conspiratorial, exciting—for about a month. Audrey's virtue, though fervent almost to hysteria, proved deficient in staying power. Or so I thought then, for now I am disposed rather to the knowledge of a conspiracy to which I was more a means than a party. Why Great-uncle wished to marry me off I have still no idea (the cousinship was later admitted to have been, as he said, erroneous). Perhaps he had meant simply to provide me with a mistress—the thing is entirely possible—and had chosen unwisely a character so strong as to find unbearable a merely morganatic attachment to all that wealth. Anyhow, whether according to plan or failure of plan, Audrey and I sailed from New London for a month's wedding trip in southern waters on a steam yacht named *Midas IV* provided by Great-uncle, who had not stirred from his wheelchair.

And what of Midases, I, II, III? I wondered, lounging idly in the sun off the Bermudas. Then, according to our implicitly yet clearly understood duty, we returned to Great-uncle

Magus. Our married life has proved somewhat less intimate than our courtship.

2 —

I will have given by now an impression of myself as an extraordinary creature—a little feeble, you know, and not a little contemptible. Yes. Let me add at once that such an impression is due to no failure in this little record, which thus far has gone exactly as I wish it to go and represented lamentable things with admirable precision.

Not in extenuation but rather to enforce this impression, let me cite an anecdote which my wife and I (reading in the *Annals and Memoirs of the Court of Peking*, a book of which we were fond) had no hesitation in applying to myself. The brief paragraph in question describes how in 1912, the Empire being newly a Republic, the editors had met with a strange little gentleman in shabby morning coat and top hat, the last prince of a noble family whose hereditary office it was to tend the extensive tombs of the late dynasty. Of course, no money was any longer assigned to maintain this function; yet this job, which in greater days might have been performed by a thousand servants, he did each day with a broom, walking twelve miles to the graves and twelve miles back to the board hovel which the charity of an old woman allowed him.

Now that little old gentleman am I, and admittedly there is little to be proud of; yet I am touched with his (and my) devotion, ridiculous as it is, to the visibility of the past, to what part of that vanished splendor (itself sufficiently ridiculous) still pokes its head above the frozen earth. There is a pathos to it the more eminent because it cannot possibly last. More than this absurd and incongruously silk-hatted dignity I do not and cannot claim, but I have to perhaps the ultimate extent a respect, even a reverence and devotion, for the past, for the dead.

Great-uncle Magus had a vegetable soul, one which without moving to hunt yet seized for food whatever came near, and thus prospered. He was a thin old man who should have been fat: his soul was fat. Let me show by a figure what I believe our relation to have been.

He, the spider, sits at the center of his web, that is, his immense fortune. The little fly, aged five, is caught on the outermost thread, but the spider does not move, for he knows that the fly to escape must move and further that every move will be toward the center. It takes the fly perhaps twenty years, or twenty-five, fully to traverse the radius, and during this time —a long life for a fly—he has forgotten his captivity simply because the web is remarkable in itself and there is nothing but the web. Presently, then, the fly is eaten by the spider, not from malice but hunger. It is the sacrifice of the fly, yes, but it is also his triumph: for now he is at the veritable center of the web, in the very stomach from which it was spun; and what nourishes the spider nourishes the fly. And when the spider dies the fly inherits all that crawls inward on the web, and is wealthy, and is happy, but he cannot even so emerge from the spider's corpse, which has fortunately, however, begun quite to suit him as a home. Is the fly alive, or is he dead? An irrelevant question. He is enormously wealthy.

"I look upon you as my son," Great-uncle would say, "my only son." And he would show Audrey and me his accountings, his corporation reports, listings of stocks and bonds, inventories of his various properties, his fabulous possessions. "You've only to be patient. You will be so rich." He would shake his venerable head slowly to and fro on this, as though it were presumptuous in him even to meditate the extent of the wealth that would be ours. Thus, and because also, I suppose, of some fundamental incompetency of my will or soul,

I was taught to be useless to myself or the world, and became the ravaged feeding ground of his immense vanity.

Toward the end the matter grew less simple. "You must never neglect me," he would say—a queer old fellow gripping my shoulder or the sleeve of my coat. "You are all I have in the world" (his brother's daughter's boy). "And I," he would sometimes say, smiling, "I am all you have in the world. Am I not? Say that I am!" I would always capitulate and say what was demanded, for I had plainly told Audrey that I planned to humor my kinsman in all things. She nevertheless would look up from her book at such interviews and smile a disturbing, melancholy smile, as though she were the audience at some rather mean problem play of which the situation was enough like her own to cause her mild discomfort.

Meanwhile we lived disgracefully in that great house so commandingly poised on a hill above the Hudson. Servants were impossible to keep for long. They complained bitterly of food and wages, both of which were indeed shabby, and when they left stole things (curious things occasionally: a small Vermeer so-called, which had definitely turned out to be a forgery; Magus's dead sister's little butterfly collection; a K'ang Hsi vase of splendid ox-blood glaze which I later found shattered on the gravel driveway): none of these people was ever caught, since the absence of what they chose to take was never noticed for weeks afterward.

When I was thirty-five Great-uncle began to fail, if that is the way to describe his gentle yet rapid descent into death scarcely so much by perceptible steps as by an inclination. I summoned the family doctor, who shook his head more with admiration than gravity. "A miraculous grasp on life," he said. "I've sometimes thought he might go on forever, haven't you?"

There was nothing *wrong* with Great-uncle; he had simply reached that venerable state of life for which the tomb is the only remedy. Moreover he knew it, and the subject of his funeral vastly occupied him from then on. Not morbidly, for it is hard to imagine the morbidity of a being so remote from the consequential weight of life and death, but in a business-like way he interested himself in the pomp of the vault.

He was fortunate in the acquaintance of the local under-taker (mortician, as he proudly styled himself), a man named Rambode, a person of intensive if purely professional culture and what I can only call zest for the elegant fripperies of his trade. Greatly willing to put himself out for his customer, this man actually came to the house eight times during the last three weeks of Great-uncle's life and sat with him for hours each time. I recall their reading aloud from *Urn Burial* with much enjoyment. They discussed the effects of damp, the possibilities of seepage, the metempsychosis, mummification, preservation to the resurrection, etc. Plans, blueprints, specifi-cations, flowed in by every mail from New York, while Great-uncle and Mr. Rambode compared styles, wrangled over terms (the figures quoted were hardly within belief) and in general much enjoyed each other's company.

For Great-uncle had, I believe, the feeling for immortality that I began by speaking of. If not an eternal life, then an eternal death or an eternal something he was determined to have. I need not describe the monument he settled on, which was kingly indeed and would have made quite a spectacle on the banks of the Hudson twelve miles from Poughkeepsie, for as it happened Great-uncle Magus found something better in the end, something much better, and this predacious Rambode was cheated because, progressive as he was, he was not suffi-ciently so. As a matter of fact, since a contract had been signed, we were forced to let the man build *something*, and build he did, a mausoleum maybe half the size of a high school, which we eventually used to house the new dynamo—

for we made our own electricity until a short time ago, when it became necessary to go on the main.

Nevertheless the man Rambode is greatly inclined to blame me, which is absurd, as I knew nothing about Great-uncle's plans until too late. On my infrequent trips to the town I sometimes feel as I pass his plate-glass window the little chill which informs me that Mr. Rambode is watching from among the potted rubber plants, and washing together his hands (always dirty, as though we were in fact made of dust) in speculative anticipation of having my arrangements in hand, and soon. I do not know whether the dead suffer in their persons bodily or spiritual indignity and damage, but I do know this, that sooner than fall into Mr. Rambode's clutches I will make some such arrangements as my great-uncle did.

3 –

A few days before the end a large closed van arrived, and from the cab stepped a portly young man in a neat blue serge suit. He carried a thick briefcase which turned out later to be full of plans—more plans! The young man represented, as he was good enough to tell me whom he obviously considered an upper servant, The Arcane Enterprises Incorporated; and he was unreasonably shocked at being asked to take himself and his vehicle around to the trade entrance (for I saw no valid cause why these formalities should be allowed to fall into disuse). Nevertheless he complied and we went through our little comedy again in the rear of the house.

What was he selling, with his Arcane Enterprises? Ah! that was a matter which personally—"intimately"—concerned Great-uncle, at whose request he came. He would divulge his affair to no lesser person, he would remain (unless introduced at once to the Presence) an insoluble conundrum over which the servants' hall, he strongly implied, would vainly vex itself.

At last he condescended so far as to show me a letter undeniably in Great-uncle's childish script, and addressed to his firm.

"You might have showed me that right away," I said as I conducted him to Great-uncle's bed.

"Our discretion," he replied, "is immense." And for this reason, presumably, I was kept out in the hall during the first part of their interview and then peremptorily summoned in.

"It is a service we can offer at present only to wealthy men," the young man was saying, "though we hope to get a more inexpensive model into production in a very few years' time. But at this moment—" he leaned forward impressively— "at this moment only a few dozen of the richest and most prominent men in the country—" he named several.

Great-uncle Magus wanted to know whether it was permanent.

"As permanent as power itself," said the young man, confidently smiling. "Dependable as sunrise." Great-uncle, scanning a brochure that lay on his lap, remarked that he rather favored model J. The young man clapped his hands in spontaneous delight. "Just what I'd have said would suit you!" he exclaimed. "The library, the nonchalant pose, leaning perhaps gracefully on a . . . a . . . golf club, for example. Certainly." They both looked excessively pleased. I began to see what was up.

"Of course," the young man said as an afterthought, "it's as well to have a dependable man with you night and day— just in case. Though the company has a regular inspection service which is surprisingly low in price."

"My grand-nephew," said Great-uncle, indicating me (the young man regarded me with amused surprise), "he will stay on after my—" They both coughed. "He is, I'm sure, able to learn the operation of the thing, if it is indeed as simple as you make out here." He tapped the catalogue against his knee.

"Of course we'll take the maintenance service as well," he added.

"Here," I said, "what is this?" Both men smiled.

"You do like this place?" Great-uncle asked me. "I mean, you would be willing to—you intend in any case, that is—to make it your permanent home?"

"I don't know," I said. "I hadn't thought."

"Ah, but you will, won't you? Stay on, I mean. To please me." These words were delivered in a wheedling tone; but to them he suddenly and commandingly added these: "I want you to remember one thing. This is my dying wish. Whatever I may say later, this is my last wish, that you stay on here permanently."

"Ah, permanently. I can't promise," said I.

"But I advise you to promise, my dear. And further, to swear." The old eyes narrowed at me and flickered once or twice, and I realized what was at stake.

"If it means so much to you, Uncle," I said.

"I'll be the witness to that," the young man said quickly. "You know," he said, "Arcane has a service—a legal service—that can make your dying wish in this matter your will, a condition of your will. Other clients," he added, looking not very kindly at me, "have had trouble of this sort."

"I will take that service," Great-uncle said.

And soon after this they signed the contract, with ample inclusion of my name, which would (as I began to see plainly) lay up Great-uncle Magus in his perishable body where neither moth nor rust would be given the opportunity of corrupting. I went up to my room and there the thing suddenly struck me. I was sick to my stomach, and afterward lay down with a headache. But before dinner I felt possessed enough to tell Audrey what I more than suspected.

"You needn't whine," she said sharply, "and you needn't

worry. Think what you'll be master of; you'll soon short-circuit all these preposterous schemes."

Audrey had been for more than a year a stranger to my bed, yet that night she came to me, her rather gaunt and haggard face lighted by a childish happiness. She lay awake until all but morning, with plans and schemes for a new life, a life based on huge sums of money, on travel, on entertainment. She proposed an immediate trip to New York, "to get servants—and, of course, friends." I took her hand in mine and looked at them both in the lamplight: both displayed, gently and embryonically almost as yet, the beginning curve of talon and claw—it was funny, our avaricious weakness. We were, I thought, growing up. Like Great-uncle.

Meanwhile the young man and four workmen who appeared out of the van had all moved in, to wait. Their wait was not long, but it was inconvenient as our one servant at once departed and Audrey had to cook for them while I, though I would not wait at table, naturally carried the dishes in from kitchen to dining room. The whole period, of but a few days, was a chaotic and topsy-turvy interregnum, and the workmen, knowing themselves to be under the protection of Great-uncle and the fortune that was still his, had their moments of insolence.

But he died, he died dramatically but with obliging celerity. He insisted on celebrating what he called his centenary— it may well have been, I suppose—and was brought to dinner dressed in evening clothes. Ancient and withered, all but dust already—but "mummy possesst" as the poet says of woman— Great-uncle sat at the head of his table and proposed a toast.

"To self-preservation," he cried in his squeaky voice. "To self-preservation—the first law of life." And his glance piercingly fixed itself on me. These were the last words he ever addressed to me (for I am sure they were above all addressed to me) and an hour later, somewhat tiddly, he breathed his last, still impeccably clothed.

The portly young man and his hirelings at once took over, with an efficiency amounting too much to enthusiasm for my taste; yet I can understand the necessity, in that profession, for a somewhat unceremonious speed. Audrey and I were, so to say, breathed aside by the wind of their monstrous haste; our well-intended if amateurish offers of help they brusquely rejected.

From the van came a glass box the size of a small room. Furnishings followed: a table, a lamp, mahogany bookcases, a desk, a rug. The bookcases were neatly stacked, the only principle of choice being convenience and what was nearest to hand, with volumes pilfered from our library. Subsequently coils of wiring, a switchboard and instrument panel, with other electrical equipment, were brought in, and a gadget whose purpose I did not comprehend until I saw Great-uncle measured, posed and clamped upon it—a kind of rack devised to insure that rigor would find the subject in a convenient posture. Even Great-uncle's mouth was subjected to the pinch of a vise—to inhibit the *risus sardonicus*, the young man explained to me.

When so much had been prepared we all sat down to await the completion of *rigor mortis*. The workmen were breathing quite hard and attended to their beer so as to quite exclude conversation; but the young man became, in the consciousness of a good job being well done, rather friendly, not to say fulsome.

"We got the idea from the deep-freeze people," he said. "Frozen foods, that kind of thing. You know."

At last, very late at night, Great-uncle was pronounced ready and they took him and set him on his feet in that glass room, by now fully and attractively furnished. They removed the scaffolding from about him and stood him up. With one hand he leaned on a fine old putter (a golf ball lay on the floor) and with the other he reached, and would reach in perpetuity, for a volume on the highest shelf but one. I looked: it was the *Legenda Aurea* of Jacopus de Voragine. On the desk near by stood a glass of whisky and soda (which Great-uncle had not permitted himself during my life) and a humidor of tobacco with several handsome briar pipes. Another book lay open there: Catullus. They were doing Great-uncle proud.

The coils and wiring having by this time been arranged, the last glass wall was sealed in place. I began to weep, and even Audrey seemed affected.

"The coldness of death," I murmured. She nodded her agreement.

"Come on now," the young man said, putting his hand on my shoulder. "It's really better this way, isn't it, than—you know—'to lie in cold obstruction and to rot'? Isn't it?" He turned away to his workmen.

"Contact!" he said in a loud voice, and looked at his watch. The loud hum of electricity filled the room. "We have only an hour or so to wait," he said gently. "Then we will leave you to your sorrow."

During this hour or so, the most delicate part of the operation apparently, he paced the floor in silence broken only by the directions he gave to the man at the switchboard. Once, icicles began to form, on Great-uncle's mouth and eyebrows, on the glowing lamp, on the edges of the bookshelves. The young man directed that the temperature should be raised again until these melted; and when the glass walls had somewhat misted over he had them install a suction pump.

"To extract the moisture from the atmosphere," he explained. "We often hit that snag on installations near water."

At four in the morning Great-uncle Magus was deeply frozen. The young man instructed me in the operation of the controls, the major rheostat, the suction pump. "We'll leave that attached for a few weeks anyhow," he said. "Then if you don't have trouble we'll take it off. Unsightly thing, that pump in a dining room."

As he was getting his equipment together and readying to leave he turned to me very seriously and said, "You mustn't go away much, you know. Your great-uncle's will has made you responsible for his safety. I feel I ought to warn you that Arcane takes a very responsible interest in the . . . ah . . . legal side of the question."

And with that he left us, he and his workmen. They chugged away in their van and left us with Great-uncle Magus, who beautifully and dutifully reached for his book. The hum and throb of power filled the hall where we stood. I turned to Audrey.

"Oh, God," I said.

"Now don't worry," she said.

4 –

But for all that, she broke first, my gaunt, mythological, late-passionate cousin from the south, and my wife. She has gone away, being unable to bear up, it seems, under the deep electrical silence that keeps Great-uncle going, or at any rate keeps him where he is.

She tried, I will say that for Audrey. Since I could not leave—because of the Arcane Regional Supervisor, as he calls himself, who shows up irregularly on an average of once in three days (our motto is Service, he says to me as I open the door)—she went down to New York alone to recruit friends, old college chums, etc., whom she brought up for house-parties. I meanwhile wrote, from her model, copies of a letter:

DEAR SO-AND-SO [a classmate, for example]:
Having recently come into my patrimony I should
like, by way of picking up old connections once
again, to invite you [and Mrs. So-and-So where
appropriate—what consultation of alumni bulletins!]
to visit. I am married [I too am married where ap-
propriate] and . . .

Et cetera, et cetera. It was all sufficiently shameful, I suppose; but we were a little beyond shame and had between us
not so much experience of the world as would have fitted us
for the society of apes.

Apes, incidentally, were more or less what we got. It was
not a great success. Balding, fatling strangers, some of them
having the presumption a little to resemble myself, they stood
about the dining room—they couldn't stay out of the dining
room; you'd always find one of 'em in there—watching Great-
uncle. At meals they kept nervously glancing about to see if
he had taken down that book. Some of them, when they went
away—which was always soon and as though in flight—took
the liberty of offering me advice. They were on Great-uncle's
side, they quite in fact admired the idea in principle; but they
could not understand, they said or implied, what could possess me to throw the house open in this way, to make a cele-
bration of mortality, to dance, as it seemed to them, in the
face of the dead: did I have no respect? With Great-uncle
not yet cold in his grave? I forbore to explain that Great-
uncle was cold in his grave, was measurably colder, in
effect. . . . I let them go. And presently Audrey went too.

I live alone with Great-uncle now. No servant will stay in
the house, and tradespeople, I understand, are becoming chary
of delivering. Superstition, of course. I am a very wealthy
man, but even so I have my worries.

These worries—do not expect from me a complaint in charnel imagery, an obsessive feeling that there are worms in my clothes and hair, that I am perpetually dusty even after bathing; no, my concerns are far more prosy than all that.

The Arcane Enterprises have wrought, I think, better than they knew. The comfortable, sustaining sound of power has become my steady companion, my silence even. Beyond this, Great-uncle looks considerably improved. His pallor is disappearing, his cheeks blush with a faint but growing pink, the liverish spots on his neck and hands are quite gone away. Am I deluded when I think that his whole carriage improves from time to time—that he is in effect no longer leaning on that putter but carrying it? Hard to tell in that deep-piled carpet, but sometimes I suspect the club head is not touching the floor.

All of this, of course, costs money. I said before that we made our own electricity. But because of the Arcane Enterprises I had to install a new, larger dynamo (which I had housed in Mr. Rambode's tomb palace) and this was supposed to take care of our greatly increased consumption—Great-uncle's, mostly, and mine. It did not. Presently I noticed that even on the cool nights of autumn the lights would waver, go down, flicker and even for a time go out, as if Great-uncle in one shallow, pathetic breath had guttered a thousand candles, or drawn the air from the whole house.

I consulted with the Regional Supervisor, and on his advice had our plant connected with the main network that serves the public. Though he was calm, or affected calmness, I felt a slight disturbance was tugging at his professional pride.

"They do sometimes suck it in quite powerfully," he admitted to me one night. "But this beats anything I ever seen."

Well then, we are on the main, on the network of all the power in the world if we need it. You've read, I don't doubt, the advertisements that tell you that you can run almost any appliance in the world "for only a few cents an hour" by electricity? That the big point in favor of electricity is that it's inexpensive? This is not always so.

My great-uncle consumes the stuff incessantly at the rate of —well, you would not believe me if I said. I have begun—in only a few years—to be seriously inconvenienced. I revere my dead as much as any man, and more than some; but I can clearly see the approach of a limit which will put Great-uncle beyond my power of sustaining and protecting him. I cannot understand what he does with this electricity, but there is no pleading with his silence, and worst of all it must be kept going without failure. I have imagined, and dreamed of, that day, the last day. I am sitting on a box in the hall. The power people come to turn the supply off at the meter. The Arcane people arrive in their van, to take back their equipment. In so short a time Great-uncle will . . . I cannot say it. But first, possibly, his face will mummify for a moment and in a moment, like that of the young woman in that picture about the paradise in the Chinese mountains—the *Lost Weekend*, I think they called it. Will he stare at me with one reproachful glance which even as I watch will decompose?

I have, you see, a great deal of imagination; always have had, even as a child. I should curb it. For really, at the present rate, I can continue indefinitely. Indefinitely. If Great-uncle taught me one thing for which I am thankful, it is that money is the blood of the world, and as things are now I can comfortably go on bleeding for years, for life.

But there is one other thing. We live, as I said, on a hill, and I am able to look down on the Hudson, the bridge, the town. It is my distinct impression, though I have heard as yet no complaint nor even a rumor, that the lights down there do not shine so brightly as before. Especially on the terrible, hot nights of August they are likely to waver and dull from their clear brilliancy to a brownish yellow, as they would at the darkening of a theater.

I look at Great-uncle then, and I sigh. Insatiable old gentleman! Where will he stop?

The Ocean to Cynthia

ALL AFTERNOON THEY SAILED beside the gray cliffs
and castles of Ireland, and the girl Elizabeth was at Mr. Bower
again with her idea that it was better to die than live. Clearly
she was mad, and he regretted having got himself involved,
though it was that quality of madness, with its hint of the
erotic behind the mortal abandon, which in the first place
had attracted him. Now she had him there by the rail, aft,
where the motion of the vessel was most apparent, and the
two of them would rise dizzily into the empty sky, then sink
as suddenly till they stood beneath the black and cresting tops
of the waves, which, only fifty feet away, seemed that they
might at any moment fall on the liner and overwhelm it in
their continuously thundering weight. It was a bad place for
the discussion of a suicide pact; the ocean, from this view of
it, exercised a frightful fascination, and Mr. Bower, with one
arm as if protectively about the girl's shoulders, kept his free
hand tightly clutched on the rail, which shuddered sugges-

tively with the vibration of the engines; it actually seemed to him that—in a careless moment, so to say—he might throw himself overboard. Also he feared catching cold from standing so long in the chill wind, with spray and a hint of rain in the air; age with its prudence rebuked the lover's recklessness, and he kept thinking of his overcoat and tweed cap in the cabin below.

"To get it over with," this bitter girl was saying. "Look, there's no one looking. Now!" She actually urged his body strongly against the rail.

"My dear," he cried. "My dearest girl, be sensible. You don't really want to; you're just teasing yourself with the idea."

"You promised," Elizabeth said, "because you 'loved me more than the world.'" The theatricality of this quotation filled Mr. Bower with the sort of self-disgust to which, however, he had long been inured, and he merely shuddered, part with cold.

"It was because I wanted you to be happy," he said. "Dearest Elizabeth, you were so sad."

"Because you wanted me to come to you last night," Elizabeth replied. The strength of the wind made it necessary for them to shout these intimacies at each other; even so the words would be whipped into fragments which flew off over the sea.

"I wanted to bring you out of it," he said, "that pathological state of mind."

"We know what you wanted," she cried back. "And now you've got it."

"Don't talk like that, my child—" Mr. Bower admired this priestly form of address, even at the top of his voice—"you know I'll always love you."

"'Better than the world'?"

The great waves smashed at the side of the ship and broke

away beneath them in dirty marble flags like the flying drap-
eries of a statue. The girl clung to him and pressed against
his mouth the cold skin of her cheek, wet and salt to taste.

"Tony, Tony," she said, sobbing in such a way that he felt
the crisis, for the time being anyhow, must be over, "don't
leave me alone, Tony."

"Of course I won't, ever," he proclaimed, patting her
tenderly on the shoulder but keeping his other hand firmly
all the same on the rail.

For a moment the cold sun broke raggedly through cloud
and shone on them: it was like the epiphany of all the movies;
and across the glinting, tossing black of the waters great white
birds, gannets, flew low and fast.

"Look, aren't they beautiful!" he cried, turning her to see
these bulky, long-winged wanderers, while the sun obediently
lighted the lonely, magical cliffs and castles of the coast as
though to tell this poor child in his embrace that the world
could be the scene after all of wonderful adventure. Presently
he was able to send her away below to powder her nose,
after which she was to meet him in the Moorish Court for
cocktails.

"We'll talk it over sensibly," he assured her, wondering
what sensible things might be said—other than "No! No!"—
on the subject of their jumping together into that loud,
insane sea.

2 —

Morbid thoughts, morbid thoughts! While Mr. Bower sat
waiting in the Moorish Court, as the tourist saloon was called,
he sipped at a Bols gin which he hoped would avert the consequences of his having stood so long in damp and cold not
merely physical in their effects—he could not help imagining
himself, embraced with that sad young lady, drifting hither

and yon in the black water, their hair streaming, their faces eaten by fish—it was all very poetical, no doubt, and he wanted no part of it.

At the same time, while his spirit was soothed by the gin as by the string quartet of the Moorish Court, which at this hour played sentimental "semiclassical" music to the tea drinkers and cocktail drinkers, Mr. Bower could not help some rather self-pitying reflections on the subject of suicide. To be rid of one's life—there was something theoretically proper (and really rather moving) in the thought, so long as it was thought in the ornate vulgarity of the Moorish Court and not outside, face to face with the wild abyss. And that this girl Elizabeth should love him, Anthony Victor Bower, of all the world, enough to want to die with him—that suggested a fascination in his very nature, which age had no power to diminish. For a moment he could feel toward her a tenderness and romantic ardor such as had not come his way in many years, which put him nostalgically in mind of the first girl he had ever loved, Cynthia, whom he had got with child and deserted at the very start of his career, which was that of a seducer of women.

But this girl, Elizabeth, was insane; she really wanted him to jump! Anthony had even thought briefly of pushing her overboard, if she so badly wanted to die—that was how far matters had gone—but had refrained chiefly because he could think of himself as a scoundrel but not as a criminal. He imagined again the huge waves of the sea, shuddered, and ordered a second gin. At this moment he was joined by a criminal.

This was a portly, apoplectic-looking gentleman who dressed as a priest of Rome and called himself Father Frank. He and Mr. Bower had chanced to travel by the same ship a number of times during many years and recognized each other as alike predators of the sea; not that they were friends on this account, for the counterfeit priest was contemptuous of Mr. Bower as an amateur, while Mr. Bower, though he did not care much for religion, felt horrified at Father Frank, who profaned the cloth with the object of blackmailing women. Still, a kind of neutral acquaintance was imposed on them whenever they met on the high seas, and Father Frank had to be invited to a chair and a glass of gin.

"Prosperous voyage, Father?" asked Mr. Bower; it was his standard joke with this colleague.

"Good hunting to you," Father Frank replied in kind, raising his glass.

"As a matter of fact, I am expecting a young lady just now," Mr. Bower said, and the priest made a conventional gesture at rising to seek another table. "No, by all means join us, do," Mr. Bower insisted. "It occurs to me that you may have the power of assisting me to avert a rather unpleasant thing."

This time Father Frank's motion to depart was not conventional at all; however, Mr. Bower clutched at his arm.

"Please," he said.

"I don't want any part of your trouble, old son," said Father Frank.

"I should be eternally indebted to you," Mr. Bower said, "for only a trifling effort on your part."

What this trifling effort was to consist in he outlined quickly.

"You see," he said, bringing his narrative after a few minutes to its climax, "she actually wanted me to jump with her."

The false priest laughed contemptuously. "Maybe one day you will," he said. "You never know."

"Never mind that," Mr. Bower said. "The point is, the poor girl is obsessed with the idea of death. She is a widow already, her husband died on their honeymoon in America, and she is bringing the body back home—she made me go down to the baggage room with her to see the casket, that's how much it's preying on her mind. We kissed first down there," he confessed in a suddenly altered voice.

"And you swore to die with her—to drown?"

"Well, you know how that is."

"Well, I don't, my dear Bower. An oath is a serious thing."

"Come off it, do," said Mr. Bower savagely to this wolf in lamb's clothing, "or I'll report you to the purser."

"That would fix us both," replied Father Frank. "Supposing I put on the show for you, is there any guarantee it would work? Is the girl religious?"

"I've no idea."

"For ten pounds."

"That's a good deal of money, Father."

"You may jump in the ocean for all of me," the other replied with a civil smile, "but put it this way—five pounds down, now, and if you drown yourself tonight, why, you needn't pay the balance."

Elizabeth appeared just as Mr. Bower was passing over the five pounds.

"It is for charity," he said. "The Father has touched my better nature—for the orphans and poor."

"Are you a Roman?" she asked. "I didn't know that."

"No, I'm not," Bower replied. "But it is a good cause. Father Frank and I are old friends. Father, this is Mrs. Brayle I was telling you of."

"May I offer my sympathies," said the Father, "in your bereavement."

"I don't believe in God," Elizabeth said.

"Now, dear, now, Elizabeth," said Bower, but the Father raised a warning hand.

"Why shouldn't she say so, if it's the fact?" he demanded. "You seem to think a priest should be protected from the truth. It's better to be perfectly frank, isn't it?" he said to Elizabeth with a lively smile, as though placing them both over against Bower. Elizabeth smiled back somewhat stiffly.

"It's what I've always thought," she said, now taking a chair between them. The fresh air had improved her color, perhaps her disposition, Bower thought, and she looked *so* pretty, there was such an appeal in her thinness, delicacy, even in the rather sober poverty of her clothing, which was bride-new and yet not quite *good*, that he wished very much to lean over and squeeze her knee in amiable assurance; restraining himself, however, as not being quite right in this wish when they were *before a priest*. For by imperceptible revisions of countenance Father Frank had now so entered into his role that Bower absurdly felt some emanation from his presence of the real power to rebuke and forgive; and this he continued to feel even despite his knowledge of the facts and his compelled admiration for a technically polished performance.

The element of reality in this performance depended, he knew, upon Father Frank's once having been a priest, though long unfrocked for reasons which Mr. Bower had neither heard nor expected to hear; consequently the details were all quite exact, being marked by a dignity both grave and jovial and by no excessive austerity, since, as the Father had said once, it would be easier to counterfeit a saint than a priest, but less profitable and far more likely to awake suspicion. In the conduct of his present profession Father Frank had two or three dangers to face, which kept him constantly alert. The first of these Mr. Bower shared; it was the risk of becoming too well known to the authorities, and they neither of them traveled by the same line more than once in two years. The second danger was that of meeting real Catholic priests; not that the Father was incapable of handling doctrine and lingo, but the Church is in some respects, to its officers, like the Regular Army, a large but intimate association in which one was always likely to be asked "What about old So-and-So who was stationed at Karachi five years ago?" etc., an embarrassment which the impostor skillfully evaded, when necessary, by getting in first with his own questions. His third peril was a personal one; he liked the drink, did Father Frank, and had to be very careful of himself while working— though, as he had told Mr. Bower, "People can think only one thought at a time, and the more they think of a real bad priest who drinks the less they will think of his not being a priest at all. It is, as a matter of fact, a fair instance of the doctrine of casuistry, whereby a venial sin is substituted for a mortal one."

That was the kind of remark which not merely shocked but a little terrified Mr. Bower, who as a tourist-class seducer was also a sentimentalist, and did not like to hear religion spoken of except in distant and poetical ways, preferring to keep unsullied by the technicalities of obedience his half-belief in a Being unspecified who would bring all things right in the end, subdue the proud and exalt the meek, and, in the intermission of these activities, find time also to forgive Anthony Victor Bower, who, whatever his faults, really did love each and every one of those women who for twenty-five years had moved across his vision like ducks in a shooting gallery.

What a disgusting life I lead! he thought, and, simultaneously, But I am really a very nice fellow after all.

They ordered a gin for Elizabeth, and soon after another round for all, Mr. Bower paying.

"My dear child," Father Frank said, after having in a few minutes got on an easy footing with the girl, "you needn't think of me as a priest but simply as an older man and, I hope, a friend." He too, Mr. Bower noted, very nearly patted the girl's knee, but at the last instant his hand remained suspended above it: the blessing of the patella, thought Mr. Bower irrelevantly, and considered briefly the polished flesh beneath the silk stocking.

"But I do want to talk to you seriously for a moment, if you will let me," insisted the priest.

"Go ahead, then. I shan't stop you," said Elizabeth with derisive carelessness, and she smiled quickly, secretly, at Mr. Bower, a loose, reather dreamy smile which he found both erotically appealing and desperate to insanity. She is gone, he thought nervously. Nothing can touch her.

"This gentleman here," began Father Frank, indicating Mr. Bower, "though he is not of our persuasion, has nevertheless seen fit to repose his confidence in me as a priest, and has told me something of your unhappy circumstances, my dear, together with that decision of yours which I cannot too strongly reprehend—but it is difficult for me, sitting in this comfortable lounge, even to believe you can be serious, or final, in thus deciding once and for all against life and in favor of the other. I tell myself that something—which you will call fear and I will call, if you like, a good angel—would always hold a person back, at the last instant, from the satisfaction of that dreadful wish."

"I really don't give a damn," Elizabeth said in a neutral voice which embarrassed her lover and frightened him at the same time with its impudent despair. To behave that way before a priest! It was precisely the measure of her childishness and distance from reality.

"I tell myself that," evenly continued the priest, "though it is true that everywhere, every day, people do this terrible thing. It is not so much to die, themselves, personally, that they wish; it is to deny life, and by a puerile obstinacy make it impossible for God to save them."

"I don't believe in a God," Elizabeth said again.

"God may believe in you," said the father with a smile of dialectical triumph. "After all, what is so insupportable about

your life? You have lost your husband—many women lose
their husbands. Sometimes, you know, life appears as not all
happiness. What of it?"

"He had left me," Elizabeth said. "He was—what you call
it?—killed trying to escape." This joke had a dreadful effect
on her, so that she was laughing with her mouth while her
eyes cried.

And I can understand why, thought Mr. Bower, you poor,
dreadful child. He felt filled with a vague, generous pity for
all the sad world, while at the same time he thought what an
embarrassment it would be if the girl made a scene here, with
the quartet playing an arrangement of "Tales from the
Vienna Woods."

"You and this gentleman," said Father Frank with a new
sternness in his voice, "have sinned. Understand that I am not
overlooking the fact—you are both at this moment in a state
of mortal sin. Maybe you don't view that as desperate, but
I do. You have come together carnally without blessing, without sanction, without so much, poor as it would be, as the
scratch of the registrar's pen. Consider, young lady, if that
in itself may not be responsible for your present despair—
remorse, natural remorse, which by mysterious ways might
yet light in your souls the beginning of grace. You know,
both of you, that you have sinned. Oh, this is not theology,
my friends; I am merely stating what you both have natural
knowledge of. I want to use that natural knowledge to help
you."

And he really does, at that, thought Mr. Bower, becoming
aware in some surprise of the depths of sincerity which must
go to the making of any good impersonation. Despite himself
he felt vague yearnings which began with the formula: If I
had my life to live over again . . .

"I hate the world," Elizabeth said, tears running down her

face. "Cruel, miserable, bitchy world where you're to blame for everything."

"That hatred of the world," said Father Frank, "is the beginning of wisdom. In it is our first awakening to the command of our Creator, who did not put us here to enjoy ourselves. Consider," he added, "that this life is like an ocean voyage, a vessel filled with delicacies—of which we become weary, nevertheless—and borne up irrationally on the waters of utter death."

"Another gin, all of us," said Mr. Bower. "And don't cry, Elizabeth."

"You are fortunate indeed, young lady," said Father Frank, "that this man with whom you have committed fornication is, after all, an honorable and upright person. Though he was tempted, and fell, upon coming to his senses he has resolved on the only right course—and it is to make his decision public and in some sense binding that he has employed a third person, myself, to say openly that he will marry you as soon as we reach Southampton—or on this ship itself, tonight, if I can persuade the officials that the ceremony will be confirmed by a civil ceremony tomorrow, ashore."

Elizabeth giggled sadly. "It's very nice of you to bother," she said to either or both of them.

"You see, dear," Mr. Bower said tenderly. "Things do sometimes come right in the end."

"I can't conceal my opinion, though," said the priest, "that you both have a great deal to beg forgiveness for. I don't at all condone your behavior but am simply making the sorry best of a bad situation."

"We are grateful to you, Father, I'm sure," said Mr. Bower.

"He won't really, will he? Marry me?" asked Elizabeth. "You've cooked this up, both of you, to keep me safe till we dock." Her eyes, glittering with suspicion and tears, went first to one and then the other.

"I put it to you, Anthony Bower, as a gentleman," said the priest.

Mr. Bower's eyes too filled with tears at the image of himself in his sacrifice.

"Elizabeth," he asked, "do you love me?"

"You ask me that?" she cried out. "You've had what I could give. I'll do anything, I don't really want to die—anything. But don't let us talk about love."

"I love you, my dear," Mr. Bower replied, and truly at this moment meant it, so that his generous nature expanded with sympathy, pity, romantic ardor—all those feelings which ran so near the surface in him that he had always been convinced, when cuddling ladies naked in bed, that he really saved them from the dire and miserable world.

"I will marry you, Elizabeth," he said outright. "I will try to make you happy." And really he believed this, seeing suddenly, unexpectedly, something like the very truth emerging from falsehood. False priest, false lover, between them they had cooked up—the phrase was Elizabeth's—a resolution which he could regard as satisfactory, at least for the time being; so that instead of going down into old age in increasing loneliness, watching the failure of his charm, he might be comforted in bed and at his board by this young and pretty girl whom by this means he had saved, in all probability, from death. In what was nearly a religious thought he saw himself redeeming the past, and silently he named a litany of names: Cynthia, Joan, Louise, Helen . . . etc., etc. It was a prayer, perfunctory and powerful.

"I'm glad I didn't die," Elizabeth said, with a return of that secret, crazy smile. She took out her compact, made a little exclamation, and began intently to repair her stained face.

"You consent, then?" insisted Father Frank.

"Yes, I do," said the girl, continuing to examine her face in the mirror.

Father Frank looked significantly across at Mr. Bower, who nodded reassuringly and framed with his lips the word *later*.

"We should have some champagne," he said, and waved at a waiter.

The priest pursed his lips indecisively and wistfully while champagne was selected. But he rose to his feet.

"I will speak to the proper authorities," he said, "and meanwhile, you two, be steadfast."

He frowned severely down at them, while his eyes twinkled with benign merriment, and off he went. In his new resolve, Mr. Bower wished that the authorities were actually going to be consulted; which was, however, too much for Father Frank to be expected to do for ten pounds.

The champagne arrived, and they drank to each other while the quartet played selections from *Midsummer Night's Dream*, the *Barcarolle* and other such pieces.

"The coffin," Elizabeth said suddenly. "I must return it to his parents. They will be waiting."

"You needn't tell them anything," Mr. Bower assured her.

"You don't know anything about me," she said.

"Nor you about me—I have not been a very good person all my life," he replied.

"Aren't we shabby, though?" she said, laughing.

"Not at all."

3 —

On the strength of the champagne they neither of them wanted dinner but decided instead to walk on deck.

"To look at the sea," she said, "without wanting to throw yourself in."

Giggling like children, they agreed to climb the forbidden passage to the first class, and cautiously emerged on a well-lighted but empty boat deck.

"They are all at supper now," said Mr. Bower, pressing his fiancée's arm. "We have the place to ourselves."

The sea had calmed, and the moon come out between clouds. Ireland had been left behind, and here, so high above the water, the scene was no longer threatening even though the waves were still moderately strong.

"My darling," cried Mr. Bower above the voice of the waves. "Be happy."

"I'll try," she cried back. The cold wind whipped at their hair and carried off their words.

They stopped to embrace, standing under the high white bellies of the lifeboats. Here there was a break in the railing, and Mr. Bower was possessed of a sudden irrational desire to carry both of them overboard now, while they were happy. He trembled with this feeling and the tension produced by his terrified resistance to it. Happiness never lasts, he thought, and pressed the girl closer to him.

"Elizabeth," he cried, "I'm so happy I could die."

She broke gently from him and stood back a trifle.

"You really mean it," she said, and then, somewhat histrionically, " 'My love is not of time nor bound to date.' "

"What?" loudly asked Mr. Bower, who seemed to hear these words flying past his ears as from a great distance and at high speed.

She repeated the verse, and drew out from her dress a locket.

"My mother," she replied; "someone wrote that to her."

They leaned their heads close together over the open locket and looked at the picture of the young man with wavy hair and bristling mustache who had written in a cramped hand beneath his face, "My love is not of time nor bound to date."

"But it was, after all," Mr. Bower said in a low voice.

"Was what?"

"The 'Ocean to Cynthia,' " he said. "A poem."

"Cynthia was my mother's name," she said. "You know poetry too."

"Yes," Mr. Bower said, "yes, I know everything."

He took her in his arms again and gently moved with her between the lifeboats. He kept his eyes shut, and seemed to hear the sound of the sea become louder.

"No!" she cried in his ear. "No! No!"

"Everything," he shouted back, and they moved together as though dancing toward the free fall and the wild marble water singing below.

The Twitch

IT WAS A BEAUTIFUL MORNING, beautiful. Near Studio 7 on the walk to his office Mr. Rumont passed a group of carpenters lounging on a pile of boards. They were smoking. This was wrong, and Mr. Rumont directed his secretary Mr. Mortimer to tell them so. Rejoined by Mr. Mortimer, he had walked perhaps two steps when he heard the voices behind him, quiet, anonymous and (though intended to be heard) hardly so much insolent as humorously pitying.

"King kike himself."

"Jesus, Flossie, do they let these yids in everyplace these days?"

And a little light laughter.

Mr. Rumont walked on straitly. Balance is a delicate matter, and may be achieved by the crushing pressure of enormous opposed forces as well as by two grains of sand, so Mr. Rumont walked on down the narrow walk. He sensed that Mr. Mortimer, a step behind, was trembling, because Mr.

Mortimer, also Jewish, was afraid of being asked to confront
the carpenters. Mr. Mortimer perhaps thought he ought to
show initiative as well as courage, and confront the carpenters
anyhow, mainly because if he did not he would tremble, alone
in his hotel room at night, and be unable to sleep. Mr. Rumont
realized this.

"Never mind, Herman," he said briskly and without turning his head. He heard Mr. Mortimer sigh, a wavering, liquid
exsufflication of fear. In silence the two men walked on,
turned a corner, nodded to the policeman at the door and entered the long corridor leading down to Mr. Rumont's offices.
These were underground, a fact explicable only by some
inversion of the common occupational paranoia that sets
movie producers—in towers, minarets, imitation frontier
blockhouses and romanesque churches—high above their empires whence they may look down on the Egyptian slaves,
the Russian troops, the crew of the Pequod, Pasteur, Garbo,
Napoleon, etc. The corridor was battleship gray, inclined
gently, suggesting a descent to an engine room, especially by
reason of the heat, which was uncomfortably intense.

"The air conditioning has broken down," said Miss Parrot
as they passed. "I've phoned the company. There's a list of
incoming calls on Mr. Mortimer's desk." She stopped as
though turned off, having delivered her information in the
exact time it took Mr. Rumont and his secretary to pass
through her sphere of influence—not a room exactly, but an
egglike bulging of the corridor (with gray silk wall coverings
and a gray steel desk) which suggested that this ugly little old
woman had somehow been born here and made room by
growing. Or that she had been swallowed by a snake too
small for her. At least Mr. Mortimer thought of these things
when he passed through. He did not know what Mr. Rumont
thought.

"See you, Herman," said Mr. Rumont, at the angled artery

which led to Mr. Mortimer's cell and, farther along, to the private theater.

"Yes, Mr. Rumont." The man seemed about to say something further, but with a sigh instead (another such soft, bubbling sigh) he turned into the twilight of his place. He was a big, flabby and light-complected person who had the nervous habit of mopping his face with a handkerchief, so continually and lovingly as to suggest that he sweated a sacred lymph which later he would wring out into the vials of some priestly and private self-love. For a man like Mr. Rumont of great powers and precarious power he was an achievement and an acquisition: a favorite from whom nothing need be feared, the exquisitely balanced weapon of another will. When people called Mr. Rumont God they referred to Mortimer as little Jesus, but Mr. Rumont simply thought, with more affection than contempt: *Schlemihl.*

In his own office Mr. Rumont sat down behind the desk and lighted a cigarette. The sad impassivity of his face gave way, and for some two minutes he cried quietly in spasmodic whimpers of outraged petulance. His hands were trembling, and he could have stopped that but did not, it was relief almost to the point of luxury. In a queer way he felt grateful to the carpenters.

Joseph Rumont was head of the corporation so improbably called Rumont-Positive Pictures; his partner Amiel Positif had died several years before, leaving, however, his name, *anglice*, to suggest (as he himself was progressively forgotten) some highly specialized virtue in the films turned out by the organization.

Rumont was a small, gnomelike man in his late fifties, about as unlike as might be imagined to the allegorical figure of the comic Jewish millionaire of the movies: frail and unhealthy in appearance, in the constant subdued St. Vitus-like motion of a compact engine racketing itself quietly to pieces in its

mountings and leaving everywhere a nervous exhaust of cigarette smoke, he yet exercised among his associates a ghostly
pale dominance with something about it of immediate mortality and imminent corruption—a silent panic of energy like that
by whose means the feeble drowning man drags down his
rescuer. He spoke a precise English in a low, rapid voice and
could not bear interruption.

What he lived on, and perfectly knew, was fear: it con-
centrated both energy and intelligence for him. By what sup-
pressions, shifts, evasions and humiliations he made profitable
an anxiety that might as easily have wrecked him, he also
knew, and wondered if it had not wrecked him anyhow.
Like any Jew who has given away his religion and received
his race in exchange, he had the sense not of betrayal but of a
cruelly unequal bargain for which he might thank himself at
least in part. His fear was complicated by the suspicion that
he was in the wrong, by the obscure guilt imposed from
within as well as without, by the deep certainty that he was
indeed that loathsome criminal after whom children (twice
in his life) cried "dirty Jew bastard." His fear, which was
not the simple longing to wear the gaberdine and be spat on,
had early implicated itself with his life as the contagion in
whose stain the world was seen: he was afraid, not physically,
but as one feeling the general atmospheric condemnation of
man, and half admitting its justice. The incomprehensible
nature of the charge against him—to have been born a Jew,
which one surely couldn't help—was aggravated and made
more sinister, he felt, because in himself was confirmed (in a
laughable way) the prime thesis of the Jew-haters: Jews are
rich and powerful (he had to smile through his tears), Jews
will control the world (the cardboard scenery, the fake
palaces, the African tribesmen from Harlem).

He stopped crying, he stopped the trembling of his hands,

he dried his face of sweat as well as tears—it was very hot. He lighted another cigarette just before the phone rang.

"Mr. Rumont, Mr. Madrilene is on the line." Mortimer's voice expressed a gentle perturbation. "They are having a little trouble—" like the last apologetic flushings of an old toilet, Rumont thought—"a little trouble with *All Men Are Brothers*. Mr. Madrilene is very insistent on speaking to you personally; he says trouble he's used to but this—"

"Put him on already." It's about time, he thought. I expected it. *All Men Are Brothers* was Rumont-Positive's contribution to the new fad for sleek, sexy pictures against anti-Semitism. The troubles to date (though in mere delay they amounted to money) had been trivial—some person with microscopic ingenuity had scratched little messages, "Down with the Jews," etc., on the walls of the sets to be pictured— or else somewhat removed from the main issue—a person named Batthoven had turned up claiming to be the only living descendant of the composer. He had just come from a displaced-persons camp in Hungary, Batthoven said, and heard they were going to use his great ancestor's Ninth Symphony; Batthoven wished it understood that there were laws, copyrights. "Breitkopf and Hartel would always give me a small per cent," he claimed over the phone. "I would not ask much." While Batthoven and his claim were being put through channels (everything was investigated) Batthoven must either have overplayed his hand or let someone else in on the racket: there came a long, obscurely phrased telegram announcing the price at which a person signing himself F. Schiller would consent to lease the rights to what he called "the lyrics."

"Listen," said Mr. Madrilene. "I didn't want to bother you, but we've been stuck on this thing for three days and I think it's going to mean a decision of policy."

"So stop being excited and tell me what it is."

"You'll see what it is; I don't want you to get the wrong impression and it's too long to explain on the phone." The director was excited (not improbably a little pleased); there was obviously trouble. A pogrom, maybe; it wouldn't surprise me.

"Now don't get anxious, Joe. It's nothing—well, nothing horrible, if you know what I mean. It's just kind of funny."

"Tell me so I can laugh too."

"I'll tell you when we get there."

"We—who's we?"

"Listen, Joe, I want to bring down Fellowes—" Fellowes was the assistant director—"and the principals. Yes, down to your office. This morning. Now, even."

"All right, all right. If you have to. I'll expect you in fifteen minutes."

"Swell. And Joe—"

"What?"

"Better have a lawyer there. Gowry's called his." Gowry was the male lead.

"Now listen," said Mr. Rumont, but the line clicked as Mr. Madrilene with his fine sense of the dramatic (and also to give the impression of speed and efficiency) hung up. Mr. Rumont switched on the interoffice speaker and told Miss Parrot to get Mr. Fine down to the office.

"At once," he said. "Tell him I don't know what it's about and it's probably nothing but he should bring Gowry's contract anyhow."

That done, Rumont settled back in his chair. He smoothed one hand down over his face, closing his eyes. This felt good, and he did it again. It was like a caress. His wife had died years ago, a blowsily majestic Hungarian woman younger than himself. Her picture stood on his desk staring with a lorn seriousness just over his head, probably at the tall chauffeur with whom she had gone away. He had worn whipcord breeches and red leather puttees and touched his cap at your appearance. Some officious person had them traced as far as a place called Kozy Kabins (for tourists) and a little farther, to the abandoned car outside a town near the Mexican border. The detective agency had brought back photographs of everything available—the car, antique and upright; the Kozy Kabins themselves, with an extra one of one of the kabins (the relevant one presumably); and finally the proprietress, leaning on a broom. Ysolt died in Mexico, of dysentery; the chauffeur was probably still around. All the photographs were still in the desk drawer.

"Of course combat," Mr. Madrilene was saying (a fat, squat man with pompadoured gray hair), "we combat cancer, we combat infantile, we combat anti-Semitism. So? So art goes down the drain." He flushed his hands away in midair.

"It goes without saying," said Mr. Fellowes, "that the aesthetic achievement of *All Men Are Brothers* will be at best nil."

"So it goes without saying, so don't say," Mr. Rumont snapped. Mr. Fellowes looked aggrieved; he was a nonentity who had not been on the Coast very long and wore his rogue shirt as though he didn't quite believe in it. Just now he slumped slightly forward in his chair, hands between his knees, resembling just what he in fact was, an ampersand.

"Anyhow the movies is not art," said Mr. Rumont. "The movies is a state of mind."

They had all been there for ten minutes and had not yet come to the trouble, preferring rather, it seemed, to begin with a general denunciation of *All Men Are Brothers*. Robert Gowry and Agnola Dole, the principals, sat together on a couch, whispering. They were both in costume—Miss Dole in a nightdress of black net, Mr. Gowry in football uniform (the plot of *All Men Are Brothers* was complicated, and its high seriousness did not exclude other attractions: the scene was a big midwestern university). Gowry's lawyer sat with Mr. Fine, and Mr. Mortimer, at the edge of the desk, prepared to take notes. A portly person thus far not identified paced up and down near the door; it later turned out that he was a doctor.

It was extremely hot, and all were sweating freely, especially the actors, whose make-up had begun to run. No one had mentioned the heat.

"And in the bargain—this," said Mr. Madrilene, flapping a hand toward Gowry. "I almost hate to say it, it sounds so trivial. But he's got a tic."

"A tic?"

"Yes, a tic, a twitch—a nervous thing around the mouth."

"He got it in the war, Mr. Rumont," said Fellowes.

"So? I don't get it. Tell me more."

"It's nothing to worry about," said the unidentified man, still pacing. "Nervous in origin. Won't affect his general health, probably."

Miss Dole giggled. "It's perfectly simple, really," she said. "Whenever he's got to mention Jews his face goes all funny —like this." She made a quick grimace.

"Not like that—worse," said Mr. Madrilene. "Absolutely impossible to put on the screen."

"Remember," said Mr. Fellowes, "that *All Men Are Brothers* has an excessively delicate subject."

"Thank you, I'll try to remember," said Mr. Rumont dryly. He turned to Gowry. "Now, Bob," he said. "You tell me what it is."

"Well, I guess it's like they say, Mr. Rumont. I like the part, and I want to do a good job, but—"

"I'm having some rushes sent down, Mr. Rumont," said Fellowes. "You'll see what it is."

"Shut up already, you. I'm listening to Mr. Gowry. Go on, Bob."

"I don't want you to think I'm being unco-operative," Gowry said. "It's only that I try to be sincere about the parts I play, I want to think myself into the character. And it seems every time something Jewish happens I get this . . . this thing in my face. I don't know much about Jews," he concluded unhappily (the granite jaw, the blond hair, eyes like little blue marbles, centered about a nose ever so slightly, so delicately, vulpine and bent—which was now, due to the heat, melting down his upper lip).

"God," said Mr. Rumont heavily. "You're incongruous." He leaned forward to Mr. Madrilene. "Well, what should I do? Give him my face?"

The director looked uncomfortable. "Now listen, Joe," he said earnestly. "Please don't get excited—"

"Do I look excited?"

"I've thought it out and there are two things we can do. We can scrap the whole thing."

"Seven weeks of work?"

"Or we can replace Gowry."

"Now wait a minute." This from Gowry's lawyer. "Bob's got a contract to cover this picture."

"But if he can't make the picture," Mr. Madrilene patiently began.

"If he can't make the picture nobody else can. That's the contract."

"But if his health prevents him, that's our out," said Mr. Mortimer suddenly.

"His health? What's wrong with his health? Ask the doctor, is he in bad health? Why, he's got perfect health. Only this little tic in the face . . ."

"So's a Hottentot got perfect health," said Mr. Madrilene. "Only we don't want the Hottentot in the picture."

"Only another thing," said the lawyer. "Only the Hottentot hasn't got a contract."

"Gentlemen," said Mr. Rumont. "Exit the Hottentot. He confuses me." He peered searchingly into Gowry's eyes. "Tell me, Bob," he said, "what do you think of Jews?"

Gowry sat uncomfortably at the center of the shocked silence, rolling the football helmet between his hands.

"I don't know, Mr. Rumont," he said. "I never thought about it much."

"Probably his mother was frightened by one," Miss Dole said; and winced extravagantly as Mr. Rumont glared at her.

"Jesus, pardon me for breathing," she said at large.

"Now, Joe," said Mr. Madrilene. "That's the wrong line, Joe, the wrong line entirely."

"Please." Mr. Rumont raised a hand. "This is between Bob and me. As man to man, Bob. Don't be afraid, be perfectly frank."

"Christ, Mr. Rumont—I don't know."

"Listen, Bob. I'm a reasonable man. They say you get this twitch or whatever it is when you're doing a take with something Jewish about it. Now there's got to be a reason, Bob."

"Let me assure Mr. Rumont," said the doctor pompously, "that the whole thing is perfectly involuntary."

Mr. Rumont continued to stare at Gowry with an undefinable and slightly absurd intensity. The young man, the handsome all-American fullback with the waxy smear of levantine nose under his nose, stared back saucer-eyed, like a hypnotized bird.

"Did you ever think," asked Mr. Rumont with final calm, "that I crucified the Saviour?"

"Jeeze, no, Mr. Rumont." The halfback squirmed uncomfortably, like a child hauled by the hair from a costume party to face an outraged father. "I don't like this kind of talk either," he said. "I told you I couldn't help it."

"He got it in the war," said Mr. Fellowes.

"Honorably serving his country," said Gowry's lawyer.

"In a USO camp show," said Miss Dole.

"Those shows were sometimes very dangerous," Mr. Fellowes said impressively. "I remember one in Naples where—"

"Enough!" cried Mr. Rumont. He got to his feet and walked over in front of Gowry. "Look," he said gently. "Look at it this way, Bob. You're a Jew, so all right. This is America, it's not Germany, there are no Nazis, no storm troopers, no nothing. You're a Jew, you've got nothing to be ashamed of, nothing to fear. You don't have to take any back-chat from anybody. This is a free country, am I right? Well? Am I right?"

"Yes, sir," said the quarterback sullenly.

"That's the idea of the picture, see."

"But the twitch," said Mr. Fellowes. "He can't help the twitch; it goes deeper than that."

"I know," said Mr. Rumont heavily. At this moment Miss Parrot rang through to say the rushes were ready in the projection room.

The twitch was everything they had claimed for it. Madrilene kept up a commentary in Mr. Rumont's ear.

"He goes into this hotel lobby, see," he would say, "and the clerk tells him there are no rooms; but he watches other people for a while, and they can get rooms—now, look, in a second now: there! Did you see it?"

Mr. Rumont had to admit you couldn't miss it. "It's a queer thing," he said.

They watched Gowry being pledged for a fraternity, standing in sweater and pipe with one arm on the mantelpiece, confessing somewhat primly to his origins.

"There it is again," fiercely whispered Mr. Madrilene, as the disgruntled fraternity members filed out of the room. The momentary convulsion wrenched at Gowry's features and was gone, so rapidly that you could never say you saw it, but only that you were sure you had seen it. Sitting in the darkness, Mr. Rumont felt the muscles around his mouth stretch in imitation of that ferocious and meaningless joviality: his mouth silently twisted and puckered as with tough meat. Struck with an idea, he leaned over to Madrilene.

"He couldn't be a Jewish war veteran with a twitch?"

"No, I thought of that too," Mr. Madrilene whispered back. "Not with that twitch."

Mr. Rumont turned in his seat and beckoned to Gowry, who put his head forward.

"How do you feel about Negroes?" he asked.

"What do you mean?"

"I mean, how about doing it with you in blackface—instead of a Jew?"

"No, sir," said Gowry emphatically. "The folks back home wouldn't stand for that."

"Besides, what about me?" whispered Miss Dole. "He marries me in the end."

"Oh, all right," said Mr. Rumont sadly. "It could have been rewritten."

At this point Gowry was shown talking to the football coach, who was telling him he needn't report for practice.

"Oh, because I'm a—" said Gowry; and there it was again. A smile on one side, a scowl on the other, a strange momentary collapse dictated from the only profundities and subtleties of Gowry's nature, which were unconscious. Mr. Rumont imitated the grimace slowly, wryly. It struck him, rather; there was something about it. The reel ran out and the lights went on.

"I see what you mean," said Mr. Rumont. He meditated for a moment.

"Look, I've got it," he said then. "We've got to waste some of it, but we can't afford to waste it all. So here's what we do. Take off the nose, cut the Jewish angle, and put it over as a straight collegiate story—football, coeds, maybe a few songs at a Senior Prom."

"But, Mr. Rumont," Fellowes objected, "his unpopularity—that's the basis of the whole story. He's unpopular because he's a Jew, so he's got a hard struggle."

Mr. Rumont was not perturbed. "So now he's unpopular for some other reason," he said. "Maybe he studies too hard or something."

"And what about *All Men Are Brothers*, and the chorale from Beethoven?" asked Mr. Madrilene.

"Keep it all," advised Mr. Rumont. "It can be a fight song between halves." If they would only leave him alone, he thought, he would practice that twitch of Gowry's. Somehow it seemed the adequate answer to everything.

Beyond the Screen

THIS IS A STORY about something that happened in the early days of television, just after the time at which it was exceptional to have a set, and just before the time at which it was eccentric not to. You will remember how in those days many people used to show an extreme ethical delicacy and sensitivity about the value of television, before they too bought their sets and settled down in front of them like the rest of us.

Andrew Stonecroft was one such, and at this time he had just achieved his object of moving out of New York and into Westchester—not the landscaped and half-timbered Westchester, though, but the somewhat ruggeder and less expensively pastoralized part nearer the Hudson. The modern house which he had had built, a long, low building of gray field-stone and board, with a steeply slanted roof, represented the closest possible adjustment between his income and the size of his family; he and his wife had one child, a seven-year-old boy named Stephen, and another at this time five months on the way. The house also had a study, den, or library, which could be used as a guestroom, or, rather, guest space, since the architect, a friend of Andrew's from college days, did not believe in the old-fashioned idea of *rooms* but saw a house rather as "organized space," "a machine for living," with adjustable partitions everywhere substituted for walls and doors. This somewhat fluid conception had much disturbed Andrew at first; he had been raised more or less in the country, in a small village in Massachusetts, and a door had for him the value of a moral distinction (he particularly remembered how his own father would shut himself away on a Sunday afternoon in a study protected from the rest of the household by a corridor and two doors), but when he raised his objections he found Janet and the architect full of rational arguments. The architect pointed out that people did not live that way any more, that it had been demonstrably an unhappy and inefficient way of "using the space," that families nowadays shared things more than they used to. When Andrew gave the example of his father, the architect laughed.

"And look at you," he said. "Do you really want your kid to grow up like you?"

Janet said, "You'll be in New York all day long, five days a week. Stephen will be in school. I've got to live in the place, and keep it swept up together." And she showed how easily the vacuum cleaner would roll from one part of the "space" to another.

The most convincing argument, though it was never spoken aloud, was that the architect was doing the job at a greatly reduced fee out of friendship, in return for which he must naturally be given the chance for a practical demonstration of his own ideas. Andrew wondered whether they were really his own; it all looked, on the blueprints and drawings at any rate, like pages from *Vogue*.

Yet when the building actually went up, and he was able to have a true impression of its cleanly and pleasant interior proportions, the crisp efficiency of furnishings and cabinets built into the walls, the easy availability of everything from everywhere within his house, Andrew became convinced that quite truly a new way of life was opening out before him; he could imagine them all, on a winter night before the fine double fireplace, Janet sewing (for instance), himself and Stephen building a model airplane or with heads bent together over the boy's arithmetic problems, the high-fidelity phonograph filling the air with good music, not loud, even a trifle distant, from three properly spaced loud-speakers; it did seem as though there were a charming harmony to be expected from all these activities thus conducted in freedom which did not require the expense of loneliness.

And so it turned out. They moved up when Stephen got out of school in June. Andrew and Janet were delighted with their efficiency in arranging everything so that they might enjoy the summer in the new place, and they did enjoy it. Stephen made friends rapidly, for the neighborhood was delightfully populous without being at all crowded; their two acres were so well screened with stands of pine and birch as to give no view at all, from the lawn, of the two adjacent houses which were, however, close enough for a comfortable sociability and in case of emergencies. By this time Andrew and Janet were aware of the fact that they were to have a new child, but when they confessed their uneasiness about "the space" to the architect, who naturally came to spend a weekend in his creation, he delighted them by pointing out an overlooked advantage in this type of construction—that an "annex" could be built on inexpensively, anywhere almost.

"It's free to grow as you grow," he told them.

Meanwhile, there was no television; Andrew, compliant

about all else, was stubborn about that, and Janet for the time being did not make an issue of it.

"Though I don't see what you've got against it," she said sometimes.

"I don't want my child—my children, for that matter—to grow up on that stuff," he would reply. "Stephen will get more out of books, like any civilized person."

"He goes down to watch almost every day with the Stennis boys, and at Joey Capes' house," Janet said. "And he can't invite them back, that's all."

"Now you're talking like an ad in the papers," Andrew said angrily. "Our child is decently clothed, properly fed, we don't beat him or even make him work around the house to teach him how tough the world is, as the Capes do with Joey. But because we don't have one of these damn boxes we are 'depriving' him, you'd think, of life itself. I refuse to be shamed into buying one, and that's absolutely the end."

And so it was, "absolutely the end," for the time being anyhow, though even Andrew sometimes wondered if he really had anything against television beyond, perhaps, an instinctive, or inbred puritanical resistance to the passivity it commanded. And those aerials, which he saw in ever-increasing numbers when he drove into town in the mornings, appeared to him as the sign of a social identity he found (and was obscurely ashamed of finding) repulsive. He clipped from a newspaper once an item to the effect that many people, it had been discovered, were installing these aerials on their roofs without buying television sets to go with them, and, showing this to Janet, he said, "That's what it comes to in the end."

2 —

If there was one thing less suited than another to the Stone-crofts' modern house, or to the style which was felt to go with it, that thing was a wheelchair, and that is exactly what they got. Janet's widowed mother had a heart attack in July, and by mid-August was established in the guest space for a convalescence of indeterminate length; there was some resentment over this, as much from Janet as from her husband, but the situation did not really allow of argument.

Mrs. Parker was a gaunt but massive woman, with hair of a color Andrew had always thought of as battleship gray. An active woman formerly, a leader in her church and community, she was now condemned to a passive life, which she endured with some difficulty. Stifled and suppressed energies emanated from her, which, with her size, made the house seem smaller than it was. The poor lady doubtless realized the somewhat stereotyped nature of her situation, and even tried to make jokes to Andrew about having a mother-in-law in the place; but it quickly became apparent that she had, and needed, an iron determination to be quiet, give no more trouble than necessary, and express none of her disapproval of modern architecture and a churchless generation which brought up its children without God. This determination, like most iron objects, would not bend, but any break would be irreparable.

The television set came as a matter of course with other of her personal possessions from the house which she had put up for sale.

"Mother is used to having one," Janet said, "and now that she can't go out of the house it's practically a necessity for her; they even have church services on Sundays."

"Now I'm depriving people of the right to worship, am I?" asked Andrew severely; but he conceded nevertheless that it would not be fair to prevent Mrs. Parker from enjoying her own television set, even though in his house.

Nevertheless, the large blond box stood in the living space, the aerial lying beside it, for several days while Janet tried to get a serviceman to install it.

"These people aren't interested in you," she told Andrew, "if you don't buy the set from them in the first place. They keep telling me they've more work than they can possibly handle, or that their own customers come first—they behave worse than the butchers did during the war."

Finally Andrew agreed to put the aerial up himself. "If you can wait for the weekend," he added, feeling somewhat uneasy about climbing up on the roof.

So on the Saturday afternoon, wearing old clothes and having assembled about his person a number of wrenches, screwdrivers and pliers, Andrew began to sort out the bits and pieces of the aerial. Mrs. Parker sat in her wheelchair watching him, and Stephen too looked on, ready to give his advice. It was a very hot day toward the end of August.

It had never occurred to Andrew that the aerial must penetrate the house at some point, and he found it gave him considerable pain of mind, after they had decided where the machine must stand, to take a brace and bit and actually bore a hole through the wall of his own home: the inner wall, the insulating wool, the outer wall. One did not realize, he thought, how thin one's walls really were, and how close the outside of things was to the inside. But he did it, anyhow, and threaded the wire through.

"Now what in heaven's name is this?" he asked, turning to his mother-in-law with an iron spike with a porcelain fitting at the end. He was already somewhat exasperated, for he had never been mechanically minded or clever with his hands, and anticipated with some anxiety having to climb up even on their fairly low roof; ladders frightened him.

"Oh, that's very important," Mrs. Parker replied. "You mustn't leave that out of the circuit—is that the word? It's a lightning arrester. You run the wire through that china bit and push the stake into the ground outside. It goes between the aerial and the set, and the man who installed it at home told me that it protects you against storms. Without it, he said, the lightning could travel down the wire and turn the set into one lump of molten glass and metal. It could probably kill anyone in the room."

"I see," Andrew said, thinking of the set fused into "one lump of molten glass and metal."

"Lightning happens when two clouds bang together," Stephen said. "They have electricity in them. The Russians store it up in bottles and use it later," he added.

"I don't think they do, Stephen," Andrew said.

"They do; it was on television," Stephen insisted. "The Black Raider stole some to give to the United States."

"Okay, Stephen," said Andrew, dragging the light but cumbersome aerial out the door.

"Don't forget the arrester," Mrs. Parker called after him, and he came back for it.

The arrester proved a simple enough matter; you merely threaded the aerial wire through two terminals which you then clamped; all you had to do after that was thrust the iron spike into the earth. Andrew looked at it dubiously; it seemed a very simple device, and very small, for warding off a bolt of lightning, but he supposed the people who made it knew what they were about.

The aerial was a good deal less simple. Janet and Stephen stood on the ground below while Andrew went up the ladder, laid the aerial on the roof, dragged the ladder up after him and propped it against the chimney. For a while it seemed as though he would need a third hand, and twice he lost his temper and told Janet and Stephen to go inside, that he would let them know when he was finished—but they continued to stand there. At last he had the contraption bound securely to the chimney, though.

"I'll leave the ladder here," he said, "till we see if the thing needs to be turned."

And, pleased with himself, he came down onto the roof, from which, on account of the slope of the land, it was not more than six or seven feet to the ground. Andrew took this in a casual jump, but his right foot came down on a loose stone, there was a perfectly audible crack! and three hours later, after Dr. Arnstamm had come and driven him to the hospital for X rays, it turned out that he had broken the outer metatarsal; a simple fracture, fortunately, which hardly needed setting, but which would keep him confined for two or three weeks at least. It hurt terribly, though, when the shock wore off, and after he had been placed with care on the bed Janet had to make an extra pitcher of martinis for the wounded, disconsolate and angered hero. But the television set, to Andrew's great surprise when he thought of it, worked very well.

3 –

Because of the simple nature of his injury, Andrew was allowed to get by without a cast—"on condition you're very careful," the doctor said, adding that the cast would be most irksome, especially in this hot weather—"it would begin to itch." For this reason it was a week before he could rise up and move around, even awkwardly, on crutches, and during this time the television had established its routine in the household. Luckily, Stephen's school began too, which kept him away from the set during most of the day, except on weekends; on account of Mrs. Parker, too, he was allowed to invite friends in for viewing only from five till six-thirty. Mrs. Parker, however, sat in front of that window on the world from early morning till bedtime, and Janet contended this was a good thing.

"It keeps her out of my hair, poor Mother," she said to Andrew, who during this week experienced the television only as a vague rumor and murmur from beyond his bedroom, which had a door but not a very thick one. "It gives her something to think about."

"And what does she think about it?" Andrew asked not very pleasantly. His week in bed exasperated him as it would any healthy man who moreover, on such occasions, begins to have guilty suspicions that his *hard day at the office*, of which he normally makes so much, is mere malingering compared with what his wife goes through, and that if he were suddenly to inherit several million dollars he would continue nevertheless to go downtown every morning, simply to get out of his own home. In short, he had begun to think, in a general way, as people do when confined much alone, about the nature of life "as a whole" and about his own place in it, and he wanted nothing more desperately than to get up, get back to work, and put these thoughts out of the way forever.

It was, in fact, to avert such thoughts that during the week following, being able to move around some on his crutches, Andrew took to watching the television set a good deal himself, though most of the time with a grudging and glowering expression on his face. He would swing through to the kitchen in the morning for coffee; then, on the way back, he would prop himself between one crutch and the wall and sneer meanly at the cheerful news editor on the screen, to whom also he occasionally would make comments.

"Don't tell me about your soap, chum," he would say, or, for instance about the weather forecast, "There you are, grinning away and giving me the word, but you're wrong, dead wrong." But he did not move away, and presently Janet would turn on him.

"Sit down and watch, if you're going to watch. Don't stand right in the way."

Andrew then would sit down, sulky and tentative, in a deep armchair right next to where his mother-in-law had already wheeled herself for the day's viewing; and, as it turned out, there he would stay, with his foot up on a pouffe which Janet brought, glumly watching one program after another.

"I knew you'd like it, dear, once you gave it a chance," Mrs. Parker said once, and her son-in-law thereupon refused to speak to her for one whole day.

"You're being ridiculous," Janet said that night. "I know it's hard for you being cooped up at home, but think what it is for me. And you don't need to be rude to Mother. If you don't like television, go into the bedroom and read."

"I don't want to read," he replied, "and I don't want to think."

The weather continued day after day the same; it had gained official status as a heat wave, and there were jokes about it on the television.

Another week, and Andrew was able to get about with a cane. His temper improved, for he rather admired the image of himself as an old man leaning on a stick, and Dr. Arnstamm had said he could probably return to work the Monday following. Then a rather terrible thing happened.

Stephen was sent home from school on Wednesday morning, near noon. He was in tears, but they were tears of rage, and he would say nothing of what had happened beyond some confused story of injury, wrath and condemnation. Janet phoned the principal, and came from the phone white-faced, nervous; Stephen had been suspended from school for the rest of the week; in the playground that morning he had hit a little girl on the head, with a rock. The little girl was seriously hurt. Oh, she would recover, probably she would suffer no permanent damage, though it was too early to tell about concussion; but there it was. Stephen had hit her on the head with a rock.

The television set had to be turned off while they questioned Stephen, who, however, would tell them nothing more than that "there was a fight." Throughout the interrogation he continued to cry, more and more sullenly.

"Listen, Steve," Andrew said a number of times, "tell me plainly, son—did you do that? Did you hit this little girl with a rock?"

"There was a fight," Stephen said. "Everybody was fighting around."

"But *did* you hit the girl—you yourself, I mean—with a stone or anything like that?"

"Answer your father, Stephen," Janet said.

"We were fighting," Stephen said.

"Children these days aren't taught the difference between right and wrong," Mrs. Parker said.

"All *right*, Mother," Janet said sharply, and Andrew gave the old lady a terrible look.

Janet phoned the little girl's mother.

"I'm terribly sorry about what happened to little Alma," she began, and had to hold the phone away from her ear; the others could plainly hear the high cackle of the other woman's views, though the words were indistinguishable.

"I'm sorry you feel you have to take that attitude," Janet was finally able to put in, her icy voice contrasting with the redness of her face, "and of course I'm deeply sorry for what happened to your little girl, but I'm not yet convinced that it was absolutely all Stephen's fault."

Another burst of outrage clattered out of the phone.

"Since you are so utterly wanting in charity—" Janet announced when she next got the chance; but she was too late; the other receiver went down with a loud clack.

Janet began to walk up and down, squeezing her hands together.

"How terrible," she repeated again and again, "how brutal, how vile—"

Andrew hobbled to the phone and called the principal of the school again.

"Look here, Mr. Blanchard," he began in a very reasonable voice, after introducing himself, "it's been hard for us to get anything coherent from Stephen about all this sad business, but surely it can't have been all his fault. There was a pretty general row; he's told us that. I'm in favor of some reasonable punishment if the boy has done wrong, but for a seven-year-old kid to be suspended from school is—"

"Mr. Stonecroft," the principal said, breaking in, his voice remote and impersonal in the black receiver, "I don't think I've ever been accused of being a severe or punitive person. We do have our discipline to keep up, and we usually keep it up quite successfully. We simply will not have behavior of this sort at the school; most of our children are good-natured, kindly boys and girls, a little rough of course now and then— but things of this nature, hitting people with rocks, simply can't be permitted to happen. If an example must be made, be sure I will make it as I see fit."

"Do you mean to tell me," Andrew said in a most quiet voice, "that you have arbitrarily elected to punish *my* son because there was a general fight in the playground? Is that what you mean by making an example?"

"Your son was undoubtedly guilty," the principal replied. "His own home-room teacher saw the incident. Let me advise you, Mr. Stonecroft, that you should take this opportune warning—you could scarcely do better than use this period of suspension to institute the kind of home discipline without which a mere school cannot hope to have any effect."

"Now you listen to me," said Andrew.

"Please listen to me first, sir. You are new to this neighborhood, and of course you're welcome here. You came from the city, and I can understand that your boy may have received a rougher sort of education in city schools than we have here . . ."

Andrew listened in silence for some moments after this before putting down the phone without saying goodbye.

"Juvenile delinquency," he announced somewhat breathlessly to Janet. "He actually used the words *juvenile delinquency*."

Janet and Andrew stared at Stephen, who was curled up in the armchair, worn out with tears.

"There, dear," said Mrs. Parker, leaning from her wheelchair to pat his head, "you can stay home with Granny and watch the set this week."

"It's time for lunch, anyhow," Janet said.

"Could you turn on the set, Jan, before you go?" asked Mrs. Parker pleasantly.

4—

The remainder of that week was horrifying. In the first place, the weather continued hot, hot and damp. Andrew twice tried to get out and limp around the grounds alone, but after a few minutes of this his foot caused him so much pain that he went indoors again and sat before the television set, which he watched now out of a kind of helpless despair, like a gambler who, having lost most of his property, hurls the rest after it with a sort of insane gaiety before shooting himself.

Mrs. Parker sat in her wheelchair, Andrew next to her, Stephen on the floor in front of them. There had been a desperate move organized at first to punish Stephen by depriving him of his television rights; but this meant, in their "living space," that Mrs. Parker (not to mention Andrew himself) was being punished; the set had to be turned off. Stephen sulked bitterly, and played father and mother off against each other until he trapped Janet into an exasperated permission to go watch the set, if he must; whereupon Andrew flew into a fit of temper having to do with the nature of discipline.

"If you keep him from the television," Janet explained wearily, "someone has to keep him amused, and I'm usually the one."

"It's just that if I say a thing," he said back, "you must not —must not—go and say the opposite."

"You and your discipline," she said; "you're punishing yourself, if you want to know. You want to watch the tiny screen yourself, and you hate yourself for it."

"Just you go psychoanalyze someone else for a change," he said, since he felt there was some truth in what she said. Then he added, in more reasonable tones, "What gets me is that the boy isn't even sorry; he doesn't seem to realize what he's done."

"Watching or not watching the television isn't connected with what he's done," Janet retorted. "And he is sorry—I'm sure he is. Aren't you sorry, Stephen?"

"I'm sorry, Mommy and Daddy," Stephen said in a small voice.

"You should be ashamed of yourselves, quarreling in front of the child," Mrs. Parker said.

"Stevie, look at me, look in my eyes," Andrew said. "Do you understand that you did something wrong, something real bad, when you hit Alma?"

"Yes, Dad."

"Something you must never do—never? You understand that?"

"Yes, Dad."

"Look me in the eyes, now, Son. You promise never to do anything like that again?"

"Yes, Dad."

"All right, then. You may watch the television."

"If the child is not being properly brought up in his own faith," Mrs. Parker said, "how can he be expected to know good from bad? I've not wanted to say anything all these weeks, because I'm a guest here and an unwanted guest, too —and an unwilling one, I'll let you know that, too. But I've seen what I've seen, and if you want to know God's truth, the pair of you, you've been punished, and you are lucky the punishment was no heavier than it was."

"I don't want to know God's truth," said Andrew savagely, "and when I do, I'll go ask God for it."

"For shame—in front of the child," cried Mrs. Parker.

"Now that is absolutely enough, from both of you," said Janet. "Just one little bit more of that sort of thing, and *I* leave."

So the television set was turned on.

5 —

On Sunday morning the weather was hot again. The news announcer predicted, however, that the hot spell would definitely break that day. Showers and thunderstorms, a cold front, were forecast for New York City, eastern New York and New England.

"You've been wrong before, chum, and you could be wrong again," said Andrew to the man on the screen.

There followed a succession of religious services, Catholic and Protestant. Mrs. Parker usually turned off the Catholic service, but today, for Stephen, she kept it on.

"It is all about Jesus just the same," she said. "The little differences can come in later."

"Jesus, Son," Andrew said in a plain, toneless, pedagogic voice, "is a man who lived long long ago. Some people believe this man was really a god. Others—like your mother and myself—think that he was only a very good man."

"Was he nice?" asked Stephen.

"Yes, he was very nice," said Janet somewhat tensely, leaning over the counter from the kitchen space.

"Jesus loves all little boys and girls," Mrs. Parker said.

"Is he dead?" Stephen asked.

"Yes," said Andrew exactly as Mrs. Parker said, "No, he is in heaven."

"Do they have television in heaven?" asked Stephen, leaving Andrew a little at a loss. Mrs. Parker replied that they had everything in heaven, and then they all watched in silence for a little while.

The Catholic service was followed by a Protestant discussion group, which talked about the breakup of the family in the modern world.

"If you're bored, Son, you can go out and play," Andrew said. "Any time, you know."

The group on the screen, two oldish men and two middle-aged ladies, congratulated themselves and one another upon a successful family life.

"You listen to that and mark it well," said Mrs. Parker to Andrew. He had left off replying to this kind of thing, out of a sense that the old lady did it only to needle him, and she had become correspondingly bolder.

Stephen did not seem to get bored at all; he watched everything impartially, with bug-eyed attention.

He doesn't understand any of it, Andrew thought. When the novelty wears off he won't bother with this stuff.

After the Protestants came a children's program, a circus, which Andrew found quite fascinating, and after that a Western story.

Janet brought a sandwich lunch in, and sat down herself.

"I think it is going to storm at last," she said. "Big clouds are piling up down over the Hill."

Another religious program, hymn-singing and a sermon, followed the Western.

"Methodists," said Mrs. Parker in some disgust.

"Almost time for the football game, though," Andrew said. It was the thing he looked forward to already; the season had started yesterday, with a college game, and today there would be the first pro game, the New York Giants vs. the Pittsburgh Steelers.

"Oh—" said Mrs. Parker, to indicate that she was bravely concealing her disappointment about something.

"Mother likes to watch 'Window on the World' on Channel three," Janet said.

"And what is 'Window on the World'?" he asked.

"Ah, well." Janet was a trifle vague. "They just show films of what various sorts of people do all over the world."

"Last week they showed pearl divers in Japan," said Mrs. Parker, "and how automobiles are made, on an assembly line —you know, all sorts of things of that kind."

Andrew had been about to make some protest concerning his right to watch a football game if he cared to. But he saw what this would involve him in: further argument, more ill temper and discontent; and besides—his deeply moral nature told him—it would do him good to deprive himself of this trivial pleasure; there would be other football games. Once he had decided to give in, moreover, it became a moral point with him to do so pleasantly, and without seeming to struggle over it.

"Fine with me," he said, smiling. "We'll have a look at this 'Window on the World,' eh, Son?"

Stephen did not reply.

"It's very good for children," Mrs. Parker said. "It's an educational program. Especially while he's out of school," she added.

"He'll get educated when he goes back to school," said Andrew with a sweet-and-sour expression.

"Yes, both you men get out of the hoosegow tomorrow, don't you?" Janet said. "Will you like being back at school, Steve?"

Stephen continued to watch the hymn-singing.

"I said, Steve, will you like being back at school?" Janet asked more sharply.

"Yes," Stephen said without turning around.

"O Lord, my rock and my redeemer," cried the mixed choir; and then, after several very rapid advertisements, expressed so urgently that the people speaking might have been jerked from the microphone by an invisible hand, came "Window on the World."

The narrator of this program was a pleasant-faced, portly and somewhat scholarly-looking man of middle age. He wore thick-rimmed glasses, which he would sometimes take off and twiddle elegantly in his fingers. He had a deep voice, and spoke softly, casually, and in a friendly way which pleased Andrew despite a determination not to be taken in by what he thought of as "this professional bedside manner." If people were really as friendly as this gent sounds, he thought, the world would be a wonderful place, the way one sometimes thought it was when one was a child.

This narrator spoke a few pleasant, random words, talked about the weather for a moment or so, saying how good it was that this heat wave was breaking up all over the eastern seaboard, how his own garden needed the rain as much as anyone's, and so on. About his garden he was humorously modest. "I may not have a green thumb," he said, "but I sure have a black and blue foot—planted a shovel right on it the other evening."

He probably lives in the St. Regis hotel, Andrew thought,

but all the same he could not help being rather charmed with the man's way of doing things.

After a little of this kind of talk, the narrator stepped aside and the screen flickered for a moment, then revealed the first episode. It was the Changing of the Guard at Buckingham Palace, the entire ceremony, with only its inactive periods cut out, so that it was not only real, it was better than real; Andrew remembered watching the real thing during the war and being bored by the length of time in which both the incoming and the outgoing guards stood at ease while their officers walked up and down whispering. But here on the screen everything was martial, musical, clipped and precise, the sound caught even the metal click of heels on the stone, and even the echo of this thrilling military noise from the stone walls of the parade yard. And there followed a parade of the Horse Guards in the Mall.

"You should see it in color, Son," Andrew said, touching Stephen's shoulder. "The way it really is, with the red coats, golden breastplates, the way those bay horses shine in the sun. You'll see it one day."

The boy turned and smiled at his father for the first time in four days. Andrew felt affectionate and grateful.

The narrator spoke a bit more, then faded out on a gracious wave of his hand, like a magician, to show them something of the life of a big farm in the Middle West. The farmer himself, a seamed, bitten, shrewd yet kindly face, showed them over his land, with not acres but it seemed miles of grain waving in the sun and then bending to a violent storm which the camera splendidly captured. It was at this moment or thereabouts, oddly, that they heard the first distant noise of thunder outside the house.

"It will storm, after all," Janet said.

"Of course," said Andrew, but with a smile. "They control it from the studio."

The narrator returned to say a few more words. He spoke again, casually, with no attempt to be dramatic—to ham it up, as Andrew would have said—about the vastness and variety of the world. Then he faded away, with the promise of strange things to come, and because these were late films his voice continued, giving the commentary informally which ordinarily would have been prepared in advance and recorded with the film.

The thunder sounded a trifle louder outside, and the image on the screen jerked, flickered and jumped with distant lightnings.

"I hope Mother's lightning arrester works," Janet said.

"We're lucky to have it," said Mrs. Parker, "or we would have to turn the set off."

The cameras now showed them a confused, milling throng of white-robed black people on an evidently limitless grass plain. The narrator said that they were privileged to witness something few white people had ever seen, the incoronation of the King and Queen of the Wabuga peoples of West Africa. And indeed the camera, evidently mounted on a truck, moved bumpily through the great crowd until it arrived at a clear space near the center. Here enthroned among dignitaries sat the monarch and his wife, both of them handsome, dignified, with shining black skins, and dressed in the richest brocaded silks or satins; the King, a young man, wore several large medals as well.

They were able to witness the whole ceremony, which the narrator explained to them: how the bishop—since this was a Christian nation for all the color of their skins—brought the consecrated crown upon a cushion, how he would anoint the King but not the Queen with the holy oil, how all the people would bow down before the Lord's Anointed.

"You will see," the narrator continued, "in a few moments —you will see a rather terrible thing which marred the religious part of the ceremony. Our cameras managed to catch this thing—this moment of history, you might call it—just as it was actually happening."

Like a field of wheat before the storm, those thousands of white robes knelt just then; the camera swung over the field to catch this movement.

"Now watch the upper left corner of your screens," the narrator said, still in a casual voice but with a touch more urgency. "Here he comes."

A boy, or a young man, was riding unsteadily on a bicycle, his white robe tucked up around his waist; he rode down an alley between crowds of kneeling people. The camera turned to look at the royal couple and the bishop, who stood poised with the crown high in the air, then switched back to the boy. A few people had risen up and were waving at him, and then some were shaking their fists, but he rode on toward the central space.

"They are warning him to get off and kneel down," the narrator said rather neutrally.

Now some people took off after the boy, and a few of them made throwing gestures.

"Those are stones they are throwing," the narrator said. "Probably you can't see them on your screens. Stones."

Now some of the white-robed figures had caught up with the boy, who either threw down his cycle or was knocked off it. He began to run.

"The outraged worshipers stoned the young man to death," the narrator said, and they watched a cloud, a wave, of white robes break over the running boy and bring him down; then there followed a violent rippling of cloth over the mob at that place; then the cameras turned back to the King and Queen of the Wabuga, there was a flickering of the film where some interval of confusion probably had been cut, and the coronation went on its way, the narrator explaining as before.

"Tch, tch," went Mrs. Parker. "That poor fellow. He should have known better."

Andrew said in a choked voice, "Mother, this really happened. They killed that child right in front of our eyes."

"Well, I know," Mrs. Parker said, "but after all, I suppose they have their—what do you call them?—taboos, don't they?"

"He said they were Christians," Andrew said.

"Is heaven like that?" Stephen asked. Andrew could only stare at him.

"He means the white robes," Janet said.

The narrator reappeared now, his grave, kindly face comforting. But he did not choose to talk about what they had just been shown. Instead he said a few words about what "Window on the World" would show them next Sunday.

Andrew got up and hobbled outdoors on his cane. He felt confused and outraged, unable to think clearly, and certainly unable to say a word to anyone in the house. He wondered if the New York Giants were beating the Pittsburgh Steelers.

There was going to be a storm, that was certain now. Great dark clouds towered high in the southwest over Appletree Hill, the brilliant anvil shining in the sunlight above them. Thunder, though still a little ways off, rumbled almost continuously, there were brief, indefinite flickers of lightning, and he felt already a few drops of rain. The heat wave was over.

Andrew hobbled slowly around the house, not much caring if he got wet or not. What did he care about? he asked himself, and replied that he surely did not care if one black boy got knocked off by his own people. Only something, something to do with his having watched this episode, this moment of history, as the narrator had called it, seemed to him more atrocious perhaps than the thing itself. To have helplessly witnessed that death on the screen in the security of his own living room—or living space, as he sardonically remembered to call it, *Lebensraum*—that was horrifying to him, and presented to him an image of his life as mean and cowardly.

The thunder banged, suddenly close, as though nearly overhead, and sudden lightning opened the entire sky, it seemed.

"O God of Battles," Andrew said with irrelevant violence. "The Lord is a Man of War," he remembered from his early days, and, from the famous battle hymn, "He is trampling out the vineyards where the grapes of wrath are stored." But none of all this comforted him or released in him feelings which remained obscure and intense.

His eye fell upon the lightning arrester sticking in the ground near the back wall. He disconnected the terminals, freed the aerial wire, and with a gay gesture of violence hurled the iron spike as far away as he was able, into the bushes.

Take your chance along with everyone else, he said to himself, and limped back into the house, already feeling both ridiculous and timid.

His family remained before the television set, which now showed for a long, still instant the image of a television set. The announcer declared that television set to be without fault.

"We won't even show you a picture on the new Universal," he proclaimed, "because you wouldn't be able to see it properly on the set you have now."

Andrew limped back to his chair and sat down.

"What's on next?" he asked, hearing the thunder crackle and roar while the air even in the room seemed to darken.

Tradition

BELOW THE VILLAGE of Ravensburg, at the edge of the woods and facing the swampy bottom lands that spread to the river, old Mr. Birch had his cabin where he lived alone and did nothing, or almost nothing. People driving the highway on the other side of the river could look across and have a glimpse of him—a faded denim shirt, flowering white hair— sitting peaceably in a rocker on his porch, one end of which had sagged; and those people, if they were just passing through on their way from one city to another, would sometimes be reminded of the firm rural virtues, frugality and toil, upon which our civilization is reared. In a flash—before even slowing down for the stop signal which marks Ravensburg's one crossroads—they would have a vision, touched by nostalgia, of the fine thing it was to live close to the soil, to be born, spend your days, and die old in a cabin beside a river. Ravensburg itself, an unenterprising and largely decaying little place, would perhaps change their minds, as they passed the abandoned stove factory with its heap of rusting iron bellies and limbs like the carnage of some robot battlefield; but by that time they would have had the vision, and for the fact that it rested entirely on illusion, on nothing, nobody—certainly not Mr. Adam Birch—could be held responsible. But that is often how it is with our edifications. People are driven to noble and desperate actions by, it may be, a lie in a schoolbook; perhaps Alexander the Great imitated in his conquests some perfectly fantastic notion of ancient virtues which his tutor had heard fables of.

Old Mr. Birch had not been born in Ravensburg but in Brooklyn. To his present habitation he had come many years ago, during Prohibition, and the rumor was that he had been a small beer baron, a rumrunner, a hijacker, a dynamiter of safes—some such thing, anyhow—who had not only evaded the law but piled up, also, a sufficiency of funds to enable his quite modest retirement to the country. We see Mr. Birch from outside, and do not know if these things said about him are true, but certainly he seems to have had some experience with dynamite.

If Mr. Birch presented no living illumination of the truth that Crime Does Not Pay, he could at least be used to illustrate the proposition that Crime Does Not Pay Very Well. If a beer baron at all, he must have been an extremely small one, for he drank nothing but beer except if someone stood him the odd glass of whisky now and then at the Blue Light Tavern, where he usually went in the evenings to read the paper. This treat happened seldom, though, for while he was a nice, friendly old man, he didn't talk much, he seemed to have little to talk about. When he had first come—and not many people clearly remembered that time, jealous as for some reason they all were about the high privilege of having been born in Ravensburg—Mr. Birch used to talk some about Brooklyn, and how good it was to have been born there, to know that you had, so to say, all that life and infinite rumbling variety behind you. But then Brooklyn dropped out of his talk, and he began to tell people that as a matter of fact he had been born right in Ravensburg, but moved to Brooklyn at an early age—that he had really, in moving to the country, come back home. People did not exactly believe this, but they did not exactly out loud refuse to believe it; partly because Mr. Adam Birch was an extremely powerful (though gentle) old person, and partly because this story of his seemed to them less an outright lie than an honest and praiseworthy ambition to have been born in Ravensburg. Also they thought him a bit queer, though not seriously so.

The Lord alone knows what he did with his days, old Adam Birch. In the good weather he sat before that shack of his and watched, presumably, the world go by; which at that place it did very leisurely, at about the pace of the Manadoc River flowing slowly from right to left in front of him. Perhaps he counted the cars going by across the river and thought it a good day when more cars went from left to right than from right to left, or vice versa. Perhaps he thought about his boyhood, about being born in Brooklyn or Ravensburg. Perhaps he watched, with slow, perceptive care, the seasons change in hundreds of slight allusions and indications which over twenty years he had come to know quite well, though probably without calling them by their names. Behind his white head lay the poky, prospectively dirty and unneat mystery of his shack, which no one but himself entered, and behind the shack lay the forest rising up over the hills and the wild country of deer and bear and badger and fox and skunk and maybe bobcat; and over his white head sailed the immense sky like a sea with turreted galleons of cloud and distant lines of surf of cloud.

One thing he must have done was watch the crows, the crows and ravens which had given his village of adoption its name long ago. Ravensburg had a huge population of these birds, not so noticeable by day when they were dispersed over the countryside as at evening, when they returned to roost, which they did all around Adam Birch's house, in the massed trees at the forest's edge, and in the lonely single elms, oaks and hickory that stood out in the swamp land between there and the river. At sundown in this place the sky would thicken with wheels of crow, their voices in deafening volume would rebound from the hills behind and fill the damp bottoms with continuous sound; then, as though by a single command, they would settle for the night into their ridiculously unkempt, huge and rickety nests. Henry Ward Beecher is supposed to have summed up the crow's reputation for wisdom, or at least intelligence, by saying that not many men, if they had wings and feathers, would have the sense to be crows; but probably any man, even without wings and feathers, could make a better-looking nest. Anyhow, there were thousands upon thousands of these crows, it was like an airport for them out where Adam Birch had his residence; so there can be hardly any doubt he must have watched the crows, though what he thought about them it is impossible to know except by inference from the things that happened, and such inference is always at best a dubious business.

Ravensburg had its name, as I said, from this circumstance of birds. No one knew any more whether the first settlers had called it so because there were in fact more ravens than crows, or whether it was from the simple consideration that the raven, even before Poe's celebrated poem, had a more attractive and high-sounding reputation. It is true that a place called Crowville (or even Crowburg) could scarcely be expected to get very far in the world; but then, neither had Ravensburg got very far in the world. At any rate, there were now many more crows than ravens, perhaps for the same reason that "more geese than swans now live, more fools than wise," and perhaps for no reason at all. But they are very different birds, the raven and the crow, the former being much larger, and flying more like a hawk, with passages of planing on perfectly flat wings alternated with passages of wing-beating, while the latter beats his wings more continuously, and in his slight soarings is observed to have a dihedral tilt to the wings. They also make different noises, the crow saying *caw* and the raven something altogether less humanly imitable, such as *krauuuk*, described by authorities as "hoarse, uncouth, dismal and prolonged," though whether they mean something entirely different is open to question. And it is doubtful that these distinctions much occupied old Mr. Birch's mind; probably to him they were all crows, or all ravens.

As to his physical appearance, Mr. Birch was tall and fat, though as a matter of fact he was one of those persons who look fat and are not, whose sagging paunches seem resting cruelly on the edges of their belts but turn out, if anyone dares to touch them, to be hard as a tire; so all the beer which old Mr. Birch had drunk in his life seemed to have transmuted itself magically, and without any particular help from himself, into muscle. His face was broad, browned and weathered, with a large, twisted nose that fattened like a root prospering in midair, with jagged teeth brown as kernels of Indian corn, with eyes of a pale blue like fringed gentians. His hair was as soft and fine and white as the silk which in autumn spills from milkweed when it bursts, and carries the seed away on the wind.

He might have been a poacher, a great huntsman outside the law, except that upon his first arriving in Ravensburg he seemed to have attempted some such thing and got lost on the hills, in the deep forest, to be found two days later by accident (for no one knew he had gone) when a couple of real poachers came across him sitting on a fallen tree with his rifle on his lap. Since then old Adam Birch had stayed away from the deep forest, and though it was thought he might be not above taking a deer out of season, or in season at night by jack lantern, that would be very likely because the deer was wandering past his front door, where it could really be regarded as a nuisance on his property and killed quite legally. But as a true poacher he exemplified something that must happen more frequently than we know, a career of crime prevented by simple incompetence. It remained true to say, when asked what Adam Birch did, that he did nothing.

2 —

Now one of the newspapers that Adam Birch used to read in the Blue Light Tavern evenings was the Hartland *Press*, and as Hartland was the county seat, that paper used to publish a page or so of doings around the county generally; one of the things they would run from time to time, just to make up the end of a column, was a little stick of a sentence or two saying how Ravensburg had got its name, and once they added another sentence to the effect that in one year the birds had been so numerous, and such a pest to farmers, that a bounty had been put on their heads of twenty-five cents per bird. And that was all it said, but it seems to have been enough. People find their destiny by the most trivial indications.

That little stick of filler could doubtless lie around a printer's shop for fifty years or more, and even be printed three or four times or more, without becoming an occasion of anxiety to any large number of crows or ravens or both, without inciting any person to the kind of large-scale activity implicit in its premises. The sensible person, the person with a business and a life of his own, skimming over the article in the first place as of no real interest and clearly inserted just to fill space, would think—if he fleetingly thought of it at all— that this bounty must have been withdrawn long, long ago.

A less sensible person might pause to think, Why, there's money in crows—why not go out and . . . But by this time even he would have concluded dismally that probably the bounty had been withdrawn long, long ago, and even if it hadn't been he would look seven kinds of damn fool out blasting away at crows, which were very wily birds; and he would think of the cost of shotgun shells (or rifle bullets if he had so high an opinion of his skill) and what his friends would say (not to mention his wife), and he would by that time anyhow be halfway through the next column of type, dozing off a little maybe, and that would be that.

Adam Birch was not a sensible person, in this sense, and not even a less sensible person; it seems likely he thought quite a lot about that stick of type (it is at least a plausible inference that he did) and that somewhere in his hypothetical background (beer baron, rumrunner, etc.) there lay the possible application of modern industrial methods to the problem of crows; there may have been also in that background the vague suggestion that ordinances and laws do not get repealed but get forgotten instead. The conclusion had to be that a bounty offered on the premise that farm boys would here and there loose off at a crow with a flintlock (or whatever they had back then) was perfectly liable to survive in oblivion, and, like so many ancient customs, traditions and whatnot, provide modern opportunities and modern embarrassments. Such at any rate may have been the mechanics of the matter; as to what were the deeper motives which caused Adam Birch to leave his seat on the shaky porch and come to be the scourge of crows, little or nothing can be said. Maybe he had come in all that time to hate crows, and needed only the slight financial incentive to get him off his behind and into action; maybe he loved the crows and sacrificed them regretfully to his well-being; or maybe the crows had never really existed for him, and he had thought nothing about them until given an abstract equivalent—that a crow was, a crow meant, twenty-five cents—which had the possibility of being thought about.

But whatever he thought—to take things in their apparent order—the village of Ravensburg did not know for some time, though there had been the following indications of increased activity on Birch's part: that he took his old Ford (which he had got when he planned on doing some farming which he did not do) over to Hartland several times; that he was often to be seen snooping around the stove factory picking up old bits and pieces (there may have been a law against that, but who would enforce such a thing?); that he got the Village Records from the clerk and spent hours going through them, his lips moving silently while he ran his forefinger down page after page looking for what ought not to be there; that finally, one day, he came into the clerk's office holding a dead crow and said he had come for the bounty on that crow. The clerk looked at him vaguely, but old Birch showed him the Records with the announcement of the bounty, and prepared to take him right through to show that bounty was still on the book. "All right, I believe you," the clerk said after a few minutes of this, and threw him a quarter across the counter, taking in exchange the dead crow and tossing it thoughtlessly in the wastebasket behind him. He remembered thinking, the clerk did, that maybe he ought to mention that bounty to the mayor or the judge, but he put it off from laziness, thinking, "If he comes in again, I'll let someone know."

The foregoing suggests—it is easy to be wise after the event —the care with which Adam Birch, having discovered doubt-less from the Records the difficulty of negative proof, sought to put the burden of it altogether on the other side; and established him a precedent with the clerk; for it followed, once the principle was admitted that a quarter would be paid for a crow, that n crows would bring n quarters.

What else followed was that toward dusk a few days later Ravensburg was startled out of its suppertime wits by numerous and rapid explosions. Everyone rushed out of doors, but it was too dark to see much, no glare of fire lighted the horizon, silence had already settled back down (though a number of crows, startled by the blast no doubt, were flying about overhead and screaming), so everyone went back inside to supper and speculation—the latter quite useless, for there were no industries in Ravensburg which would go off with anything like that effect; so people finally began to declare it must have been over to Hartland, and sounded so loud on account of echoing from the hills. Anyone out walking the highway, however, would have seen, probably without tying it to the explosions, a lantern bobbing ceaselessly and jerkily up and down as it moved this way and that around the swamplands by the river; this lantern was attached to Adam Birch's belt. The milkman saw this light next day at dawn; it was still bobbing up and down, but he did not give it much thought because of the gloom and mist of morning which made all else impossible to see.

Full sunlight disclosed a horrible mess, there on the marshes before old Mr. Birch's house. Trees, split and fallen, lay every which way, and between the trees the ground was covered with crows. Among these crows still strode Adam Birch, the lantern at his belt still jerking up and down (it was still lighted, as a matter of fact) as he methodically and according to some definite pattern he had laid out in his head moved about bashing at the black bodies with a baseball bat in his right hand and a length of lead pipe in his left. Here and there a crow still feebly fluttered or cawed, but mostly those crows were through. Mr. Birch must presently have thought so, or had enough anyhow, for just as he was he got into his Ford and drove to the office of the clerk.

It was still quite early, the clerk had only just got there and

was occupied rubbing the sleep from his eyes, when in came
Adam Birch covered in mud, sweat, blood and feathers, with
pieces of bone and crow's eyes sticking to his clothing, his
hair all bloody and black with mud where he must have
pushed it back out of his eyes with a gory hand—in came
Adam Birch and said that so far as he had reckoned he was
entitled to the bounty on about two thousand crows, and a
hard night's work it'd been.

The clerk, as soon as he recovered from the terrible fright
the sight of old Mr. Birch had given him by coming in covered with blood and so forth, realized that the matter was
beyond his competence, and so he told Mr. Birch that nothing
could be done until the mayor came in, which would be in
about half an hour. "I'll wait," Mr. Birch replied. And so he
would have, had that clerk not been greatly taken with his
own cleverness and after a moment said, with a slight, civil
sneer, "We don't pay no bounty but for crows in hand; crows
in the field is not enough." That, he thought, would discour-
age the old man.

But Mr. Birch was not discouraged; he acknowledged the
logic of what the clerk had said, so he simply turned back and
loaded his Ford up to the roof with dead crows and came up
to the office again while the clerk was out at the barbershop
telling everyone what had happened; with the result that
when the mayor arrived at the Town Hall the floor of the
outer office, where his clerk worked, had on it a substantial
first load of dead crows, Adam Birch having meanwhile gone
back for more. "Clerk!" shouted the mayor, in a voice that
could be and was heard clear down to the barbershop; and
the clerk came running back to be denounced by the mayor.
Before this clerk could get in a word edgewise, back came
Mr. Adam Birch with another load of dead crows, which he
began dumping slowly, two by two, on the floor in the office.

When the mayor finally understood what had happened,

he used his wits. First he told the clerk to tell Mr. Birch to get those crows out of there. They would count the crows on the field, he said, and (with an edge in his voice) Mr. Birch would get everything that was coming to him. Mr. Birch obediently began removing the crows, which he put back on the field in front of his house to be counted. Meanwhile the mayor, after instructing his clerk to wash the floor, summoned to a conference the chief of police, the judge and the game warden. This conference lasted into the mid-morning, and when it was over all these officials drove out to see just what had taken place; by that time the whole town, more or less, was standing around with hands in pockets, smoking and making remarks. It was a public holiday.

It was clear by now that what Mr. Birch had done, with great effort and at some cost, was to manufacture a number of bombs from sticks of dynamite placed in stovepipes and packed from end to end with fragments of iron stove. These bombs, wired to storage batteries, had been placed quite high in the trees where the crows most numerously nested; there on the ground lay the ladder which Mr. Birch had evidently constructed himself, a very crude ladder; and from the group of batteries on the porch wires still led away everywhere. And there on the ground were all those crows. It was a sickening spectacle. Among the crows, when they came to be counted, lay a number of innocent victims—presuming the crows to have been in some way guilty: squirrels, rabbits, a brace of pheasant, three woodchuck, a few dozen sparrows, starlings, robins, three or four jays, and there was even one doe lying dead at the edge of the wood, a piece of stove door in her head. What was more, several fragments of a bomb incautiously planted too close by had gone through the side window of Mr. Birch's cabin, breaking the glass, a hanging bulb and the mirror on the far wall. It looked probable, as this window was but a few feet from the porch, that Mr.

Birch himself might easily have destroyed himself with the crows; and some people were of the opinion that this would have been a good thing.

But this kind of indignation came from a very small minority, inspired perhaps most of all by the clerk, whose motives for indignation could not have been purely in favor of the crows. Most people were a little dazed by the whole affair, did not know what to make of it—for it seemed unlikely that the appearance of so much blood could be unconnected with some sort of crime—and were waiting for someone to take an official view. Mr. Birch by this time, whether to avoid questions or simply because he was tired, had gone into his cabin and shut the door. It is noteworthy that practically everyone among the confused majority had gone over to look at the dead doe and remarked on the pity of that, as though a certain size and distinction of gender were necessary to make innocence visible. Apart from this, though, many people were inclined to laugh at the whole business—if they had had nothing against crows they did not know so much in their favor either —and to make the outstanding thing the "unholy mess" that Mr. Birch had caused. Some said he was mad, and most likely all would have agreed that his action had been at least queer; yet there was also, to such as imagined it in any detail, something ludicrously yet frighteningly Homeric and titanic in the idea of the brute old man with the white hair slaughtering wounded crows the whole night long by lantern light. It was not the Vale of Roncesvalles, nor the Valley of Ajalah where Joshua made the sun stand still, but remotely it parodied such scenes, and Mr. Birch implicitly had the sort of reputation from his deed that the tailor had in the fairy tale, who slaughtered six at one blow. As for the old man's being in fact and in law mad, there had to be set over against that the irreproachable cold sanity of his having done all this for money; and in some people's minds the question of his madness resolved itself into two more basic questions: was it enough money? and would he get the money? It should be added that a few people, looking at the ground, became sick to their stomachs.

The remainder of the morning was taken up with an official tally of the crows. The clerk, carrying a writing board, moved through the field marking off each crow which Adam Birch, summoned from his house, placed in a pile until there were twenty-five; then they would both, followed by the mayor and the judge and the chief of police and the game warden, move a few feet over and begin again. The crowd spread raggedly around them.

It turned out that the number of crows came to 2,102, or, translated, a bounty of $525.50. Allowing the odd dollars over for expenses (the dynamite, the batteries) Adam Birch could be said roughly to clear five hundred dollars. The mayor was almost in a stupor from the sun and indignation.

The Village of Ravensburg did not have five hundred dollars to spend on this old man, and was not certain (in the person of the mayor) if it would be morally right to spend it so granting the money to be available. Legally, legalistically, it appeared to be old Adam Birch's just reward for ridding the village of such a number of crows which for all practical purposes it had not even known it had. There was not such a deal of farming around Ravensburg any more, the land being mostly poor and worked out, and besides, as the game warden had assured him that morning, the modern view of crows, rather different from what had been believed when the bounty was established, held them to be as useful as they were destructive, inasmuch as the contents of their stomachs proved they ate not merely corn but so much else besides that the corn scarcely mattered: all sorts of offal, refuse, carrion, garbage; young birds, adult ones now and then, eggs, mice and snakes. A neutral sort of bird, in the modern view.

To a reporter who had come from Hartland the mayor said (again) that Mr. Birch would get everything that was coming to him.

At his conference that morning, he had found the other dignitaries of the village entirely agreed that something must be done, though no one was altogether sure what it would be. But the chief of police (and fire chief) had been reassuring when he said, "You can't make that much noise and not commit a crime," while the game warden, echoing him, had said, "You can't kill that many anythings and not commit a crime," and the judge had said, "We'll see to it that the man eats crow," at which all four of them dourly smiled.

So when old Adam Birch showed up, by instruction, to collect his reward—it was now midafternoon, and he had cleaned himself up and changed his clothes—he found waiting for him not only the clerk but the mayor, and not only the clerk and the mayor but also the chief of police and the game warden and the judge, all of whose offices gave off the clerk's room, and all of them were standing in the doors of their offices smiling.

The mayor congratulated Mr. Birch upon ridding the village of all those crows and asked him to step over to the clerk, who would make him out a check for five hundred and twenty-five dollars and fifty cents. When this was done the chief of police tapped him on the shoulder and said, "Adam Birch, I arrest you in the name of the law," and brought him over to where the judge was standing.

"This man is charged with disturbing the peace," said the chief, "also with the unlicensed possession and use of explosives."

"Guilty or not guilty?" asked the judge, and old Adam, who saw very well where things were tending, replied that he was guilty.

"Fifty dollars on each count," said the judge. "Case dismissed. Pay the clerk as you leave."

But, before he could even pay, the game warden had arrested Adam too, on four charges. First, killing a deer out of season. Second, killing a deer by illegal means. Third, killing a doe. Fourth, as some of those crows had fallen in the river, polluting a stream. To all these charges Adam Birch had to plead guilty, and was sentenced to pay a total of three hundred dollars in fines. He also lost his hunting license on this account, and it was a lucky thing he had one, as the officials were planning to get another fine with the charge of killing a deer without a license.

Because they could not get this other fine they were puzzled for a moment; Adam was handing the clerk his check and would have received $125.50 in change. But the judge spoke up in time and said there was the matter of destruction of public property; the trees were public property: fifty dollars. And this inspired him to add that the crows also, inasmuch as the village was named after them, or after the ravens anyhow, no difference—the crows also were public property. That would be fifty dollars.

There was a great chance, now, of Adam's escaping with $25.50 in pocket, to pay him for the dynamite. But the mayor, at this moment, became very clever.

"Of course, you could plead innocent to all these charges," he said, and Adam turned toward him looking bewildered.

"I mean, nobody *saw* you do all those things," insisted the mayor. "Maybe you didn't do them?"

"In that case," said Adam Birch, "I plead innocent."

"In that case," said the mayor, "you didn't kill those crows, so there will be no bounty."

"Sonofagun," said Adam. "There's no justice. I plead guilty."

"Profanity," said the judge cheerfully, "which is in contempt of court. Twenty-five dollars."

"And fifty cents, Judge," the mayor reminded him.

"And fifty cents."

After Adam had gone, leaving the check on the clerk's counter, the mayor sighed.

"Thank God for that doe," he said, or perhaps it was "dough."

3 –

But the history does not end on this sordid consideration. No one knew what Mr. Adam Birch thought about all that had happened, for he answered to no laughter and kept his own ideas to himself, sitting on the porch before his place, surveying the field of killed crows. When the chief of police came by next day to tell him to clean up and get rid of all those birds and so forth, or there would be another fine, Adam nodded and set about it. By that night, in a true bonfire, a great pyre of crows soaked in kerosene began to burn, and burned for three days. The smell at first was quite good, and led some to say he might have sold the birds for eating, but after a while it became oppressive, and on the third day a downright stink. There might have been another fine imposed for this, but the mayor did not want (he said) to go beyond justice into tyranny, he pitied the poor old man (in a way), and the fire would soon be over. Besides, there were some who thought that Mr. Birch had got a raw deal, and sympathized with him. It seemed better to let the whole episode die away. Perhaps the only person who did not fully agree with this judgment was, again, Mr. Birch.

Though at the heart of the fire his crows were burned to indistinctive ash, all around the edges and a certain way in their skulls and their bones remained, intact and beautifully white. These Mr. Birch collected all of the third day, and also thousands of feathers which lay scattered about the field; he even rescued from the periphery of the fire a fairly large number of crow's feet.

Of all this material he patiently began to make souvenirs: quill pens at first, and feathers for hats, and feather Indian headdresses; then, more ambitiously, little lattice houses of bone, a tray of patterned crow feathers under glass, reflecting brilliantly blue-black lights shot with green; the skulls of the crows were left as they were for macabre stamp boxes, or the little hole in the top of the skull allowed it to be filled with dirt and a violet or other small flower planted there; the lacquered legs and claws, mounted on rocks (later on polished hardwood), made attractive paperweights. In all this Mr. Birch displayed considerable ingenuity and manual skill; and by midsummer he had made a stand by the highway over the river and was selling these objects, with a certain small success.

Or was it the objects, exactly, which he sold? Each person who stopped at his roadside stand, whether he bought or no, was given a throwaway which old Mr. Birch had had printed in Hartland. This consisted of a single sheet of paper, narrow but about a foot long, on which was printed (in the horrible green type such things often use) an account of the entire incident; or not of the entire incident, for there was no mention of fines or injustice; or more than the entire incident, considered in another way, for what the account omitted at the end it made up for in the beginning; Mr. Birch had placed the massacre of the crows back in the last years of the nineteenth century and assigned it to his grandfather (also named Adam Birch), who was described as one of the earliest settlers of Ravensburg Village. The head of the sheet bore a green picture of this grandfather, a majestic and bearded old man who resembled (and happened to be) John Greenleaf Whittier. The account itself described the crows (and ravens) of

Ravensburg as, in those days, a menace to farming, a plague comparable to those in the Bible, which the relatively primitive methods of the times had no way of stopping until Grandfather Adam singlehandedly, by the ingenious use of dynamite bombs, made the great massacre of crows and became thereby the benefactor of his native place, in witness whereof hardly a crow (and it is true there were now very few) could be seen today in Ravensburg. A final paragraph described the souvenirs offered for sale as family treasures, made by the grandfather and sold now out of absolute necessity.

So that it may have been not the sale of crow relics at all which Mr. Birch had in mind; the crows were possibly but a means to the sale of a certain idea which he had entertained for some time, an idea of himself as born in Ravensburg and native there; born, moreover, of an old established stock. For how long might he have entertained this idea? That is easily answered, for it was many years since he had begun to speak of himself as born in Ravensburg. But it leads to another question not so easily answered, and rather dreadful even to ask—with what intensity had he held this idea? The crows, of course, were killed for the five hundred-odd dollars he did not get—or were they? On the night he waded about in the squawking flesh of crows, beating at them, was the further motive already in view? But the mind boggles worse at that than at the bounty of five hundred dollars.

At any rate the scheme more or less succeeded, if that was indeed the scheme. Not that the crow relic business ever really flourished—though it went on—but that a notion of old Adam Birch, grandfather or grandson, got put about and more or less accepted, as people will negatively or implicitly accept something that they do not believe worth disputing; so that when Mr. Adam Birch died, without remaining kin to claim the bits of nothing that were left, those green-print circulars got just so much in the way of the reality that the Hartland

Press referred to him as "the last surviving member of one of Ravensburg's oldest families," and had a line or two about his grandfather ("a colorful figure of earlier times") and the crows ("who were then so numerous and so destructive . . .") and so on.

It may rightfully be objected that Mr. Adam Birch could not have seen this obituary. But a man who can, even in so small a way, change the past so that as it were he grows back into it, and now has a publicly attested being where he had not it before—such a man might have stumbled on some trivial secret of time, at least enough to know his own obituary, and perhaps so much that, becoming a legend, he does not die but after his human death is made the king of the crows, who will one day lead them back to Ravensburg, where indeed a few are beginning to return even now.

The Amateurs

"OF COURSE SOMETHING must be done. That could have been said six months ago." Anna jingled her golden bracelet, pulling it by one of its bangles around and around her wrist. "You all sit there and say something must be done, somebody has to do something—no wonder his life's a mess, for he does get to hear about it, you know."

"Will you stop rattling that bracelet, please?"

"Does it make you nervous, Osmin? You've been very easily upset, since you started working for *Time*."

"Me—nervous? Ha! I've noticed that compulsive little gesture of yours with the bracelet, Anna; I've seen it for a long time now. You're sure you're all right? I mean, quite certain, are you?" Osmin, a lean young man, dark-complected and with silky black hair, settled back in the corner of the sofa. His insolent smile seemed to suggest that he had scored a hit, a very palpable hit with his remarks; but no, it was only the smile he automatically assumed after every sentence, and his friends had long since stopped looking for the profundity which, it was implied, lay hidden in every trivial observation.

"Why not beat me, dear," said Anna, twirling the bracelet. "I only do it to annoy."

"If you would only stop it," said Malibron, turning as he always did a silver ring on his fat little finger, "we could get back to the question of Allan. While it's certain that nothing will be done," he added, "I think our concern for our friend is kind and amusing, in a grubby sort of way."

"A wife, or a mistress—or even a job . . ." Nancy suggested vaguely. She frowned, then smiled and shrugged her shoulders.

"Oh, yes, indeed—" Malibron picked up her words—"but that's typical, absolutely typ-ic-al. The wife, the mistress, the job—or the needle, the bottle, the grand tour. And let me say I've seen it happen before. You don't know, none of us know, what would be good—really good for him. So like a shop window, we offer the stock solutions, the ready-made things that are available in case of troubles like his. And like the manager, well disposed on Christmas Eve, we come out, very grand, rubbing our hands together, and we say to this poor, poor urchin, who is rubbing his nose on the glass, 'Well, Son, what do you want? Just say the word, anything at all—for we are God, you know, we are very grand and we want to treat you right.' And the poor bloody little urchin—"

"I think, somehow, we've heard this before," Anna said, pretending to yawn.

"In somebody's book, wasn't it?" asked Osmin.

After a silence, Anna said, "We might give him Angel. Would you like that, Angel? You've never met him, have you?"

"Never met Allan Hastings, Angel?" asked Osmin. "My God, you've got a treat coming. Do you like simple people— I mean, but really simple?"

Angel uncoiled herself slightly at the other end of the couch. "I don't know," she said. "It's so long since I've met any." This got a laugh, for Angel was still "new" enough in this little circle to be taken for a wit, a phase that would not last long, since she was undeniably as serious as she was beautiful. Also she was younger than the rest, and already their appreciation of her began to give way to their somewhat fussy pedantry, which they called "introducing her to things" and "making arrangements."

"Well, you'll meet one tonight," Osmin said. "Presently he'll come in through that door—"

"Osmin will now favor us with a 'character,' " muttered Nancy, getting up. "I'll go in the kitchen, Anna, and fix drinks." She turned to Angel. "When you've heard this as often as I have, dear—"

"He'll come in through that door," said Osmin loudly. "Handsome as a somewhat decayed Greek god, neatly and not at all originally dressed—you won't suspect in the least, until he slides on the throw rug in the entrance—" he pointed to the rug. "He won't fall down, not quite, but as he recovers he will smile apologetically, take off his hat and look at it as though it had suddenly been invented in his hands. He will say nothing. He will sit down, still with that smile on his face, and he will listen. Like a spectator at a tennis match, he will turn his face to the person who has the ball at every instant. The quality of his listening is respect, even devotion, coupled it seems with the most imbecile lack of understand—"

"That's about enough, Osmin," said Anna.

"Oh, no. Enough? Never. He is simple—exquisitely—but *deep*, you know, profound. And when he does say something, everyone attends, deeply, profoundly. 'What about death?' he will say, possibly, 'What about that?' And this, in our complex little group, is a triumph, is a success. 'Ah,' someone will say, 'why didn't I think of that?' Oh, he has, Hastings has, the secret, the key, to all things. He calls Satan by his first name, whatever that may be; he appears the confidant of angels—no pun, darling, was intended—the familiar of princi-palities, thrones and dominations, the friend of seraphim, the toady and sycophant and courtier of God himself—all because he has said, What about death."

"Aren't you getting somewhat bitter, Osmin?" asked Anna. It was true that Osmin had become very serious in delivering his "character"—more, even, than serious. His breath came faster, his little smile broadened disclosing sharp, even radu-late teeth—altogether his expression seemed fit as much for biting as for speech.

"And after all," said Nancy, who had come back from the kitchen in time to hear the last remarks, "he *is* so right. What about death, indeed?"

"But when Nancy says it," Osmin laughed, "it's not nearly so impressive, it hasn't got that *je ne sais quoi*." He kissed his hand mockingly up at the ceiling, and said in a basso pro-fundo, "What about death, what about that? That's the way it should be done."

"My God, Osmin," said Nancy quietly, "how I should en-joy watching your death agony." She set down a tray of drinks on the coffee table, conscious that everyone was staring at her. That sort of remark, everyone silently agreed, was carrying things just too far. After all, you had to know where the game leaves off and becomes something entirely different.

"Well, really," said Osmin at last, "*that's* a revelation, isn't it?" Osmin had always, if the truth be told, been frightened of Nancy. A year ago, he had been "very serious," as the phrase goes, about her. But something—no one of their friends knew just what—had happened to break that up decisively and in an instant. And what it was, actually, was that Nancy, who was taller and stronger than Osmin, had hit him one evening as the climax to a disagreeable interview which he had intended for a seduction. The blow had been more ways damaging than he cared to recall. Her ring had torn his cheek slightly—but worse, she had stood over him and dared him to strike back. A matter for quick decision, and he had decided for prudence and regretted it nightly ever since.

Now he stood up. "You have that quiet bestial charm," he said, and his smile stretched itself to its automatic suggestion of the greatest profundity, "the sort of thing that Orpheus was able to tame, O virgin and brute." And before any reply could be made Osmin bowed slightly and retired to the bathroom, where he noted without surprise that his hands were trembling terribly.

Of the friends, only Nancy fully appreciated Osmin's remark as referring not to the immediate scene but to an evening fully a year removed by time; thus through her local resentment she admitted a gratitude almost tender to him for this insight—deeper for being accidental—into the heart of another, into, as she put it, a "foreign power." She saw at this moment, she felt, deeply into Osmin.

"Like certain saints," she said with prim lightness, "who posthumously reveal the image of the Virgin imprinted on their livers, in color." This, too, was very imperfectly understood by the company.

"You see," said Malibron to Angel, "this is entirely the result of talking about Hastings. We never behave this way when we talk about other people."

Angel, however, looked very serious and said, "Why did you say that, Nancy?"

"Oh, why does one say anything? I don't know."

"But it was unkind. He might just be very frightened of dying." Angel made this remark with the most unaffected simplicity of voice and manner.

"God," Anna said softly. "Another one."

"The perfect match for Hastings," said Malibron. Angel

blushed. "How charming," Malibron said. "To blush, I mean. When was it, Anna—ten years ago at least—the last time someone blushed in this room?"

"Oh, please," Anna cried in a kind of disgusted supplication. "Please stop." And then, to Angel, "You don't understand, I know. But it's a fact that no one else understands either, and I think no one really wants to."

"About Hastings?" Angel asked.

"Yes, about Hastings," Nancy broke in. "And that's enough. Night after night, and week after week, for six months now. Soon he'll walk in. And then next week Angel will have something to say, she'll have her opinion of Hastings too. Then will you be happy?"

"You see," Anna said, still to Angel, "he was, well, a quite ordinary person until one night—"

"Oh, nonsense," said Malibron. "He was never ordinary. He simply did the things you expected from—"

"How absurd. Are you going to pretend he was some kind of genius, then?"

"No, simply a person who—"

"Well, what's wrong with the word *ordinary* then?"

"Oh, never mind. Go right ahead."

"*Critic*," Anna threw him the word with fastidious loathing. "As I said," she went on, "a quite *ordinary* person. Then, one night . . ." She paused and looked at Nancy and at Malibron, with a look that seemed to say, I hadn't really intended to go through all this again.

At this point Osmin came in again, apparently as perky as ever. He sat down next Angel, took her hand and said in a conspirator's hoarse whisper, "Whatever they tell you will be a lie. You see, I really know him."

And now the doorbell rang.

While Anna went to answer the door, Nancy stepped back into the kitchen. They could hear, now, deliberate steps upon the stair, ascending, Malibron looked steadily at Angel, who had simply let her hand remain in Osmin's possession, but entirely as though unaware. She was, he considered, a remarkably beautiful girl, tall and thin, with a serious face and golden hair. For a moment Malibron, who was not usually sensitive to such things, felt a tension in himself, an anxiety, a perturbation, a fear. It was indescribable. She is so ... uncontaminated, he put it melodramatically to himself—so unknown. For what, after all, do we know about her?

She came—so much they knew—of a rich Boston family. She had run away to New York, and Angel was not her real name. She lived with another girl in what must have been the most unmitigated poverty, and gave lessons in needlework where and when she could get them. Nancy had met her through friends whose children took lessons of her, and under these auspices Angel had been introduced into the circle. But that was all. No one, except perhaps Nancy, knew where she lived, she never met any of them singly but only in the group, where she seemed invariably affable though slightly abstracted, as if thinking of something that had to be done later, when she left them.

Just now it seemed to Malibron oddly important that the scene should be as it was, with Osmin holding Angel's hand, with the heavy steps coming up the stairs, with Anna impatiently twisting the door knob, waiting. If I knew, now, he thought, I could say to them, This is the last time that—but though he felt this with almost obsessive intensity he could not make out what it was that seemed so ominous, what sort of "last time" he meant. With a sigh, between boredom and desperation, he threw the whole situation (whatever that meant to him) away. I don't want anything to change, he thought finally. I know we're trivial, and foolish, and even bored a good deal of the time with each other's company and talk: but I don't want anything to change. When people open doors, the world walks in. It tracks dirt on the carpets, doesn't remove its hat, sits heavily on pathetic little chairs, says the wrong thing at once. You feel you've been accustomed to insolence, but this is new. Compared to this, Osmin is a harmless child. Having said so much to himself, Malibron felt rather stupid. One knows so well, he added, that nothing will change.

Osmin meanwhile looked down at Angel's hand, which rested so limply in his. He noticed with revulsion that the nails were dirty—not much but a little, which to him was worse than if they had been coal black. He could not repress a shudder. Then he saw the red weal of a recent burn that went the length of the girl's thumb, and this seemed to him pathetic, beautiful, he wanted to weep over it. He really did, very much, want to weep. But as the scream of a man wounded and in agony may, out of control, issue in a sound like laughter, Osmin knew himself for one capable of producing, from the deepest and most genuine feelings, only some cheap travesty, a sneer perhaps, immediately to be misunderstood. Angel had made a lucky guess about his fear of death: it was true, and every slur, every embarrassment, the slightest sign of violence, at once related itself for him to his own death, which was a confused vision in his mind both of a time when he should not be, when his body should rot in the grave, and of the terrible last moments when he should feel the sheets grow cold around his legs, and be scarcely able to breathe: this last scene appeared to him with terrible intensity and frequency in dreams.

Our hands, he thought, are like feeble monsters that we send into the world, to get, and be damaged. How they take the beatings that our greed deserves!

Anna pulled open the door, and Allan Hastings stood in the entrance, smiling uncertainly. Angel could not for the moment see what the fuss had been about. He was indeed

fairly good looking, quite tall but not slender—almost powerfully built in fact. And he did not, as he came in, trip or slide
in the least, though he did hold his hat somewhat (she
thought) apologetically for so large and masterful a person.
In his left hand he held a brown paper bag, clutched it really
as an object of the utmost fragility and importance. Finally,
still smiling, he gave his hat to Anna—it was funny actually,
she curtsied mockingly as she took it, but he didn't notice—
and said, "Hullo, Richard," to Malibron, then, "Hullo, Osmin,
I hope you're well." And then his eyes, which seemed to
Angel somehow vague and unfixed in their regard, took in
and tried to focus on her hand in Osmin's. She felt, guiltily,
at this moment, that meanings were being drawn, alliances and
divisions made, all very falsely, but it would have been too
much, now, to take her hand away. And it did not last long;
in a moment Anna had come up and introduced them. If he
was surprised at finding a stranger there, a new person, it did
not show. Unless, she thought, he's just a shade *too* normal,
too ordinary; and she called to mind some ridiculous bit from
a farce, about a half-wit who was coached for the first minute
of an interview—the hello, the how are you, the delighted I'm
sure—and kept repeating these formulas while his vis-à-vis
became more and more desperate.

"How are you?" Hastings said to Nancy, who had just
re-entered the room; and Angel, as soon as he had turned
around, removed her hand abruptly from Osmin's, while he,
also, moved decorously farther away.

"You're quite late," said Anna.

"Yes, I've been walking." A slight emphasis on the last
word made the reply seem to Angel the least bit pompous,
as of a person who, without saying so much, wished you to
understand that all his activity was significant and remarkable.
Osmin possibly felt this too, for he could not resist saying,

"from going to and fro in the earth, and walking up and down in it."

"Forgive our literary man," Malibron brought out after a space of silence. "What's in the paper bag?"

"Oh." Hastings seemed surprised and pleased that it should be noticed. "I'd forgot. A present for Anna." And he gave it to her. "It's best to bring presents," he said. "I know how it is. Times are hard."

"Thank you, darling," Anna said, opening the bag. She looked inside, then around at the company but especially at Osmin. Just one word, just one smile, her glance said to him. Then she took the bag into the kitchen. It contained a dozen eggs, six fresh sprats and about a pound of chopmeat. She put it all back in the bag, which she stuffed into the refrigerator. Then, shrugging her shoulders helplessly, she returned to her friends. It was nothing, really, nothing. *Times are hard.* Well, what was wrong with that? Times were hard. But people didn't bring you eggs and fish and meat, here, to your house, did they? So plausibly, so naturally, with such an air of humble apology for the times, which were hard? They brought, others brought anyhow, cakes, pastry if they came to dinner, brought something excessive and luxurious which you wouldn't have bothered with; they didn't come with the basic elements, did they? Picturing, perhaps, the eggs cooked morning after morning for the sullen, lonesome breakfast, the fish— she hated fish—staying till they stank and had to be thrown out?

"You forgot the bread," she couldn't help saying as she passed his chair. But he was listening to Nancy, and didn't hear. Osmin heard, though, and looked sharply at her.

Nancy had been talking quietly but intensely to Hastings. In general silence they heard her say decisively, "You've been wasting it, all of it, letting yourself go—it's like a living death.

If you don't want it, if holy poverty is what you're after, give
it to us—do something with it."

"How nice!" said Osmin bitterly. "How lovely."

Nancy sat up straight and said, "He must realize the position. I don't care how you interpret it. What he's doing is a
crime."

"And what is he doing?" This from Anna.

"His money. He gives it to people, strangers. He's just confessed as much."

"And whose business is that?"

"Nancy's, obviously," Osmin said.

"I think we'd better leave this subject," said Malibron.
"Interesting as it might prove to be."

Nancy got up. "You don't any of you understand," she
said. "Not just little money. Big money. Hundreds of dollars,
thousands in a day—all to people in the streets, to anyone."

Everyone now turned to stare at Hastings.

"Obviously," said Malibron, "we must all try to run into
you on the street as often as possible."

"And quite possibly," Osmin added, "one or two of the
people he meets in the course of a day belong to the deserving
poor."

Then a strange thing happened. Hastings took out his wallet, opened it and handed Nancy a hundred-dollar bill. He did
this gravely, without the least irony or condescension.

"Oh, Jesus," said Osmin. "This is too much. Nicely begged,
Nancy, well whined for." He turned to Hastings. "Who are
you, anyhow? God? St. Francis feeding the birds? You're
mad, you know. I suppose you do know that? Do you think
I'm going to ask you for a hundred dollars? That would suit
you, wouldn't it?"

Quietly Hastings opened the Wallet and extended a bill
between his fingers. Osmin looked at it without moving. He
laughed.

"The eccentric millionaire! Mass-produced loaves and mechanized fishes!" Then, more quietly, "What is it you're trying to buy, Allan? Give me that." He snatched the note from the extended fingers and, with the elaborate motions of the stage magician, bowing and smiling to the audience, he began tearing it up. Pieces fluttered to the floor, while all stared and were silent.

"Don't, please," whispered Nancy. Osmin laughed again, tore up the last of the note and ostentatiously washed his hands in the air. "I come," he said, "at a higher price."

Malibron stared at the floor. "It was a thousand dollars," he said quietly.

Osmin looked as if he had not understood, then turned very pale and began to shudder uncontrollably. Then, "It doesn't matter," he said. "Not in the least." And he spat on the floor where the torn note lay.

"Bravo, bravo," cried Angel.

"Oh, shut up," said Anna. "I've had enough. These are my rooms, you are my guests—either behave or get out." She turned away and spoke more to herself than to them. "One of them spits and the other yells bravo," she said with vast resentment.

This summary made the whole episode modulate quickly into absurdity. Malibron laughed uncertainly, then Nancy, then even Osmin. Finally they all laughed, except Hastings.

The laughter was succeeded, nevertheless, by a prolonged and uncomfortable silence. Then at last Malibron spoke, with effort and obviously painful sincerity. "Maybe it would be a good thing, Allan, if you told us—tried to tell us—what all this is about. What it means to you. I was going to say that we're all your friends, but since a moment ago I've had some doubt of that. Still, if we could . . . *do anything* . . . understand, even—if we could . . ." He left off helplessly, making odd gestures as if weighing things in his hands.

"It would be better if we forgot all this as quickly as possible," Anna said.

"No," Nancy said. "He owes us an explanation."

"He owes . . ." Osmin laughed once, in her face.

"Well, why not!" Nancy turned on him. "If the hundred dollars is what's bothering you, remember that you tried to buy me for less. You think it's greed, I know, and to you that changes everything. Well, it's not greed, it's not. It's something . . . it's . . ." Her tone of controlled fury gave way to vagueness. "It is greed," she said in a faint voice. "It is, oh, it is."

"That's right, tell me your troubles," said Osmin. "Right this way, folks," he declaimed, "this way to the sin eater's, where you will see wonders worked, miracles performed. Come, Allan—slip that camel through the needle's eye."

The sarcasm of the invitation seemed quite lost on Hastings. He sat with his head slightly bent forward, hands on his knees, and began to speak.

"It's hard to explain," he said. "You'll probably laugh. I don't mind that, and I can't argue with you." He took a deep, labored breath. "I'm quite well off, as you know—"

"You surprise me," Osmin sniggered.

"And that may have been a lucky thing," Hastings imperturbably continued, "because as you also may know, I'm not very quick or clever—I haven't anything like your mind, Osmin."

"A tribute! Thank ye, kind sir."

"Because I'm so slow, then—ah," he cried, "it's nothing to be explained. I just, one day, woke up. You people, you're clever enough—when someone says to you, 'The World' in that awful and disapproving voice—you know?—why, you're able to surround it quickly with thoughts. 'Here's a dissatisfied creature,' you say, or, 'Why does he tell this to me? Why not to the priests, or the kings, or the senators?' But I couldn't get all that on my tongue. And besides, really no one *said* anything."

It was comprehensible. That, to them, was the worst. Despite his incoherence there could be no pretending that he did not make himself understood. And it grew worse. Hastings rocked gently back and forth in his chair, as though wrestling to bring up some poison that sickened him inwardly; but all that issued was the word, the jagged, uncut phrase which landed among them as though he spat rocks.

"I saw a blind man. My own blindness, I said to myself. Blind men are angelic, they have merciful faces. I always thought that. He tapped his stick in the gutter, and his face was malicious, was guileful. The evil—innocence of the face, like some awful child. Very fat. This was a rainy day, and I stood there. As if somebody had said, 'The World,' in that disgusted voice, and suddenly you felt it. You would never forget, never.

"I can't explain. It was an infection. Everything I ate tasted hot, wicked and dirty. For weeks I could only take water and a little bread. I went to doctors. But it always came to this: that they were puzzled, and I had to explain. Then I knew they were laughing. They sympathized, but they were laughing. And I too, I was laughing at them because they were so helpless. We never said anything, but they must have known."

Speech seemed to become more and more difficult; his breathing, even, was rapid and unnatural.

"I said, we must cut it out, cut it away, get rid of it all. Burn all the junk and go down in the waters, I said. Burn. I said—"

He stopped, seemed to search for a word. His mouth hung open helplessly. "I don't know, I don't know . . . I don't know."

Although Hastings had been speaking quietly enough, what he said was evidently costing him much, in strength, even in humility, since as so often occurs, the belief that was held with such courage and modesty, such chastity in silence, became in speaking of it outrageous, vulgar and illogical, even absurd.

"But you don't *stop*, do you?" cried Nancy. "You don't kill yourself?"

"It's difficult to explain," he muttered. "I said that before." He had been sitting with his head somewhat bowed. Now he raised his face to Angel, and it could be seen that he was passing into some phase of crisis. The muscles of his jaw were set as though in paralysis, there was sweat on his forehead. His eyes, Angel thought, might have been a blind man's eyes, unfocused as though in irrelevant and universal concern.

"You mustn't ask me questions," he said, "because I'm not good at explaining. I only know what is right . . . for me." The last words were spoken in a whisper.

"Into the fold," said Osmin with a triumphal sneer. "The bloody Catholics have got him."

"Now that's good," said Malibron heavily. He stared at the little crucifix on the wall, and stared at it until the others turned to look. Anna said nothing.

"Osmin, you're a cheap miserable little bitch." This from Nancy.

"But it's not enough!" Hastings suddenly said, and got to his feet. He stood there and repeatedly struck his fist into his other hand; yet it was not a gesture of anger or even of resentment, but rather somehow of the completest helplessness.

"Something definite, final, conclusive . . . the end." He began to walk up and down among them repeating "the end" at every step. He came to a halt finally before the crucifix— almost he clicked his heels together or made a slight bow, but this might have been unintentional. "Some *pain*, some pain," he said, with the utmost emphasis.

Malibron got up and stood behind him, expecting obviously

that he would collapse in a moment; and Hastings did in fact look like a person on the edge of some hysteria: he seemed to struggle for breath, and his whole body trembled slightly and incessantly.

"Some—conclusive—pain." He brought this out with difficulty. The others were frightened now, not knowing what to expect. Eccentricity had definitely gone over the edge, but into what land, what territory, none of them wanted to say or know. It was very well to talk of madness—he's mad, absolutely mad, they said—when a person did something quaint and amusing; but this eccentricity and odd humor of the blood was a joke they had no taste for. So that at first they were curiously grateful to Osmin for laughing.

"Pain—you talk about pain," Osmin cried. "That's a different thing, a pain, a real pain, you understand—not just the sharp sting in the pocketbook which is the morbid essence of your affair with Lady Poverty. But pain—" he stood up and pointed at the crucifix—"the spear in your side, Allan, the nails. Do you think you could stand up to the nails, Allan?"

"Yes, pain, what do you know of pain?" Angel cried, and Osmin glanced gratefully at her. "Or poverty either? Have you ever been poor? Answer me, have you ever been poor?" She too seemed struck by a curious enthusiasm, elation, difficult to understand or explain. There was such an excitement in her voice as she threw him her question.

"Believe me," Osmin went on. "Believe me—I know pain. I know how to bear it."

Nancy said something aside, obviously vulgar.

"It's not bearing it—that's not the thing," Hastings said in a low voice.

"I could stand that pain, even that!" Osmin said. "Even His pain." Obviously he meant it, theatrical as he was. "You could —truly—drive a nail through this hand." He held up his right hand, pointed to the palm with his cigarette; then, with no

more ado, drove the burning tip into the hand and ground it
out there.

"Schoolboy stuff," said Nancy distinctly. "We did it for
amusement, winter nights at Vassar."

And there the thing might have—should have—ended. Osmin was so absurd, standing there with his burned hand still
raised, but looking otherwise white and drawn and ready to
faint.

But Angel said, almost in a whisper, her eyes burning,
"That was wonderful. How many of you could stand that?"
Her voice was intense with admiration, even with love.

"If you two damnable little perverts will stop—" said Anna,
just as Nancy struck Angel across the mouth.

"Look, please!" said Malibron. "That's about enough, isn't
it? Here, Osmin, I'll get some burn ointment. Where is the
burn ointment, Anna?" He hurried into the bathroom.

"Damn the burn ointment," Osmin said. "I meant every
word."

Hastings took a slow step toward him.

"You would?" he asked. "A nail?"

"I've said so," Osmin replied.

"Bluff," said Nancy. This word did it. Or would it perhaps
have gone on anyhow? At any rate, like a vault that opens to
a password in the owner's voice alone, Osmin swung to
smoothly and at once.

He knew (he said) what they thought of him; he knew
especially what Nancy thought of him. He was a buffoon, he
played the fool, he let her beat him—yes, all this came out,
greatly exaggerated—it was because they were unchristian,
had no charity in their hearts, they didn't realize how miserable life was, how often he had thought of ending it, how he
endured pain like Prometheus (yes, this famous comparison
also was used), how he studied, learned pain, was one of its
graduate students, its proficients, because in charity, in humil-

ity, in self-loathing and abasement, turning the other cheek . . . and so on. "You all measure your pride in pains inflicted," he said. "You count it a good day when you come one over another person; but I am proud of suffering pain. I *will* to suffer pain."

"Sexy little brute, isn't he?" said Nancy with critical admiration, as though she were, in some proprietary sense, exhibiting him.

"Do you mean it—the nail?" Hastings asked harshly.

"Yes, of course I mean it. Are you frightened? Look, people," Osmin said, "I will take the pain, but he is the one who's frightened."

"You will teach this lesson?"

"No," Anna said decisively. "No."

"Oh, yes, yes," cried Angel almost gaily. "I know where there's a hammer and nails." She ran into the kitchen before anyone could stop her, if anyone had proposed to do so.

Anna shook Hastings by the arm. "You don't mean it, you don't mean to do it." He did not reply. "I won't let you do it."

"Do what?" Malibron had returned. "I couldn't find any ointment." Just then Angel came in with a small hammer and a nail. "Oh, my God!" breathed Malibron. "Is this still going on?"

Hastings took the hammer and nail without looking at Angel. Indeed he and Osmin had all this time simply stared at each other across a space of perhaps five feet; and this silent regard began almost to hypnotize the others.

If it had been simply drunkenness, Anna thought, it would be easy. We'd take away the hammer, we'd have a little fight, but it could be done. Everyone would be relaxed. But no one is drunk, and there's nothing childish about it. They are going to do it.

The realization had by now struck them all; and it seemed to produce a paralysis. Malibron said, plaintively, "What will it prove? What is it going to prove?" and sinking into a chair he continued to say just this, this formula, in a voice that was becoming no more than a moan. Angel was evidently and horribly ready to enjoy herself; she accompanied Osmin, holding his uninjured hand, as he backed to the wall. Anna looked away, looked at the crucifix. Only Nancy seemed either unaware or incapable of believing in what would happen.

"They won't do it, it's a joke," she assured everyone in confident tones; then she too began to repeat the phrase as if it were a prayer.

Allan Hastings towered over Osmin. His face was impassive, his eyes dull and without expression. He held the nail in one hand and, in the other, the ridiculously small, dainty-looking hammer.

Osmin put up his right hand to the wall. He was smiling, for this scene represented, perhaps, an ultimate ambition with him. His smile was strained, grimacelike, but the intention to smile was unmistakably there.

"For you, I do it for you," he whispered to Angel, and she whispered, "Yes, I understand."

"Begin, then," Osmin cried with an awful insolence. "What are you waiting for? I forgive you, you know. I forgive you, I forgive all of you." More quietly, he said to Hastings, "You called it a lesson. That's right. My God, how you will learn from this. And me—" he brought back his hand and touched his breast dramatically—"a minute of pain, and then I'll spend my lifetime laughing while you learn about pain. I'll even let you give me the thousand dollars again—for the tuition."

"Stop," Hastings said. "We'll talk about that later."

"What is it, hate? Do you hate each other?" Malibron groaned. "What will it prove, even if he does stand up to it, what will it prove?"

Osmin threw his hand back against the wall, and Hastings set the nail against it.

He struck gently at first, and the nail went in easily enough. Then it hit a bone, and Hastings seemed to go completely to pieces. He smashed with increasing force, sometimes not touching the nail but letting the hammer thud directly on the flesh. Osmin's eyes were open and very bright.

But it did not take long. Soon, with three final blows, given with more strength and less accuracy than was needed, the nail was driven fully in.

"All right," Anna said, as firmly as she could. "That's enough. Now draw it out."

"No," Osmin said. "Let it stay a minute." He was evidently in terrible pain, perhaps only now (as his elation subsided) realizing the pain. "Let him look. Look, Allan. The nail. Look, damn you."

Hastings had turned away, shuddering terribly. The hammer fell to the floor.

"It's not a claw hammer," Malibron remarked. "It's not got anything to draw nails out."

"Oh, Jesus." Nancy began to laugh. It didn't seem a hysterical laugh; but rather brilliant, cold and pertinent. Anna went to the kitchen to get—Lord knows what, pliers perhaps. But before she got out of the room, the plaster about the nail gave way and Osmin simply fell in a bundle on the floor. The back of his hand was bloodied and raw. Angel went at once to her knees and began to fuss tenderly over him. Now that the crisis had passed, her fierce and perverse exaltation seemed to have gone too; she was almost matronly, there on the floor, and when she raised her face she was crying.

"I'll phone a doctor," Anna said. But Malibron looked intently at her and she stopped. "You mean—"

Hastings was standing in a far corner—a neutral corner, Anna said later—with his back to the room. His fists were clenched at his sides, his posture rigid and strained, his head thrown back.

"He's dead," Malibron said. "Anyone can see he's dead." He knelt by Osmin and took up the wrist, with the nail still in the hand. "He's dead." The wrist fell stupidly back to the floor. "Obviously dead."

They all looked at Hastings. He turned around to face them. He seemed gripped by some spasmodic internal constriction, his face was red, he struggled to breathe, to speak. "My God. Six hours, until the ninth hour! And this. Oh, my God!"

And now, unbelieving, they saw what it was inside him that struggled, that had perhaps struggled all evening, or all his life, to come forth. Laughter. It came up chokingly at first, then in stronger surges it poured forth like blood from the mouth. Helplessly, holding his stomach as if in pain, he roared with deep, healthy laughter.

A Delayed Hearing

MISS MINDENHART'S TASTE in personal adornment, Mrs. Haxton's taste in religions, these may be said to have done the damage. Miss Mindenhart, a large, graying woman who may once have been statuesque but now was merely dumpy on the grand scale, affected ornaments of a style to match: brooches big as saucers, earrings which reminded you of doorknobs and alarmingly had stretched her lobes; and especially to the point of this story, a handbag which she now carried, whose clasp came in the form of a huge silver or chromium arrow serving also as a handle and extending, feathers and tip, a goodish way beyond the limits of the bag itself, which was not tiny. Great is Diana of the Ephesians, and great was Miss Mindenhart; whereas Mrs. Haxton was a small, slender woman, likewise graying, with soft, large, brown eyes, an appealingly wistful or martyred expression, but (as everyone knew) a shrewish temper and stubborn will, qualities she was at present seeking to allay by the study of

Indian religion; she preached nonviolence, or would have if she had preached to anyone except her husband and a few friends, who were not under ordinary circumstances violent anyhow.

These two ladies, with their lawyers, some members of their families, and some mere hangers-on, met before the courthouse one February morning. It had snowed, and was snowing, and though everyone else wanted to get inside in the warm, Miss Mindenhart and Mrs. Haxton stopped to glare at each other; or the one glared while the other, reminding herself no doubt that her principles forbade glaring, merely looked. They stood there for a moment beside the stone Civil War hero who, his rifle at the ready, appeared about to run across their heads; he had an extra cap of snow now, and snow had stuck in patches to his body; at the foot of his pedestal lay a neat pyramid of snowy cannonballs.

"You'll see," said Miss Mindenhart, "justice will be done. You'll see."

"Then we need not discuss it between ourselves," Mrs. Haxton returned.

"I only wanted to tell you personally, to your face," Miss Mindenhart persisted, "that the fault is entirely yours, entirely. I saw it all," she added with judicial vehemence.

"You could scarcely have seen it all, or any of it," Mrs. Haxton said, "since if you had been watching where you were going it would not have happened."

"You watch out what you are saying—when they put you on the stand you won't dare say any such thing. You'll perjure yourself, if you don't mind."

"Now, ladies, ladies," said Mr. Julius Porter, a large man of much florid geniality who here showed his belief that the disputes of women were to be settled by saying, "Ladies, ladies." He was Miss Mindenhart's cousin, and a lawyer, though of course he was not handling her case; he had only come, he put it, "to be there in case of need." He winked now at Mr. Haxton, who looked the other way and said in a low voice to his wife, "There's no need to argue with the woman, dear."

"The woman!" cried Miss Mindenhart, who usually overheard what she could not hear. "Listen to him—the woman!" She waved her handbag somewhat ferociously, and her lawyer Mr. Lovett stepped out of its path. "Some people," she declared at large, "had better be more civil, or they will have a suit for defamation on their hands."

"She *is* a woman, isn't she?" inquired Mr. Haxton of the company. "Did I call her anything else?"

"I heard you," Miss Mindenhart said menacingly.

"My dear Miss Mindenhart," said Betty Haxton in what was meant for a pleasant way, "it's only a muddle, that's all it is. If you had only kept up your insurance we should be friends right at this moment." This was improbable; they would never have met again; besides, Miss Mindenhart was sensitive to the other lady's tone, which seemed to her such as would properly be used to servants and clerks in shops.

"The poor are to pay," she announced in a high voice, "for the stupidity of the rich. I never heard of such a thing." She bent, and thrust her face close to Mrs. Haxton's. "Don't you my-dear-Miss-Mindenhart me," she said furiously.

Mrs. Haxton stood absolutely still, her eyes blank to the face before her; instead she watched, in blurred concentration, a few snowflakes falling between them. Patience, patience, she thought—wrath, fear, desire, go away, free me from the folly of being, make me as nothing, make me free.

The large face remained, though blurred, before her eyes, and despite herself she began to see details: the thick eyeglasses, the fat, white cheeks which, to a close view, were threaded with veins, the thick lips parted, breathing smokily past teeth so large, even and white they must assuredly be false. I must not hate, Mrs. Haxton thought, and in her des-

peration, casting around for something neutral and objective
to say, she suddenly brought out, in a voice irrelevantly light,
these words:

"Are you sure you ought to be driving at all, with those
glasses?"

"Don't you dare say such a thing in the courtroom," grimly
said Miss Mindenhart, "or I will sue you for defamation of
character."

The Buddha, the Mahatma, Nirvana itself—all these suddenly fled away, yet Mrs. Haxton even so did not appear
wrathful, only the somewhat cold and assured person she
really was, confronted with someone clearly her inferior in
every way that mattered, whose words be they never so wise
(which they were not) she would later report to her friends
as "so much nonsense."

"Of course you must do just as you please," she said as she
turned away.

"Now, Virginia," said Mr. Julius Porter, taking his cousin's
arm and trying to lead her inside; she really looked, he
thought, as though she might have a stroke, as though, in fact,
she were paralyzed right now.

"That woman should be put in jail," said Miss Mindenhart
heavily.

2—

Nonviolence or not, these two women had done each other
violence in the usual manner, by means of automobiles. Like
two medieval knights, excepting only that they had no intention of giving battle at the time, they had hurled at each other
their several tons of metal, glass and upholstery, the lists being a lonely country lane on an icy, snowy morning like the
present one. Miss Mindenhart had been out driving for the
Aid, something she did a couple of mornings weekly before

going to work (she was a waitress in one of the local restaurants), and the back of her gray old Plymouth was half full of food packages to deliver to back-country families; at the time of the accident she had, according to her custom, a sandwich from one such package half in her hand and half in her mouth. Mrs. Haxton, on the way home from shopping, had taken the long road around because she liked to meditate while at the wheel of her car, a new Buick of shining pastel blue and cream which made a fine frosty effect of its own in the deeply cut and snowy road. As there is no other account but those of the ladies themselves, it is impossible to say who was to blame, Miss Mindenhart eating, Mrs. Haxton meditating, when they so rudely came together.

The personal damage, by good luck, was slight. Both women were shaken up, Mrs. Haxton received a bump on the forehead from the steering wheel, Miss Mindenhart a bruised knee from the dashboard. Food, of course, went flying over the interior of both cars, and a bottle of maple sirup most unfortunately broke all over the floor and front seat of the Buick, so that the upholstery, even as late as the day of the hearing, was sticky and smelled appallingly sweet, and Mrs. Haxton had to sit in the back on the way to the courthouse.

The damage to both cars was trivial though spectacular; in each, the bending of fenders and grill, the smashing of the nearside headlight, produced a kind of snarling expression combined with the half of a sinister, chromium smile from the undamaged side. It was the sort of breakage which meant nothing automotively essential, perhaps, but looked very ignominious and humiliating and would cost a fair sum to straighten out; a matter of appearances, for the most part.

The two ladies took it all calmly enough, at first. They were correct, if not amiable, and for all their natural nervousness remembered to exchange license numbers, names, addresses and phones. They waited in the cold road, smoking cigarettes, for fifteen minutes or so during which no one came by; then, their tremors having somewhat subsided, they prepared to go their ways.

"It might have been much worse," said Miss Mindenhart.

"Yes, if the bumpers had locked," Mrs. Haxton said, "we should have been here all day."

"I did not mean that," the other woman replied. "I might be lying there dead. You might be screaming with agony, and no one there to help you."

Betty Haxton resisted a shudder. Fear, desire, death itself, nothing can touch me, she thought. All those things are the self. Thou art that, that art thou.

"My husband will call yours tonight," she said as they parted.

"I have no husband," Miss Mindenhart said.

"Oh, of course—*Miss* Mindenhart, isn't it? I'm sorry. He'll call you then."

"There is nothing to be sorry about," said Miss Mindenhart sternly.

But by the time of the promised phone call that evening Miss Mindenhart's temper had veered, and with it her view of the accident. This began to happen from the moment that, arriving home, she walked around and stared at the front of her automobile, which leered at her, she thought, in an intimate and knowing fashion, as though to say, "We both know what this will cost." Miss Mindenhart made a fist and thumped the car heavily on its hood so that the metal bounced loosely; but its grin did not change. She went upstairs and kept an impassive dignity till she had phoned the restaurant to say she would not be coming to work; then she sat down in her deep leather armchair and cried for an hour because her Plymouth had turned on her with a mean look.

She was in any case a lonely and unhappy woman, Miss Mindenhart, and because she was a stupid one as well she hung grimly, silently, to a view of the world which had been popular in her youth, as a struggle between the insolence of the rich and the sufferings of the poor; whatever the merits of this picture, the rest of the world around her had been educated to a different one in the course of twenty years or more, leaving Miss Mindenhart increasingly confirmed in her loneliness as time passed and she added details to the portrait of herself as a woman meant for nobler things (though uncertain what these were), and bearing on her own the martyrdom of a poverty whose essential tone, if not its fact, had long been deserted by the army of the truly poor, who now had refrigerators, television sets, and pastel cars which they had to finance for three years. The sufferings of the proletariat and her large, platterlike costume jewelry had been fixed upon her irrevocably in youth by episodes semi-artistic and semi-political of which no other traces remained.

The accident, then, in the course of her musings (which occupied the whole day), went through such extensive symbolic transformations that, as sometimes happens, the reality of it, in one repetition after another, became pleasingly plastic and accommodating. So when Mr. Haxton called up and politely, as one stranger to another, reminded her that she had not mentioned the name of her insurance firm or broker, Miss Mindenhart was not content merely to say that she carried no insurance ("That changes everything, then," said Mr. Haxton gravely), but felt forced to add, "Insurance is a racket, anyhow."

"Oh, now, I don't know about that," Mr. Haxton's voice told her, with a kind of wheedling reasonableness such as one uses to a child.

"I know about it," Miss Mindenhart firmly declared, and gave one or two illustrative anecdotes from hearsay, concluding with, "They won't get any of my money."

She must have spoken in a loud voice for some time, when

at a pause she heard Mr. Haxton say, "Here, Betty, you talk to the woman. I can't make anything out of her at all." Miss Mindenhart not merely resented, then as later on, being called "the woman"; she also took the second half of what he said to mean, clearly enough, that these people were scheming to *make something*—money—*out of her*. To Betty Haxton, then, she repeated the gist of her views on insurance.

"I'm afraid I mustn't agree with you there," said Mrs. Haxton with a friendly laugh, "since Harry—my husband—is in the insurance business."

Miss Mindenhart laughed loudly in a way which the other woman was unable to interpret.

"I've been thinking over what happened," Miss Mindenhart said, "and it seems to me the whole thing was your fault."

There was a silence, either from shock or because Mrs. Haxton was relaying this to Harry.

"You were way over on my side," Miss Mindenhart continued, "and you couldn't have been watching the road. Those big cars like yours ought not to be allowed, anyhow; they are too wide. Besides, I was on a charity."

This last statement was puzzling to Mrs. Haxton, who was not at all clear what it had to do with the matter, and failed to realize that in Miss Mindenhart's imaginings during the day her having been "on a charity," that is, driving for the Aid, had become the most significant point in a parable, as yet vaguely developed, of the poor (with their food packages) being ground under the blue and cream juggernaut of the careless rich.

"I'm sorry you feel that way," Betty Haxton nevertheless said in the politest fashion. "And I forgot to ask how you were. All better now, I hope?"

"Ah, no, I'm not well," Miss Mindenhart said, "not a well woman at all. I think the knee cap may be broken, maybe.

And I'm missing a day's work. A day's work is a day's pay," she added.

"Well, I'll talk it over with Harry," Mrs. Haxton said, "and call you tomorrow."

3 —

The courtroom was hot and crowded, the morning very long; it seemed that numerous cases preceded theirs on the calendar. Quite early on, Mr. Lovett leaned over to warn Miss Mindenhart, "They might not be able to squeeze us in today." Miss Mindenhart, however, her mind scarcely on the proceedings at all, took this remark as obliquely reflecting on her girth, and scowled back at the lawyer in a way he found incomprehensible. Miss Mindenhart, lost in the distances of her mind, was making speeches to the court: "I am a poor woman, your honor, and not ashamed of it. Twice a week I deliver food packages to those even less fortunate than I am. I work hard every day in my life, I do not drive a blue and cream car as wide as the whole road. And if I do not carry insurance that is because I am a responsible driver with never an accident until now, and also because insurance is against my principles."

Betty Haxton, much as she resented the ridiculous inconvenience (as she called it) of being in court at all over this triviality, was fascinated at first by glimpses which the hearings afforded of other lives. There were two automobile accidents not so unlike her own—one of them with far more serious consequences, though—and there was a suit for debt, and even the beginning of an action for breach of promise, which barely got started when it was announced that the young lady still felt unable to appear, so that the hearing had to be postponed, Betty gathered, not for the first time. The magistrate, indeed—a man named Happel, whom she had met

once at a bridge tournament—seemed loftily bored and abstracted, making notes on a pad before him, once in a while
delivering himself of some such remark as "Come now, let's
get on to the main point," or "I haven't all day," or "Perhaps
you don't consider this court a serious place?" She also
thought after a while that he must be hungry; he kept rubbing
his stomach and grimacing. But presently it began to disturb
her, not only that her own case was not being heard, but that
none of the others seemed to end; they were all, for one reason or another, postponed, delayed, continued; and she fore-
saw that she might have to attend sessions of this sort
indefinitely. She wished she had brought a book along; there
was a new one by Sri Silkenanda called *Breathing the Mind;*
she could see it on her night table at this very instant.

Anger, desire, fear, Mrs. Haxton felt, she could cope with;
these passions were perhaps less powerful in her than she had
imagined, and it was against boredom that she wanted a remedy. Yet what was her religion in the first place, in secular
terms, if not precisely a great boredom with the world, with
the tumult of *sangsaric* existence (as it was called) whose trivial processes she was witnessing right now, in the courtroom?
She began to stir about uneasily on the hard wooden bench,
and felt herself perspiring. If they only would get on!

Even Miss Mindenhart's hostility would not have made
Mrs. Haxton go to court; that had been Harry's doing. To
run into someone in one's car, that to Harry was fair enough
(if not the very bread of life), but not to have insurance was
to sin against the nature of things.

"She is very fortunate," he had said of Miss Mindenhart,
"that insurance is not mandatory in our state." And with a
surprising firmness he had put it to his wife that an example
be made of Miss Mindenhart. "We don't in the least want her
money," he said. "I would pay to have the poor woman's car
fixed, do it in a flash, only I cannot encourage that kind of

attitude. It is not cruelty, it is plain sense. I don't want her money, I want a judgment, that's all. If only the court will clearly say to her, 'You are responsible for half the damage, and this will teach you the wisdom of carrying insurance,' I'll tell you what—I will pay for repairs to her car. But you can see I can't do that unless such a judgment is given."

Mrs. Haxton quite saw, indeed, and admitted Harry's wisdom in sending a doctor around to the other woman the day after the accident, at the company's expense. This doctor reported that there was nothing wrong with Miss Mindenhart's knee except a bruise, and that otherwise she seemed in perfectly good health—"and perfectly evil temper," he added cheerfully.

Poor woman! Yes, that expressed it. The religion Mrs. Haxton had taken up included a belief that the soul, in many incarnations, occupied every possible human form, achieved every possible human experience. Confronted with the thought of *being* Virginia Mindenhart, Mrs. Haxton felt uneasy. Of course, she thought, if one were, then one would not know about being—or for that matter about not being Betty Haxton, which suddenly in itself appeared to her as a horrid possibility.

In the weeks between the accident and the hearing, from the time that it became clear she was to be taken into court, Miss Mindenhart began to call Mrs. Haxton on the phone nearly every day, and this was much worse, more serious, in Betty Haxton's view, than the accident. The woman had an idea, clearly, of becoming close friends—that was part of it. She would say to Betty, "I'm having a cup of tea here by myself—why don't you come over?" somehow implying that they two had been doing this sort of thing for ages. Once she said, "There's an excellent film at the Palace," and the expression *excellent film* instead of *good movie* had caused Betty to wince with embarrassment in a way which must have been reflected by her voice when she said ever so politely that she was sorry she couldn't make it.

These overtures, so one-sided, became pathetically definite in a short time. Virginia Mindenhart would speak, over the phone, of "our accident," "when we first met," and so on. And one night, sounding a trifle drunk, she said, "You never invite me to your house."

To this question there was no answer. Betty imagined Miss Mindenhart in her home, among her *things:* books, furniture, reproduced music and art, all representing successive strata of a cultivation fraudulent enough (as Betty sometimes suspected, herself) but precious for the lost enthusiasms of which they were the archaeological record; she imagined talking with Miss Mindenhart of rhythmic breathing, mandalas, wisdom, the peace that is not of this world.

"You don't know how lonely I am," said the voice on the phone, into her ear.

Now, sitting ever more impatiently in the stifling court, Mrs. Haxton remembered this voice not for itself alone but as an emblem, anonymously summing up the sufferings of the world; and she had rejected it. For an instant she saw herself unusually, as suburban, trivial, empty and dry. But no, she thought, it is too late.

For after that crisis, Miss Mindenhart's phone calls had served another purpose, that of denying the confessed weakness. She became vituperative, mocking, angry, began to speak of her lawyers (in number and tone as if legions of angels arrayed themselves at her back), and, with a terrible, abstract anger, of social justice.

"You atheist Jews are ruining the country," she said once, though Mrs. Haxton neither was nor looked Jewish, and, despite her private beliefs and studies, attended the Episcopal church on Sundays.

Finally, for almost a week, Mrs. Haxton left the phone off

the hook, a privation which suggested she was living in a state of siege. Harry spoke of getting an injunction, but his wife wearily said, "No, no, poor woman, she will stop after the hearing."

And then, by one of those utter accidents which nevertheless suggest some purposive force in life, Betty Haxton, returning from an interview with her lawyer, stopped for lunch in the very restaurant, and at one of the tables, where Miss Mindenhart served. By the time she realized, it was too late. The two ladies stared at each other, and Miss Mindenhart said, in the gentlest, most sighing sort of whisper, "Oh, I'll punish you for this." After which she served with the most elaborate courtesy the food Mrs. Haxton felt compelled to order, though quite unable to eat.

The voice in the court droned on, the air became more unbearable than before. Mrs. Haxton, her resignation gone, was squirming continuously on the bench; Miss Mindenhart, her body moving from the waist in a rolling, hypnotized motion, harangued the faceless magistrate of her mind; when suddenly the real magistrate rose from his place, his hand cupped over his mouth, and vanished through some curtains at one side of the room; the curtains billowed emptily behind him, and were still. After a few minutes during which everyone talked in low voices, a young but bald man appeared through those same curtains.

"The Court will recess for lunch," he cried impersonally, "and there will be no afternoon session. Owing to the indisposition of the Court, the Court will convene again tomorrow morning at ten."

4-

Outside, it was snowing harder than ever, and there was no wind. The snow fell thickly, straight down, heavy and wet, in long lines almost like rain. Both parties to the unheard dispute stood around on the path, beside the snowy stone hero, simply from a feeling of purposelessness and wasted time. They should have moved, they should all have gone home, but after that courtroom it was a relief to be out in the pure air, so they stood there like people just out of church on a sunny Sunday with children in white frocks and blue suits decorously playing, the minister smiling, the grass green, all conversation grave and yet cheerful—that was the way, anyhow, that Mrs. Haxton saw it, for an instant, before coming back to the snow, the damp cold, the feeling that nothing, nothing, nothing would ever be accomplished.

"Let us keep the two ladies apart," Mr. Julius Porter came over to say to Harry Haxton, who looked at him coldly.

"My wife does not go in for street fighting," he said, and turned away.

Virginia Mindenhart approached Betty Haxton, who could not help shuddering a little, as if with the cold.

I must be nice, Mrs. Haxton thought, I must be terribly nice, it is for only a minute, it is for the last time. She intended to make Harry call the whole thing off, to do, at all costs, the generous thing, and never mind principles—his, that is, for her principles, were they not precisely those that enjoined generosity at all costs?

Miss Mindenhart overflowed with those sentences and sentiments she had not been able to express during the whole of the stuffy morning, and would not in any case have been allowed to express to the court, though she perhaps did not realize this. She had, in fact, the strange idea that the adjournment of the court meant simply that there would be no hearing; perhaps that Mr. Haxton had fixed the judge.

Mrs. Haxton smiled gently. It was the worst thing she could have done.

"You think you're so smart," Miss Mindenhart sneered angrily.

"Now, Virginia," said Mr. Julius Porter, coming up behind her; and Mr. Haxton turned again to stand behind his wife protectively. Mrs. Haxton's face bore a rapt, meditative expression, still gently smiling a smile from which all meaning appeared to have been withdrawn, like the smile of Buddha flowering in stone.

"I was on a charity, a charity," cried Miss Mindenhart with much force, and raised her large handbag menacingly, with, it seemed, an intention of smiting little Mrs. Haxton right over the head. The bag, heavy all by itself, was later found to contain a large bottle of blue rinse, a quantity of silver coin and a cast-iron toy pistol, which would have made the blow a dangerously heavy one in any case. But instead the unreckonable happened.

If Mr. Julius Porter had not grabbed at his cousin's arm, slightly deflecting the trajectory of the handbag; if Mrs. Haxton had only put up an arm to ward off the blow, as Miss Mindenhart assuredly anticipated she must do, a trivial battle of this sort having been, in Miss Mindenhart's encounters with the world, no such unusual thing; if only Mrs. Haxton had not at this moment confirmed herself in a religion of suffering nonresistance; if only, above all, she had not worn that smile . . .

But as it was, the silver- or chrome-plated arrow of the handbag pierced her left eye, and there was a grotesque instant of silence and motion arrested everywhere; then she began very slowly to fall, the entire episode taking perhaps two seconds; and there she lay in the snow.

Everyone stood still, and over them, perpetually on the run, the Union soldier stood still. Then for a minute or so Mr. Julius Porter had his hands full, and the lawyers did too, trying to keep hold of Virginia Mindenhart and at the same time prevent Mr. Harry Haxton from taking any desperate action. In the course of the general turbulence Mr. Haxton, a small man, was thrown roughly to the ground beside his wife, where he lay in the snow and started to cry. Then officials of the courthouse, policemen, clerks, came running out, alacritous enough now, and took charge to restore order, as they officially said later, though really there was not a great deal of disorder, but only a few drops of blood which the falling snow soon covered; many people standing immediately around were unaware for some time that anything at all had happened.

Mrs. Haxton's body was carried away in one direction, as from a stage; and in the other, led between policemen, went Miss Mindenhart, bewildered to silence, and still clutching by its arrow handle what was referred to once at her trial as "the fatal bag," an expression which elicited titters from even the soberest spectators, until the judge commanded them to order again.

An Encounter with the Law

IN INDIAN SUMMER, while the sun still blazed and the trees began to turn, Samuel Amram drove up through New England to view the colors of the fall. He made this journey every year, driving by ways he had never been before; it was like a pilgrimage with no object but return.

Amram, in his late forties, formed a picture of peaceable though maybe insolent power. His face was fat, yet subtly expressive by means of folds and wrinkles emphatically cut, results of years of smiling and frowning and grimacing at this, that and the other as life went by; his skin was deeply tanned, indeed naturally dark and somewhat oily like his now grizzled hair which lay in thin, wiry ripples over his scalp; and his eyes were dark, piercing, yet sorrowful. It was in profile the head of an Assyrian king, such as one sees on tablets brought from Nineveh to our museums; with a boldly arched, thick nose, and wearing in repose (in which it seldom was) a look of ritual dignity combining cruelty and sorrow in a strange sympathetic way. This appearance at present was becomingly set off by a red and white striped sport shirt, and as Amram idled his open, powder-blue Cadillac through the white wooden villages, his naked, hairy, powerful arm hung over the side, cigar in hand, he left behind him some impression of exotic, levantine repose; he was like a man reading in a magically moving bathtub all of a Sunday afternoon.

He was, in truth, not a peaceful man at all, but much troubled by both the outward confusions of life and inward feelings of being doomed. He was on his third wife, having divorced two, and from all these women had a total of seven children of various ages up to twenty-three; it should have been eight, but his firstborn son was destroyed in Korea. There was, no doubt, a feeling of satisfaction to go with his life's achievement, and even some pride at being able to sustain the whole burden year after year as it grew in weight and complexity; but he was carrying by now a system of branches and outriggers and remotely cantilevered embarrassments so large as to be ridiculous; the lawyers, the doctors, the dentists; the accountants and tax consultants; the twelve kinds of insurance; liabilities as distant as his eldest daughter's husband's father, who had a back injury and no savings.

"I should live in a place like this," he said heavily to himself as he drove through a white village in a spruce forest beside a river. "I should live here alone," and he thought how he would hunt and fish and wear an old felt hat with a hole in the front of the crown for the pipe which he would smoke instead of cigars. "In a week I'd be ready to go home again," he acknowledged wryly, "or I could go crazy from trees."

Superficial as this thought had been, Amram seriously viewed insanity as possible; he had terribly frightening dreams: his entire family, or all his families, fell with silent shrieks, a tangle of arms and legs, into a great crack in the sidewalk, or a tall pile of hats in his haberdashery leaned from the shelf and ever so slowly began to fall on his head, or he stood in a lonely place while from a farmhouse on a far hill people came ominously toward him and he could not run away. In this dream, so many times repeated since the death of his boy James, he was paralyzed with fear but even so, and at the same time, thought the place most peaceful and pleasant. And sometimes James would appear in the dream—off to one side of it—his face disguised in goggles and cap (for he had been a pilot in the air force when he died, and Amram had a picture of him looking this way, smiling over the high rim of the cockpit). And he had another dream, too, which consisted of one image: a great tree, whose trunk forked in a Y of black, leafless branches, the arms of the Y held at a desperately flattening angle by a single strand of wire; he was that wire.

"There is no doubt about it," he told himself sensibly, "this life is a terrible strain, it's bound to tell on a man in time."

His cigar was half smoked; he let it drop over the side, and after a few minutes, driving down the black road which led between forests at the top of a long hill, lighted another.

"It is not your dreams," he said, speaking aloud, "but life itself is very tough." And having said this, he himself at once felt as tough as life, able to meet all challenges, much at ease, his own man. "Until you die," he said, shrugging his thick shoulders. "Who cares?"

At this moment he heard somewhere the thin whine of a siren, and a few seconds afterward the mirror showed him a motorcycle cresting the hill he had just passed. The siren sounded again.

Amram's first response was to push the accelerator to the floor; his leg simply stiffened that way from anxiety. Even as the car thrust ahead, though, he realized this to be, of all moves, the one not to be made, and like the obedient citizen he had been for all his adult life he slowed the Cadillac and drew in to the side of the road and stopped there to watch the cop in the mirror; it seemed to him that, whatever his offense, it would be an aggravation of it to turn boldly around for a direct look.

The sun blazed down on Mr. Amram in his sudden silence and loss of motion; the trees around waved their highest and lightest branches delicately in a warm breeze; the leaves, the green, the yellow, the red, made little papery noises overhead. Amram's palms began to sweat, his heart beat hard and strong. "What have I done?" he asked himself, for like most citizens he kept a life-long terrified contempt of the police, based not on any crime committed by himself but simply on a prospective feeling of being found guilty, in any confrontation of the kind.

The policeman took a terribly long time coming up from behind the car where he had parked his cycle. On losing sight of him in the rear-view mirror Amram still did not dare to turn around but traced the man's deliberate progress by the scratching sound of his boots, as well as, in a curious way, by a slight tremor between his own shoulderblades, as if they had become the object of a stare so physical it could leave a mark.

Amram's fear, his anxiety, were involuntary; his conscious and willed feeling was one of contempt for himself and the officer, "this hick cop," and he already planned to give the man ten dollars for himself rather than stand around pleading innocence, whatever the charge. Nevertheless, his hands trembled and would not stop trembling as he got out his wallet and opened it to show, in the first place, his license, allowing to be seen at the same time the edges of a few bills.

"What is it, officer?" he asked, trying to make his voice both casual and friendly.

The policeman did not answer at once but leaned over the door in such a way that Amram had to move away on the seat. Except for mouth and chin, the man seemed to have no face but to be all blue-gray cloth, black leather and green glass; even his skin was leathery, red, rough, and his peeling nose seemed to incorporate itself somehow with the sunglasses which in turn fitted closely, concealingly, under the visor of his cap. He wore great black gauntlets going nearly to the elbows, and his belt sagged to one side under the weight of the holstered gun. The black, gauntleted gloves reached like robot hands and clumsily, impersonally, took over Amram's wallet, but it was impossible to tell what his eyes were looking at behind those green walls of glass.

"You didn't stop right away, why?" he finally asked, in a tone which was neither mean nor civil but quite simply *there*.

"Oh, well, officer, you know how it is," said Amram, and when there was no reply, added, "I stopped as soon as I realized you meant me."

The policeman still said nothing, and after a moment more those hands of his merely let the wallet go so that it fell into the car, on the floor. Amram picked it up.

"I can't have been doing anything very bad," he said. "I wasn't going over thirty. What's your trouble, officer?"

The policeman said, "Follow me," pointing back the way they had both come.

"Oh, now look—this is ridiculous," Amram said. He flicked the edge of a ten-dollar bill so that it showed over the corner of the wallet. As the man said nothing, he got out the bill and pressed it into the palm of one of the wrinkled black gloves, experiencing for some reason a twinge of revulsion from the touch of the leather deeply seamed with dirt.

"Here, officer," he said, with an attempt at careless cheer. "A little treat for the family."

The black glove, mechanical, autonomous—one would not have thought the man himself involved at all; he might not even have been looking on—crumpled the bill; the black fingers seemed to ruminate it, like a cud, for an instant; then it dropped like a leaf on the floor of the car.

"Come with me," the officer said, a trifle more imperiously than before.

To turn the Cadillac on that road took some maneuvering, which Amram, under the policeman's eye, performed clumsily enough, scratching his right front fender on some bushes as he swung back on the road to follow, at a respectable pace, the fat, hateful rump of the law.

"Cossack," said Mr. Amram between his teeth. "Storm trooper." He began now to remember that as a citizen he had rights which he might have invoked, though he was not sure just what they were or how one made the appeal; and already, by trying to bribe the man, he had got himself in a little deeper —deeper? and into what? He really had no idea why he had been stopped, or, for that matter, where they were going now; the little village by the river, probably, where he had thought momentarily of himself as living alone; that was already six or seven miles back.

But the motorcycle stopped again in front of him just a short way over the brow of the hill, on the other slope, and Amram stopped behind. The policeman again came very deliberately to his side and pointed into the road. Amram did not at first see what he meant, and when he finally made it out was so relieved that he laughed.

It was the cigar he had thrown away, lying in the middle of the road, still vaguely smoking.

"You think that's funny?" inquired the policeman.

"Oh, no, officer. I admit that was a wrong thing to do," said Amram civilly. "Danger of forest fires, and so on. Yes, I quite understand I am in the wrong." Had there been wrath, this soft answer might have turned it away, but there was none, only a watchful neutrality, or, worse than any wrath, inhumanity.

"There is a law in this state against littering the highway," said the policeman.

"Yes, I see—what can I say? I'm sorry, officer."

"Pick it up."

"What?"

"I said, *pick it up*."

"Oh, now—" said Amram, and stopped. He did not move, except for the trembling of his hands, which continued all this time. What most appalled him was the impossibility of expressing to this leathery robot beside him—this servant of the people, *his* servant!—the ethical delicacy of the position. He was willing to agree, not merely to having committed a trivial fault, but also that the smoking butt should be picked up; even that, there being no one else present but himself and the law, it was clearly his duty to pick it up. But that he should, in doing so, be forced to humiliation, to compulsion, like a child, and the abnegation of his will and personality, to the sense of his utter powerlessness—this struck him as conspicuously unfair. But, looking for a moment at that masked and emblematical face, that brow which was nothing but badge, he recognized the impossibility of his ever putting across, or even being given the time to state, a plea so humanly complex and problematic.

"Fascist," he muttered deeply as he stooped to pick up the cigar.

"You said something, mister?"

"Nothing," said Amram, who felt himself near tears.

"Give it to me."

Amram placed in the outstretched black palm the cigar—like a little turd, he thought—which was still smoldering.

"Now you'll follow me. We're going to the station."

"Isn't there any way we can settle this now?" Amram asked. "If there is a fine, couldn't I pay it to you right here?"

"In a hurry?" asked the officer. "There is a fine—fifty dollars for throwing things on the roads—but you'll pay it to the court. Let's go."

Again they set off in procession back toward the little village in the spruce woods. The policeman led the way, and Amram felt that even this expressed contempt for himself; it meant that the idea of his trying to escape—it did indeed sound ridiculous, put that way—had never crossed the man's mind.

Amram felt that his outing had been quite spoiled. Something more serious, too, his idea of himself, had been spoiled. His privacy, independence, liberty of action—call it what you like, it had been infringed on and even, for an instant, destroyed. Power had reduced him, and he had suddenly a very odd sense from this of what life must really be like, and of certain deep connections between humiliation and death. These were hard to express, but among their difficulties the following elements stood out: that one began in a small way with a haberdashery, one worked like hell—life broadened and deepened itself, and filled with intricately related riches, among all which, however, one kept one's head, or kept, at least, the sense of one's own being. . . . These riches, he saw, were themselves his being; they conferred, beyond what other, less essential satisfactions they brought, an identity guaranteed and witnessed with ever-increasing unanimity and authority by documents, signatures, possessions, relatives, friends, acquaintances, associates: that this, all of it, was Sam Amram, an ever-larger looming centrality to which all else was contingent. And now all this, by an encounter on a country road, demonstrated its true value, which was that of a canceled stamp. One might better simply not *be*, than be at the mercy of that cheap assemblage of emblems sputtering away down the road before him.

These thoughts Mr. Amram had, as befitted his character and station, in moderation; they had, perhaps, little enough to do with the sequel.

As they approached the village to which Amram presumed they must be going, the highway widened, the terrain opened out into farmland, the hills flattened in long, rolling sweeps to the sky at either side. The policeman on his cycle leaned to take a curve going left; at the high point of this curve a narrower road plunged straight on, forming a Y with the main road; Mr. Amram's Cadillac, as if by an impulse more its own than his, went straight on down that narrow road between high grassy banks. He had a last impression of the policeman turning to look back over his shoulder; then he was lost to view and, as a fugitive from justice, Amram entered an entirely different world, one which was, apart from his being in it, pleasant and peaceful.

He was horrified, of course; yet physically exhilarated. His heart was beating faster, and his car was going faster, even while he knew that in a moment he must slow down, stop, wait for that dreadful cop, to whom explanations of any delicacy, involving such things as the nature of personality and impulse, would be impossible.

Whenever Amram read in the newspapers of people who, flagged down by a speed patrol, simply tried to get away—a trick which generally ended in the wreck of their car and their own death—he always asked himself incredulously why they did not stop, the damn fools, since no encounter with the law could be worse than what they had let themselves in for. Now he was one of those people himself, and rushing down a lane (it might turn out to be a dead end) at forty-five, which was probably all the speed the lane would take.

The end of all this was extremely sudden. Amram did not see the policeman, could not have seen him, indeed, until the motorcycle swung in under his nose at the next crossroads; the man had taken another lane, connecting the arm of the Y farther up. The last view Amram plainly had of what was happening showed him the policeman, hand flung up in the hieratic, authoritarian gesture of riders since the world began (but which in this instance meant only, Stop), skidding his cycle around to resume his station in front of the Cadillac; which, however, plowed into him before the skid could be straightened out. It all went with the gadgety speed of an old movie, and with a rending and scraping noise of metal. The agglomeration of chromium and steel thus forced crunched and shrieked its way down the road for maybe a hundred yards before Amram could bring it all to a stop, in sudden and frightening silence.

Mr. Amram, shaking all over, got out of his car. He found he had bitten through his other cigar, and he spat the shreds from his mouth.

There was something his grandma used to say to him when he was a child: "Stop crying, or I'll give you something to cry about!" It seemed proverbially applicable just now, for that policeman was dead. He lay there like a military doll, his right arm still flung over his head.

Mr. Amram, seized as he was by a terror so absolute that all action would be irrelevant for the time being, yielded to a strange curiosity. He took off the man's cap and sunglasses; the face beneath was younger, softer, than what he had expected. But then, he wondered heavily, what did I expect? He took off also those terrible black gauntlets. The left one was clenched and his cigar butt, the beginning of all this dream, still held within it, no longer burning. The hands were perfectly ordinary hands, with bitten nails which gave them a commonplace though brutal appearance, and on one of them was a high-school graduation ring. The youthful face stared up at Mr. Amram with the expression it might have been wearing in life a moment ago: imperious and exasperated and grim, yet, with the life gone out of it, somewhat softened, and altogether meaningless.

Amram, sickened though not physically sick, stepped back

and looked around him. High on a distant hill there was a farmhouse; the aluminum roofs of silo and barn shone blindingly in the sun. No human being anywhere to be seen, and no other houses. A car might come at any moment. Someone might come walking.

He got in the car and started the engine with a roar, threw it into reverse and tried to back away. Nothing moved after a first instant in which the Cadillac, which had more or less climbed atop the motorcycle, scraped all that metal backward with a shriek and then came to a stop.

Amram got out and went around to the front end. In terror and rage he tried, absurdly, to lift his automobile by the bumper. When this did not work, he kicked the motorcycle as though expecting it simply to spin free and down the road, which of course it did not do; instead, he hurt his toe and had to dance up and down with tears in his eyes till the pain eased.

The car, seen from the front, looked to him like a monster with a chromium mouth which had just crunched the lesser monster, the motorcycle; it seemed to wear a satisfied look.

What might he do now that from being a wealthy citizen who had thrown a cigar on the public highway he had become a cop-killer (as the newspapers called them) and a fugitive? Where might he go? It was hopeless to run, if he must leave behind that huge automobile holding not merely the evidence of his crime but all the complicated evidence as well of his identity, traceable in so many ways.

Amram stood still and looked around him in every direction. Up at that farmhouse, so far away, a tiny figure had come out of a door and stood waving his arms; someone, no doubt, who had heard the noise.

His only means, and a poor one, was by fire, he now thought. That weight of useless metal contained at least the means to its own destruction, whereby it might be made unrecognizable for long enough to let him get over this hill and the next one, though even in his panic he did not consider a permanent escape at all likely.

With a pair of pliers from the trunk he began to tear away the license plate; there was no time to unscrew it. Fortunately it was cracked and rusted in one place, and he was able to remove a substantial piece, bearing half the numbers; and then the rest. These he stuffed into his pocket, tearing it. Before going to work with the matches he stopped for another look around. No one on the road. But the figure at the farmhouse had been joined by several others; as he watched, all of them began to come down the hill toward him.

What he wanted to do was, he realized, absolutely danger-ous; probably the car would explode and involve him in both blast and flame. Nevertheless . . .

As a precaution compromising between safety and the need of doing the job, he did not drop the matches in but ridicu-lously tried to toss them from a few feet away into the gas tank. He wanted to use the crankcase port, where the oil was poured in, as safer, but somehow the hood was stuck shut. With every match that did not go in, Amram moved some-what closer, in gingerly yet intense concentration; he began almost to forget, first why he was doing this, then what in the world it was he was trying to do; it seemed a game, trying to toss the match into the black mouth at the back of the car. One match after another; one failure after another. His own death, in any case, would likely accompany success. But he went on trying.

When the people from the farmhouse arrived Amram no longer was in any condition to notice them; his world had narrowed until it excluded everything but this little problem of getting the match into the tank.

The spectators saw quite well what had happened. They saw the policeman lying dead by his motorcycle. They said nothing, and on the observation of this madman tossing matches at an open gas tank they kept a pretty good distance back and away, on the bank above the road, and ready to run. This wary posture and space they maintained even after it was quite clear that Amram was not lighting the matches but simply taking them from the box and, ever so delicately, throwing them; even so, these people waited until he had used up the entire box before going down to take him into custody. He surrendered peaceably enough.

Visiting the Sick

I WENT AROUND to see Brewster Holloway one night not so long ago, because I'd heard he was laid up with a bad back. Not that I have any great love for Brewster Holloway, but I had a bad back myself a few years back, which the doctors couldn't figure out, and I had to lay around for more than a week, whining and groaning, till it cleared up. So naturally I was interested. Poor guy, I thought, probably could use a little company, and I thought back how we used to be good friends until gradually it had begun to come through to me what an unbearable son of a bitch he was, and we didn't see each other so much any more. Thinking like this what a comfort I was going to be to Brewster Holloway in his sickness made me feel quite good, and before leaving the house I rummaged around in the medicine chest and dug out the bottle of testosterone pills Doc had made me get for my back. "You'll know right away whether they're any good for you" was the way he put it. "If the first one doesn't produce a definite

improvement you might as well throw out the whole bottle."
The first one didn't, but I didn't. Three dollars for that bottle
of pills, and now I was turning them over to Brewster Holloway in his trouble, in case they would do him some good.
That was pretty fair of me.

"I'm taking these pills over to poor Brewster Holloway,"
I said to my wife Doris while I was putting on my overshoes.
"He's laid up with a bad back, and maybe these pills will do
him some good."

"Be careful and don't drink too much," said Doris.

As a matter of fact I had just had two drinks, or else I
wouldn't have thought of going out, probably, and certainly
I wouldn't have thought of going out to see Brewster Holloway, because I can remember a row we had once a couple of
years ago where I distinctly said I wouldn't drink his liquor
any more, and I wouldn't drink with a guy like him any more,
and he said things of the same kind. Of course, we'd had each
other over for drinks since that time, but not so much as we
used to, and in a more formal manner, like for bridge, with the
wives, and so on, not just dropping in the way it had been
before.

It was a mean, snowy night, but I walked anyhow instead
of taking the car; it seemed to me it was more of a gesture,
walking and coming up to the door covered with snow, and
probably Brewster would appreciate it more. It was only a
few blocks, anyhow.

When I got near the house I could see him right away,
sitting in front of the picture window in one of those leather
lounge chairs for heart attacks, smoking a cigarette and holding a glass. He couldn't be so damn sick as all that, was what
I thought, and I nearly turned around and went home, but I
rang the doorbell instead.

Nobody came to the door, and I rang again, and again nobody came to the door.

All right, you crumb-bum, if that's the way you want it, I thought. I know you're in there. Then I figured out that on account of his back he probably had trouble getting up, and I rang again. It was funny if by this time the wife or one of the kids didn't answer. I leaned over to my right, where I could see through the picture window. Brewster was trying to get out of that chair, but the chair was winning. He'd lean up, and the chair would tip forward the way they do, and I could see his lips set tight and then writhe up as if he was howling, or trying not to howl, and finally he made it, so I rang the bell again.

"Come in," he shouted a couple of times, but I waited for him to open the door anyhow. It was his house, and we weren't *that* good friends.

"Harry, boy, good to see you," said Brewster, when he had got the door open. "Come in kind of quiet; the kids are asleep."

"I heard you were having a little trouble," I said. "I just come over to watch you suffer."

You could see he didn't take to that so well, since we weren't so buddy-buddy any more, but he let it pass and made a smile to show he knew it was a joke and that I was welcome, and that he was suffering, and that I needn't think anything I said got by him.

"Here, let me have that," he offered when I took off my coat, but I said I knew my way around all right, and hung it up myself, and took off my overshoes sitting down on the stairs in the hall, and then he led the way back into the living room, hobbling before me to show how bad it was, and saying nothing to show how well he was taking it. I brought out the pills and held them in my hand; then I thought it was too soon for that and put the bottle back in my jacket pocket, where it made a big bulge.

Brewster eased himself down into the lounge chair, breathing hard. At his left was a low table with two open packs of cigarettes and a loaded ash tray and a cheese glass; on the floor there he had a gallon jug of sherry with a fat monk grinning on the label and patting his stomach; this jug was about two thirds full.

"Sorry I can't offer you anything but this or beer," he said. "Beer's in the refrigerator, bottom shelf."

"I don't drink beer, Brewse, you know that," I said. "I drink more than a glass of beer I fart the whole next day."

"Get yourself a glass in the kitchen, the cupboard at the far end," he said. "Damn sweet of you to come over, Harry."

"If I'd only known, I would have brought some booze," I said.

"There's nothing wrong with this crap," he said about the sherry. "Get a glass."

In the kitchen, getting the glass, I suddenly felt real sad. It was from seeing Brewster Holloway drinking that god-awful cheap sherry. Brewster was going down the hill, I could see that right off. He had gone as high up the hill as he was going to, to this comfy suburb in a good part of town, and he had stood there for a while looking at the view, and now he was starting down. But what made me sad was, I wondered if maybe I wasn't going down the hill myself, just like Brewster, even if I wouldn't have a gallon of that sherry in the house for Doris to cook with. Maybe it hadn't to do with the sherry, only with getting on. I went back in the living room with my face braced up in a smile; after all, I thought, the poor guy. . . .

"Where's Maxine?" I asked.

"Out," he said.

"Oh," I said, and poured us both some sherry. I filled his glass and was going to put only a little bit in mine to show that even if I was ready to be friendly I really wasn't the kind of man who drank stuff like that, but then I thought, Oh, what the hell, and poured my glass as full as his. He raised his glass, and I raised mine.

"To your very good health, sir," I said, grinning to show that under the circumstances this had to be a joke, and I bowed. Then we both drank. I filled the glasses again and settled down in the upholstered rocker opposite him.

"Pretty bad pain, eh?" I said in a sympathetic voice but impersonally, as if I was a doctor, or a priest he was going to confess to. Not that Brewster is a Catholic, any more than I am.

"Pretty bad," he said. "It's all right as long as I keep still, but when I move—"

"I know," I said. "I know just how it is. You been to Stemple?" Brewster and I had the same doctor.

"Yes, I went to Stemple a couple of times so far," Brewster said.

"What's Stemple think?" I asked, rocking nicely back and forth, getting comfortable.

"He doesn't seem to know yet."

"Slipped disc, maybe?" I suggested. "Often happens that way at our age. Fellow, Sanchez, at the office, was laid up six seven weeks—slipped disc."

"Might be," said Brewster. "I've had X rays, but they don't show anything."

"You have the deep heat?" I asked.

"Up at the hospital? Oh, yes, I had the deep heat and the massages both," Brewster said, "and that's some kid that Swedish masseuse that gives it to you."

"Some kid?" I said. "She's seventy crummy years old."

"That's the one I mean," said Brewster. "With the biceps." He thought that over for a minute. "Made me feel real good all over, that massage," he said. "Except my back, that is. It didn't do my back any damn good at all."

"I know how it is," I said.

We sat still for a minute or so after that, while I rocked back and forth. I really enjoy rocking, I don't know why. It feels like you're getting somewhere, not just sitting on your can.

"Look," I said finally. "I figured you might be having trouble with that back, I had the same thing once a few years back, so I brought you something." I wrestled around in the chair and brought out the bottle of pills.

"What's that?" asked Brewster.

"This is testosterone," I said. "It's what was prescribed for me then, when I had the same sort of trouble, trouble with my back."

"Oh, testosterone," he said, and sort of vaguely leaned forward and reached, till I got up and gave him the bottle.

"I figured it might do you some good, relieve the pain sort of," I explained.

"Yes." He looked a little dreamy. "Matter of fact, Harry, I've got some already."

I hadn't expected that, it was the last thing I expected to hear him say, and I had nothing to say back, so he went on. "Doc Stemple prescribed some for me the other day. 'You'll know at once if they're for you,' he said to me, 'and if the first one doesn't convince you, well, that's not it—you might's well throw out the whole bottle.' "

"How did it work?" I asked.

"Didn't do anything at all as far as I could make out," said Brewster.

"You too, eh?" I said, sort of grinning.

"Yep," said he.

"Jesus, three bucks a shot," I said.

"Three-sixty now, Harry," he said, and we sat quiet for a minute.

"Still, it was nice of you to think of it, Harry," he said.

"Don't mention it," I said, and got up to pour us more

sherry. That sherry was really warming my stomach, rotten
as it was. I was beginning to feel like the fat monk on the
label already.

"My God, boy," I said after a while, "how long've you been
guzzling this stuff tonight?"

"Since about five, maybe," Brewster said, like a man who
is going to tell the truth if it hurts.

"You mean steadily, right through supper?"

"Didn't have supper," he said. "I didn't feel like any."

"You mean all the time Maxine was getting the kids their
supper and putting 'em away, you were in here—"

"Maxine's out," said Brewster. "The kids got their own
supper and went to bed when I told 'em to."

"Oh," I said, and we sat there a while, smoking, drinking,
and I was rocking.

"It's real good of you to come around," he said then.

"Hell," I said. "It's what I'd want someone to do if I was
laid up."

"We've really been pretty good friends, Harry," he said.
"Give and take a little, I'd say we'd been good friends."

I didn't have much to say to that one, so I rocked a bit
faster and said, "How's the world been treating you lately,
Brewse?"

"Fair, Harry, pretty fair. I can't complain," he said.

Oh, so you can't complain, can't you, you crud, I thought.
Sitting here with your ass in a sling and consuming dee-licious
California sherry, you can't complain.

"I'm glad to hear it," I said.

"I wish these doctors had some idea what it was, though,"
said Brewster. "Stemple, and this guy at the hospital. They
don't seem to know what-all about it."

"Well, it's a pretty complicated thing, the back," I said.
"After all, at a certain age, you know, Brewse, the whole
machine begins to go."

"Boy, when the back goes," he said, "when your back goes and you haven't got that old push any more—then you know it's beginning to happen to you."

Brother, I never thought you had that much goddamn push, I thought, but naturally I didn't say that.

"It helps if you put hot compresses on it," I said, "if you get Maxine to put hot compresses on it at night."

"If you would—" he said, holding out his glass, so I got up and poured us some more. After he had it in his hand, he looked at me very level and serious.

"Harry," he said, "we've always been pretty good friends, one way and another. We've had our scraps, all right, but there's always been something there. You know that."

"You bet I do, Brewse," said I, beginning to see that along with everything else Maxine had taken off, and he was going to unload the works on me. "Something on your mind, boy?" I added.

"You don't mind if I talk just what's in my head?" he said, and I said sure, go ahead.

"Well, then," said he.

But I ought to mention first about this Maxine Holloway that I was just as glad she was not present. Maxine was always kind of a gay girl, and back when we were all friends I'd several times made some passes at that ass in a tight skirt which were not exactly what you would say rejected. I don't mean we ever went all the way, Maxine and I, because in the first place if Doris ever found out about anything like that, oh, brother. And besides, I don't go for that kind of monkey business. It isn't right. Still, we had now and again got close enough, Maxine and I, to get a fair idea what it might be like. This was at parties and things, where there were a lot of people around, but this Maxine had a way of operating even so, which you might have to pay money for at other places I've known. At one point, when Brewse and I were still good friends, I seriously thought of saying something to him about his wife's behavior, because God knows I wasn't the only one. All this, though, as I say, was a long time gone so far as I was concerned, but it still always embarrassed me a touch to look Maxine in the eye when there were other people in the room, and especially Brewster, which is why I was glad she wasn't around just now. I only mention this to show that the idea of Maxine leaving him was not going to be any great surprise to me.

"Well, then," Brewster said. "I don't know how to say it, exactly, but it's about, sort of, life as a whole."

"Yeah, sure," I said, thinking that after all Maxine was a pretty cute kid, and that Brewster Holloway, even if some people, like Doris for instance, did say he had married beneath him, was not such a much for a cute kid like Maxine who had kept her looks and what you might call her style well into the thirties with three kids, so that Brewster's back, if that was what had done it, might easily be, for Maxine, the straw that broke the camel's back. For a minute there I thought how it might have been me she had gone off with, and I thought about Doris sitting at her goddamn triple-mirrored Milady dressing table from Monkey Ward, weeping like the bejeesus. But really I was just as glad it wasn't me. What an armful. But what a handful. And with the three kids, besides. It was just a little bit goddamn unfair for her to leave poor old broken Brewster with the three kids. So, as I say, I was real sympathetic.

"You know you can trust me, kid," I said, leaning a little forward, still rocking.

"It's like this, Harry," he said, kind of rutsching around in that lounge chair and snarling with pain. "I've been thinking about love, and friendship—and caring about the other person, you see what I mean?"

I said I saw what he meant.

"I mean," he said, "I mean, we go through life killing each other. Knocking each other off, like savages, you know? What's good for me is going to poison you, but I'm going to get what's good for me anyhow—and maybe I'll like it better if it poisons you on the way. And the thing is, society wants us to do that, Harry. Society likes it."

What's the guy, a goddamn Communist as well as everything else? I thought, and it wasn't the first time I had thought that about Brewster Holloway. But I held my peace.

"The way we live now," Brewster went on, "we're shut off, we shut ourselves off, don't you feel that? It's the same everywhere, business, friendship, love—we can't ever seem to reach the other person. Take you and me, Harry. We've been pretty good friends, and I suppose I know you about as well as anybody, but do you think we really love each other?"

"I don't like that kind of talk," I said, thinking that if Brewster had been a fairy all these years and had just found it out I didn't want to hear about it.

"What other kind of talk is there?" he asked. "What else counts but that? I mean, after all, Harry, what do you care about in life, what do you think life is for?"

"Well, hell," I said, giving the rocker an extra hard push, "I care about living decently, about giving my family a decent life, about getting enough to eat and drink and getting along decently with people—you know, the usual things."

"The usual things," Brewster said with an odd little smile. "Suppose you stopped caring about the usual things?"

"Suppose? All right, suppose. Then I'd be dead."

"Suppose you were dead, Harry," he insisted, and I could see that supposing this didn't cause him any great pain. "Suppose you died tonight. Would anybody care, do you think? Would Doris care? Or the children, really?"

I could just see Doris, when he said that, sitting in front of her dressing table and smearing cold cream into her tears.

"What I mean is, Harry, do you love anybody? Anybody at all in the whole world?"

"I love my wife and kids," I said, getting a little heated because someone inside me had just said "I love me" and giggled. "What right do you have to go around asking questions like that, Holloway?" I said. "Who do you love?"

"I don't love anybody," Brewster said, and I poured us both some more sherry. "And I don't care, I don't care, I don't care." He didn't seem to be crying or anything, and yet these tears started to stream out of his eyes; it was just as if the sherry level had risen up over his cheeks and overflowed.

Then the front door opened and in walked Maxine covered with snow.

"Hiya, gents," she said. "How's *la vie?*" She took off her coat and shook it out over the rug and let it drop. Underneath she was wearing a tight black sweater and those what they call toreador pants. Harry and I may have been sort of sodden with the sherry by now, but Maxine was weaving, though very gay. It also made me a little uneasy that she didn't pay us any attention at all, after her first words, but just waltzed over to the record-player and put on the first dozen records that came to hand.

"Brewster and I were just discussing his slipped disc or whatever it is," I said, just to say something. Maxine turned to me with her hip stuck way out and her hand on the hip like she should have had a rose in her teeth.

"Oh, were you?" she said, and waltzed away into the kitchen as the first record began to play.

"Turn it down a little, will you, Harry?" said Brewster, and I did. So Maxine hadn't left him, but I began to get the idea she maybe had turned pro on him and been out on the streets, or in a bar, that is, all evening, for what she could pick up. Boy, these people had gone down the hill since we were friends, that was for sure.

"But I do care," said Brewster in a loud voice, with the tears still dripping down his face, as though nothing had interrupted our conversation at all. "I tell you what happened to me, Harry," he said, leaning forward in order to be intense, and not succeeding on account of the pain in his back.

Maxine danced into the room, twirling around and holding a frosty can of beer like a dancing partner. On the record somebody's piano was rumbling away, just the left hand, over and over, and Maxine crooned to it in a fake Negro accent.

> *O you takin' a risk*
> *When you slip mah disc,*
> *But honey it don't matter*
> *If you only spin my platter.*

"I've been having this affair with this married woman," said Brewster. "This married woman, someone in the neighborhood."

Well, Jesus! with his wife prancing around not ten feet away he says this. I mean, the record was playing, but it wasn't playing loud.

"Ssh!" I said, and I said it again, and I winked at him and screwed up my face and shook my finger to show he should knock it off, but he wasn't paying any attention.

"She's a very nice person, and respectable," Brewster said. "I don't mean any kind of cheap lay; I mean a nice married woman. She's someone you know, too. She was unhappy, see."

Well, Maxine was still dancing around, taking a swig of beer once in a while and crooning away not bothering any with us. It made me nervous as hell, though, because if she suddenly did hear him and take it in her head to start something, I've seen enough scraps of this kind to know it's the friend of the family that gets hurt first.

"Have another drop of sherry, Brewse," I said, pouring it for him, "and relax." As I leaned over next to him with the jug I whispered in his ear, "For Christ's sake, save it. Your wife's right here." But it didn't stop him at all. Was he unconscious or something? I don't know. He just went right ahead.

"What I wanted," he said, "what we both wanted, Harry, was just to love someone once for no other reason but loving someone, without the house and the car and the kids and the schools and the insurance and the whole damn rest of it. We talked about it a lot. In the good weather we'd meet out in the park, by the river."

This I could really see. The Secret Love of Brewster Holloway, in Technicolor. Walking in the park, under the falling leaves, old Brewster and some horse-faced dame, probably a schoolteacher, talking about love. I mean, if you need it that bad, go out and get it. But why be silly?

"Then we'd take a hotel room once in a while, way downtown near the harbor," Brewster said sadly. "We tried her house one time, but it was no good. It felt dishonest."

Damn right it felt dishonest, thought I. It *was* dishonest. But I said only, "I see what you mean, Brewse."

"The thing was, Harry," he said, beginning to whine a little now, "the thing was there was no place for us. There was only this terrible sense of guilt we had."

Well, if you're guilty, I thought, the least you can do is have a sense of guilt.

I looked at Maxine, dancing away into the kitchen. A record stopped; click; another record fell and began.

"Worse than that," Brewster went on, "was that we never really made it, finally."

Aha! I could see that coming a mile away. Since Maxine was still in the kitchen I took a chance instead of trying to stop this line of conversation, and I said, "They've got things that can fix that up, nowadays, Brewse. Miracle drugs, and things. You see Stemple about that."

He waved his hand at me in a tired way.

"I mean we didn't love each other after all," he explained, "or not the way we began with. So after all the fuss and fidget, there we were feeling we had done something just unforgivable. I don't know, Harry," he said, "you begin by wanting to love somebody, to feel that there's somebody you really exist for, and then you end up as usual, eating each other."

"So?" said I.

"I guess it's over now," he said. "I'd like to try again, but I don't dare. We meet once in a while, at parties now and then, or out on the street, by accident, and we just say hello. Nobody will ever know. But it's sad, Harry, it's so sad."

"Just so nobody's going to know," I said, thinking that if he went on this way Maxine was going to know and then he would really have something to weep about. "You've had your time and you didn't even get caught," I said, "so I don't see you've got anything to go pissing and moaning about."

Brewster flipped his hand at me again, sadly, as if to say I would never understand in a million years. And he was right. I won't. We're past the age, I figure, past the age when we can afford to talk that way, about love.

Maxine came back into the room with another beer, which is another thing I will never understand, why a pretty woman will drink beer, which is for slobs.

"Let's liven the party up a little," she said, making the music much louder. "Let's dance, Harry."

"You'll wake the kids with that noise," Brewster said. "Please turn it down a little."

Maxine snapped her fingers like castanets.

"Oh, turn down the volume, On that ole spinal colume," she sang, but she turned it down anyhow, a little, as asked, and spun around to me with her arms stretched wide.

"Go ahead, Harry," said Brewster. "Don't mind me. Give the kid what she wants."

I didn't much like the sound of that, or the sick kind of smile that went with it, but I couldn't think of any way of saying no to the way in which he had put it, so I got up and went into Maxine's arms.

I was fairly well on the way to being just a touch tight by this time, but I knew enough how things were to want to keep it respectable. Maxine, though, slid under my guard and fastened herself to me more or less from knee to neck. Drunk as she was, she was still a fine dancer, light and quick. But after a minute it was clear that what we were doing was not just social dancing, and I felt my spirits begin to rise and my face get red. Around and around we went, Maxine and I, stumbling a bit from being drunk if not from being so close our legs got mixed up; with Brewster sitting in his chair looking at us, nodding his head, the tears drying down his face. What is the guy, I wondered, some special kind of pervert or something? I could see him every time I came around in that direction, looking and nodding. It made me nervous, and when the end of the record came I laughed and said, "I guess that's enough for an old gent like me," trying to make a joke of it, and let go of her.

"Carry me back, To the ole spinal colume," she sang, and laughed, and fell on the floor.

"She must have been drunker than we thought," I said, making sure to get Brewster in on the act right away by saying *we*.

"Well," said Brewster, as though something had got itself settled.

I turned off the machine, which hissed and clicked for a minute until the tone arm raised itself up and very slowly moved back to its place and settled down. It was awful quiet in there.

"Listen," Brewster said. "Harry, do me a favor, will you? Take her upstairs and put her on the bed."

"Now, listen, Brewse," I said.

"You know where it is," he said, "head of the stairs to the left, where you leave your coats when we have a party."

I knew where it was for a slightly better reason than that.

"I can't do it on account of my back," Brewster said. "You'd be doing me a real kindness, Harry."

I looked at him for almost a minute, and at Maxine on the floor, and I said, "Okay, Brewse, if that's what you want," which then struck me as a pretty stupid thing to say, making more of the whole business than what he meant, and I started to pick Maxine up off the floor.

She was a light little chick, but when people are passed-out drunk, like they say when people are dead, they seem to get awful heavy. Still, I got one arm around her shoulders and hoiked her behind up with my knee till I could get the other arm under her legs. Brewster was watching all this and breathing as deep as though he was doing it himself, the way people do when they watch someone else doing what is their job, and I turned toward him to make sure he could see that my hands were way out in the clear. I began to stagger over toward the stairs.

"Thanks a lot, Harry," he said behind me as I went up.

"Don't mention it," I said, grunting, and for some fool reason almost added something like "Maybe you can do the same for me someday," but caught myself in time.

Before I had got Maxine up to where I could just let her drop on the bed, I was breathing pretty hard. I stood there looking down at her for a minute, but she didn't wake up or even move. Her mouth was open and she smelled like a rathskeller, but she was still a cute-looking kid. I didn't figure Brewster meant for me to undress her, but I did take off her shoes and unbutton those tight pants down the side so she'd be comfortable. Then something flashed into my head all of a sudden.

It flashed into my head that all this palaver of Brewster's about another dame, he meant Doris, and he meant I should know it. This was some kind of crazy revenge for the monkey business between Maxine and me, which he had somehow come to know about. God knows how people like Brewster think, sometimes, but did he maybe expect, sending me up here with his wife on my hands, that I would take advantage of her? What kind of a laugh must the moron be getting out of that?

Or was he maybe not laughing at all? I could just hear him saying, "Suppose you were dead, Harry, suppose you died tonight," in that gentle and sort of sad voice of his. And now, hearing a noise downstairs, I remembered pretty clearly that Brewster Holloway still had his service automatic. He kept it in the upper-right-hand desk drawer in the living room. I knew, because he showed it to me once.

I swear to God, as I stood there by the bed I began to sweat cold, hearing him begin to hobble and limp on the stairs. I could almost see that great blue-black gun in his fist. And then I could hear him breathing as he worked his way up the stairs, and everything about that evening, all that he'd said and how he had said it, and the way he looked at me, fell into place, and I saw that he was crazy. At the same time I saw that, the way the cards fell, it was going to look like he had a perfect right to kill me, finding me upstairs in his wife's room with her drunk and beginning to be undressed on the bed. Maybe he would kill her, too. No one would know what had really happened. I could hear him at the top of the stairs.

"Brewster," I cried, "Brewster, stop, for Christ's sake, don't," or something like that.

In another room a child laughed in its sleep and said something in a low voice.

"Don't what?" asked Brewster, coming into the room. No gun.

"Nothing," I said, trembling and breathing hard and beginning to be terrible angry, the way I can get sometimes.

Brewster looked down at his wife on the bed.

"The poor thing," he said gravely, like a priest. "Poor, sad thing." Then he turned to me. "It's very kind of you, Harry," he said, and put his hand on my arm.

"Get your hand off my arm," I said. "You criminal, you pervert."

"What?" said he, rearing back with his mouth open.

"You heard what I said," I said. I was quivering all over.

"I don't know what you mean," he said.

"You know damn well what I mean," I said, and pushed him aside and ran down the stairs, and got out of the house as fast as I could, with my coat slung over my arm and my overshoes clutched in one hand. I didn't know whether I was madder than scared or the other way around.

The snow was still falling, and before I had been out a minute my feet were soaked and I was starting to get cold. All that sherry had lowered my resistance. But what had led me on to yell to Brewster Holloway that he was a criminal and a pervert? I mean, maybe he was, but you can get along with people without having to say just what you think of them, can't you? What would life be like, if everybody came out with remarks of that nature?

Of course I had been scared, because I figured Brewster had gone insane brooding about what might have taken place between his wife and me some time back. I figured this was his big chance, tonight, when his wife passed out, and he was going to take it.

And then, too, I thought when he made that grand spiel about loving one another, he meant Doris. I wouldn't put it past Brewster Holloway, either, to go that way with his friend's wife. Mind you, I didn't really believe he had, not really. But he might have, and he had better remember that I have my service automatic too, in the upper-right-hand drawer of my desk at home, and it's just as big and just as blue-black as his. And, oh, brother, if I ever saw any reason to suspect that what took place between Brewster Holloway and some nice respectable married dame in the neighborhood, took place between Brewster Holloway and my wife, I would give that Doris something to remember me by the rest of her life.

Thinking this way, with the heat in my head and a chill everywhere else from the snow, I got home. I went in the kitchen right away and had a glass of Scotch, to keep off a cold and rinse the taste of that sherry out of my mouth. Then I went upstairs and got undressed and crawled in beside Doris. I turned on my bedside lamp and she turned over, groaning something.

If she wakes up, I decided, I'll put it to her did she or didn't she.

She didn't wake up, though I stared at her hard for about two three minutes.

The hell with it, I thought, and turned out the light. But lying there in the dark I felt uneasy and wakeful. Also I got the idea my own back was beginning to ache again, and I hoped whatever Brewster Holloway had it wasn't catching. Finally I turned on the light again.

"Doris," I said softly, but she didn't move, only puffed out her lips with a long, slow sigh.

"Doris, dear, you're asleep, aren't you?" I said, still very softly, and she didn't move.

"Doris," I said, "you went with Brewster Holloway, didn't you, and you walked in the park when the leaves were falling, and you went to bed with him in hotel rooms, didn't you, you nice respectable married woman, and you brought him up here to this bed, too, didn't you, you bitch, but it didn't work because you were all so goddamn pure you didn't want to be dishonest, did you, you common thieving low-down whore?"

Doris didn't move.

"You were unhappy, you poor sad thing, you," I said, and my voice was getting louder. "You wanted love, because you were so unhappy at home and you couldn't stand your poor damn fool husband you married, so you laid to Brewster Holloway and spread out your legs and that was love. Bitch-woman!" I cried, "I'll give you unhappy." And I slapped her across the face. She sat up with a jerk, just like that.

"What?" she said. "What?"

"I'm sorry, dear," I said. "I must have poked you with my elbow, getting into bed. Go back to sleep now."

"I just had a funny dream," Doris said, rubbing her face. "We were in this car, and—"

"In the morning, honey," I said, "tell me in the morning. It's late now. Go to sleep."

I turned out the light again.

The Sorcerer's Eye

AROUND THE CASTLE where I lived with my parents was a moat, half overgrown with weeds, where wild birds waded and swam. A corridor, which I liked to think was secret, led to a door at the water's edge, and there I used to go, against my father's absolute command, to meet the girl from outside. We spoke across the water.

"What is that you wear on the string around your neck?" she asked me once. I drew it from my shirt, a golden spoon it was, and showed it to her.

"Why a golden spoon?" she asked.

"Oh," I said, "it is something that happened long ago, a kind of family joke, though not a very good one. You wouldn't be interested."

"You're a sad boy, aren't you?" said she. "Do they really joke, in your family? Tell me."

"When I was little," I said, "my father once told me, he seemed angry about it, that I had been born with a golden spoon in my mouth. That puzzled me, since I didn't know it was a proverb, and I tried to think what it was like to be born, and why one would have a golden spoon in one's mouth at that time, and finally, seeing that my father really meant something, which it made him angry to mean, I started to cry. My mother then, to turn it into a joke, took a real golden spoon from the dinner table, tapped me on the shoulder with it, and said I was her knight of the golden spoon. So I have kept the spoon."

The girl smiled. She was dressed in black rags, and so beautiful.

"You love your mother, don't you?" she said.

"She is sick," I replied. "She lies on a sofa all day, and has little heart-shaped white pastilles, for her heart ailment. She reads novels, and sometimes I read them to her, though Father does not like me to be reading novels."

"There's a great lot your father doesn't like."

"He doesn't like at all for me to meet you and talk to you."

"I know," said she. "We're both lonely."

"I am so lonely," said I. "For I read in books about how people live, out in the world, and meet others, and make friends, and love another. I love you, I think."

"I love you," she said, "but it would be better not to talk of that."

"Because of your father?" I asked.

"Because of him, yes."

"I know about your father," I said, "for my father told me the tale on my eighteenth birthday, only a while ago. I have even seen your father, through the telescope in the tower room. He sits in the woods, in a clearing in the woods, a mile away. He sits on a throne of sorts, I think, and stares at our castle all the time. He is a sorcerer, isn't he, a kind of wizard?"

"He is," said she.

"And my father is frightened of him," I went on, "for he

built this castle of ours by magic, before I was born, and my father fears that if he is offended he may tear it down, also by magic."

"That's true, he could," she said. "Your father must have been in terrible trouble, to need my father's help."

"My father used to live in the world," I said. "He was a captain in one of the great regiments, and he had epaulets of silver, high boots, silver spurs. But he lived too well, and gambled, and was in debt. One night, when he was drunk and losing everything, he bet against a brother officer and on his side the wager was that this man, if he won, might spend a night with my mother."

"That was a bad thing to do," said the girl.

"It was," I said, "for he lost. Everyone knew then that it was not only a bad bet but an impossible one, and they left him alone until sunrise, with a pistol on the table. My father was to shoot himself because of his dishonor; that was the understanding, in the regiment. But instead he went out and walked in the streets of the city until, near dawn, he met your father, who brought him into the deep forest, far away, and raised him up this fine castle which you see—all by a look of the eye he did this, and by a gesture of the hand."

"My father has a great and terrible power," the girl said. "There was a condition."

"The condition was simply this," I replied, "that we live here, that we never go outside."

"You are safe, at any rate."

"Yes," I said, "we are safe enough. But my father is unhappy, and that makes us all unhappy. He is unhappy because, I think, he believes still that he might somehow have got out of his desperate position and gone on to a grand career, and because my mother is ill and not much of a companion to him, and because she despises him, having never forgiven the wager. Finally," I said with some hesitation, "because he suspects, and fears, that after all his fellow officer might have taken advantage of his winning, on that night, so I would be not my father's child but his. About this, he has never asked my mother, as fearing her reply, as not wanting the burden of the knowledge, I don't know."

We were silent. The waters of the moat glittered between us. Behind me the castle stood towering in courses of great blocks of stone, behind her the trees flickered their green leaves in the light wind and the sunshine.

"I never knew my mother," said the girl at last.

"I'm sorry for that," said I.

"Nor have I been in the world," she said. "I am as much a prisoner as you are, and perhaps my father is as much a prisoner as yours. The keeper is always bound to his charge, so neither can be free."

"I should like to go into the world," I said, "but only if you would go with me."

"My father has two eyes," she said, musingly, and as if not replying at all, "of which the right one, of flesh and blood, is the eye of action, and the left one, a glass orb, is the eye of thought. With the one, he does; with the other, he knows."

"That is a strange division," I said, "and yet, after all, quite appropriate in its way."

"I have been thinking," she said, "that as my father's eyes are fixed upon the castle, so that you and I are beneath his notice, we might go together, one time, and come up behind him, and you with your golden spoon could quickly remove an eye—"

"But that would be terrible," said I, "in itself and in its consequences."

"Terrible, how?" asked the girl. "I do not love my father."

"Nor I mine," I replied, "though I should be sorry to lose my mother. But the castle would fall."

"Not if you removed the glass eye," she said. "It would not

hurt him to lose it, since it is glass, since it is the eye of knowledge he would never know he had lost it, so that it follows, surely, that he must keep the eye of action turned, as always, upon the castle, to keep it as it is, in being."

"That's true," I said, beginning to be fascinated with the idea. "But dangerous."

"You are afraid?" she asked, smiling again.

"I have never been afraid," I said, somewhat sternly, but yet not pridefully, for the fact was that my existence until this time had magically excluded the awareness of fear.

"When it is done," she said, "we shall go out into the world, away from castle and forest, and I promise to love you for as long as you will love me."

"I will do it for that promise," I said. "I will do it for you."

"Tonight," she said, "meet me here again, and I will lead you where he sits."

So we parted, agreeing to meet in the hour before dawn.

2 –

"You've been seeing that girl again," said my father during the course of the evening.

"No, sir," I said, looking him steadily in the eye. I thought that he had not seen me down there by the moat, but said this simply from a sad propensity, almost a wish, to know the worst, at all times, about everything.

"I hope you are not lying to me," he said, frowning. "You know how I regard a lie."

He had come to a stop facing me, but now he resumed his usual occupation of pacing the long hall, with his hands locked behind him. Whenever he turned toward me, however, he thought of something else to say.

"It's for your good, as well as mine, that I warn you" was one of these remarks. And another was "Don't imagine I shan't know what you do." And another: "I don't like to have to keep an eye perpetually on what my own son is up to; but I will, I will if it is necessary, make no mistake about that."

My silence during all this was meant to be respectful, though it was also shamefaced because of the lie; it seemed merely to provoke him further, so that at last he came to a definite halt in front of me, but spoke rather to the ceiling, or the walls, than to me.

"What difference does it make? What can I keep? What have I to defend? A merciless bargain. Are you my son? Are you?"

"I don't know," I said, though he still seemed to be talking at random rather than to me. "I cannot know if you don't, sir."

"Ah, I know you'll do as you please," he said roughly, and then, "If you see that child once more—once more—let me tell you, lad—"

"Yes, Father," said I meekly but by no means humbly.

"I will . . . I will . . . ah, what will I?" he rather groaned than said, and stalked away leaving me there. I felt sad for him in his merciless bargain, but undisturbed in my resolve. The bargain had not been mine, and perhaps what I was about to do had, in some way, been included in the pact to begin with, before I was born. He was an elegant, lean man, my father, still young looking, and I had always thought him strong. But I now saw that his strength was of the sort which is purely for display and is always defeated in action; that is why it could continue to look like strength, because there was really for him, poor man, no world in which he might expend it.

My mother, though, was the image of a continuously victorious weakness. Fragile and lovely, with her romances and her little medicated confections for the heart, she lay there year after year, not so much indomitable—that was the qual-

ity she had lived on, and used up—as simply undefeated. I told
her nothing, that night; but she felt a foreboding.

"Something . . . something . . . will happen, soon."

"Oh, Mother," I said quite boldly, "all will be well, you
will live in your castle still. Whatever happens, trust your
knight of the golden spoon, who will never let anything bad
happen to you." For I believed at this time that I was going
to be their savior as well as my own. I should free myself,
and go into the world, and love another, while they would
possess their fine castle unconditionally, when I had removed
the glass eye of knowledge from the sorcerer's head, so that
it might never revoke the action of the other eye which kept
the castle standing. So all would be well, with them and
with me.

I reassured my mother, and then for a while read to her, as
I sometimes did, from the novel she happened to be reading
at the time. Because she read these novels far more when I
was not there than had them read when I was, my impression
of the life in them was flickering and discontinuous: someone
would be happy at one reading, on the point of suicide at the
next, married at the next, then dead, and so on; also, different
people would have entered while I was away, and the people
I knew from previous readings would have disappeared; I
never knew, even, when one novel left off and a quite different one replaced it.

In the chapter I read that night a man abandoned his wife
and child, on account of something he had done which doubtless had been described in an earlier part, but which I knew
nothing of. As he left the house at night, he stood at the end
of the street to look back once at the little light above the
door, emblem of a happiness lost and a security decayed, so
that the author, a woman, was moved to exclaim to us read-
ers, "The gleam of that lantern would illuminate his mind
for many years," and, an instant later, "how far that little lan-

tern threw its beams!" expressions which, sentimental as they may have been in that place, I have been unable to forget. At the time, however, I affected to regard them slightly, and may even have read these phrases with a tone of mockery, for my mother said to me, as I bent to kiss her good night and, as I thought, goodbye, that when one day I had gone into the world and married and knew what it was to be a father, I should perceive the bitter truth at the heart of those words which I now found merely sugary.

3 –

Before dawn, by the black waters of the moat, without a moon to silver them, I stood shivering. At her low, long call I dived as deep and far as I could, felt for an instant the weeds cling and grasp about me, and came up at her feet. We set off roundabout through the forest, she holding my hand and leading the way with a great certainty, though nothing could be seen.

"You remember what you have to do?" she whispered once. I whispered that I did, though really what went through my head was scarcely a thought, so much as the mere image of my bending over that high and crooked shoulder from behind and suddenly, violently, digging with my golden spoon.

We reached the glade in the forest at first light, when a few birds were beginning to cry out. The girl, my girl, was pale, pale as stone in this gray light, and, though I was not afraid, something of what fear was began to make itself known to me through her hand, sweating but coldly sweating, which clutched mine always more tightly as we crept into the clearing behind the old man's high throne, above which reared back his great shoulders cloaked in black and his massive, steady head, which never moved.

"Now!" she whispered, letting go my hand and pushing

me out toward the figure in the glade. I took the spoon, tearing the cord which tied it to my neck, ran forward, and leaped up, grasping that head by its white hair so that it fell back while with my other hand I did with the spoon what I had come to do.

Oh, I saw his face at that instant, and it was terrible, and I knew now how to be afraid. The air was split by his one cry of anguish, which endured while I dropped to the ground and began to run. The girl caught me by the hand again; in my other hand I held the spoon, and in the spoon was held the eye, and his mighty voice screamed behind us as we ran, "I know you! I know you!"

"Not that way," that girl began to bicker at me, "not that way, that leads back to the castle."

"I know," said I. "I took the wrong eye."

"I know you!" screamed the voice behind us. "I know what you have done."

As we ran through the forest the sun rose before us, and its red and gold light flickered through the leaves in a rhythm like that beaten by my brain: I know you, I know you. The eye stuck to the spoon, the spoon was clenched in my hand. Now I was the leader, and I was afraid, while the girl tagged on behind me, and the great voice of agony wakened the forest and the whole world.

"I can't run any more," she began to cry out after a time, and when despite my terrible impatience and fear I turned to attend to her weakness I saw no beautiful young girl, whose white flesh peeped at the shoulder through her rags, and whom I loved, but a thickened, sallow, blotched creature dressed in a somewhat elegant gown which was, however, badly ripped and stained.

"I can't go on any more," she cried chokingly, and sagged to the ground. As I took up my flight again I heard her for a time begging me not to leave her, but I could not stop.

The castle, when I reached it, was a silent ruin. The moat had dried up, and in the dry ravine where it had been was a tangle of bushes and vines and tall grass. Great trees had fallen, it seemed centuries ago, against what was left of the castle walls, brought low now and with the contours of the great stones softened by moss and lichen. One of these trees I was able to use as a bridge, and in a moment stood atop a heap of marble slabs mingled with granite blocks. Before me, in a kind of pit formed by the inward collapse of battlements, my mother sat on a stone, with my father standing beside her. He held her by the hand. I saw that they were old, quite old, and wrinkled, with dry, papery faces. And I was frightened anew, even before my father cried out to me, in a shrill voice, "What have you done? Monster, what have you done?" And my mother said, in a dull voice as though she cared for nothing in the world, "What is that in your hand?"

I looked at my hand, at the spoon, at the eye which quivered there like a jelly. In that instant I knew all the fear my childhood had been denied, all the fear, I think, of children all over the world when in their sinfulness and shame they stand before the mighty parents whom they are bidden to destroy. And as though by this means I might rid myself of the evidence of my guilt, I raised the spoon to my mouth and swallowed down the eye.

"What's done is done," I said to them sternly. "Come, we shall leave here at once."

And that is what we did, with nothing in our hands except my golden spoon. My parents opposed me no more, and we walked out into the forest, in the heat of the day, where I could still hear as it were the leaves of the trees shaking in slight sound: "I know you!" And this great forest, which from the castle had once seemed of illimitable extent in every direction, proved to go on for a few miles only. By midafternoon we had come out on a highway, with rails sunk in it, and on the rails was what I later understood to be a tram car. Of course, as we had no money, it was necessary to walk. And when, some time later, we came into the city, it was hard at first to find food and lodging. But I was now the owner—despite himself!—of the eye of power and action, and it is enough to say that I soon found work, which enabled me to provide for my parents while they lived.

It was not long. My mother was very shortly afterward taken by a fatal attack, and then my father, stealing money from me in order to do so, bought a pistol and with it one night blew out his brains, just as though he were a gallant young captain still, and nineteen years had never passed.

Since then, I have gone about my business in the world, preferring travel to residence, being, as you might say, an *entrepreneur*. I have done quite well with my life, following my many concernments from one town to another, living always in hotels, a long succession of them so that they seem to become one in my memory, with their marbles and potted palms and ancient elevators of open grillework in which the passengers arise and descend like angels in trousers and spats or in tea gowns and pumps. All those towns seem a single town in the flickering rhythm of my brain, Nineveh, perhaps, that great city which the Lord spared, as I read once, although there were therein so many persons that could not discern between their right hand and their left hand.

I have never married. And I have kept my golden spoon, for a watch charm. I used to eat my breakfast egg with it, but gave that up many years back as being bravado. And somewhere, in a small clearing in my busy brain, the black-robed magician sits still in his high chair and cries out in an anguish undiminished by time or by his impotence that he knows me, he knows me.

ABOUT THE AUTHOR

HOWARD NEMEROV *was born and reared in New York City. After graduating from Harvard College, he served in the Royal Canadian Air Force (1942–1944) and in the United States Army Air Corps (1944–1945) as a pilot. Since the war he has lived most of the time in Vermont, where he is a professor of English at Bennington College. During the present academic year (1958–1959), he is a visiting professor at the University of Minnesota.*

Mr. Nemerov's stories and poems have appeared in about a dozen magazines, including The New Yorker, The Atlantic, The Nation, Poetry *and the* Hudson, Kenyon, Partisan *and* Sewanee Reviews. *His published books include four volumes of poetry and three novels, the latest of which,* The Homecoming Game, *has been adapted into a play.*